THE DEATH DEALERS

Jack had just reached the spot where he'd left the ponies when he heard the first shot. Before he could turn, two more shots followed. He leapt up the rock wall and saw the camp in total confusion.

Men on the ground grappled with others. Jack saw Teeah running down the trail, headed for the lava wall at the far side. One of the outlaws was aiming his pistol at the fleeing girl. Hardly believing it, Jack heard someone scream as he stood there frozen. Then one of the killers pointed to where Jack stood, above the level of the camp.

"Git that red bastard on the rocks . . ."

⦸ Signet Brand Western

SIGNET Westerns For Your Enjoyment

Massacre at the Gorge

Mick Clumpner

A SIGNET BOOK

NEW AMERICAN LIBRARY

TIMES MIRROR

PUBLISHER'S NOTE

This novel is a work of fiction. Names, characters, places, and incidents are either the product of the author's imagination or are used fictitiously, and any resemblance to actual persons, living or dead, events, or locales is entirely coincidental.

Copyright © 1982 by Mick Clumpner

SIGNET TRADEMARK REG. U.S. PAT. OFF. AND FOREIGN COUNTRIES
REGISTERED TRADEMARK—MARCA REGISTRADA
HECHO EN CHICAGO, U.S.A.

SIGNET, SIGNET CLASSICS, MENTOR, PLUME, MERIDIAN AND NAL BOOKS *are published by The New American Library, Inc.,* 1633 *Broadway, New York, New York* 10019

FIRST PRINTING, AUGUST, 1982

1   2   3   4   5   6   7   8   9

PRINTED IN THE UNITED STATES OF AMERICA

Preface

The history of the cattle movement in eastern Oregon began about 1859, with travelers coming in from the Willamette Valley who knew of the rich grasslands there unoccupied by Indians or white men as yet. Most tribes located their semipermanent dwellings near fishing streams and rivers and used the adjacent hills and prairies only for hunting game. Men who owned or coveted cattle began to move in, increasing during the 1860's as demands for meat mounted with the opening of mines in Idaho, Oregon, Washington, and British Columbia.

By the mid-sixties, Indians began raids from all sides on the pioneers' scattered ranches and homesteads. Place names on earlier maps and even those of the present day attest to the tragedies. Burnt Ranch, Murderers' Creek, Skull Creek, Bloody Canyon, and Hangman's Creek all give mute testimony to what occurred in that long-ago time. The bitterness of whites who survived the Indian depredations can be found among their descendants today.

For many years a mixed breed was scorned and held in contempt. In writing Jack Tate's story, I have recalled half-breeds I have known from the Cariboo country of British Columbia south through Idaho, Oregon, and California. Knik and his wife, Marie, were guides and

friends of mine in Canada. I knew Joe Good-
reau and his beautiful half-breed wife, Cindy,
in the Umpqua country where Joe worked for
me as a foreman. Stukes, part Coeur d'Alene,
worked in the Forest Service with me as well as
Wagila Loehine—Thunder Boy—also known
as John Damon, Sr., of the Blackfoot tribe of
Montana. Others, casually met, became em-
ployees and later friends. Last but not least,
there was Jasper Palouse, who claimed he was
the last of the Umpquas, he himself crushed to
death under a loaded log truck on the Umpqua
River.

M.C.

1

"Well, feller, we got 'em all, I guess. That red bastard went down when I drawed a bead on his back. How come you missed him? You had the best chance."

"It weren't a good shot, him skinnin' in an' out, dodgin' like a rabbit ahead of a greyhound. I bounced one clost enough he got splattered with rock, I kin vouch fer that."

"What we goin' to do with the carcasses?"

"Do what the boss figgered on afore we started this little sashay." The red-bearded man grimaced. "Take what we kin use offen 'em, then load 'em on their plugs an' pack 'em over to that canyon. The river's a half-mile down there. We'll sling 'em over an' the buzzards'll take keer of the rest!"

"Yer a heartless brute," the second man grated. He hitched up his rounded belly. "Too bad the boss kilt the squaw. She could cook and give us something to fool with when night come. Why'd he do it, anyway?"

"Nothin' but trouble with wimmen, red, black, er white, he says. They squall an' bawl, somebody gits to feelin' sorry for 'em, and then there's a shootin' or knifin' to settle. Nope, long as we work with him and ride together, no woman, red er white, goes with us."

The two ragged outlaws loaded and primed their rifles, looking long at lava rock, sage, and scattered juniper trees along the distant Oregon hillside where their quarry had been seen and shot down, before they turned back toward the scene where their crimes began. Both men were bearded, their clothes a combination of buckskins, rags, and greasy cloth. The red-beard wore a flattened black leather hat; his stocky companion had a blue forage cap, filched from some soldier's outfit, atop his bullet head. Many others wearing such motley garb as these two followed trails west from distant eastern and midwestern settlements.

"I got a hunch those sod-stompers had more gold with 'em than the papers in Lewiston said. How we goin' to split it up? Straight across the board?"

1

"Have to. The boss won't go fer any other way."

"You and me'd have a purty good stake, split between us."

"Don't get them crackpot ideas in yer noggin. That hombre kin read a feller's mind afore he even thinks up what he might do. If he figgers we might bushwhack him, he's already got started on what's goin' to happen to us. Only way is fer you to watch out fer me, an' me keep a weather eye out fer yer hide." The red-beard glanced sideways. "Not that it's worth much on the market," he added.

The two walked down the broken lava hillside through scattered junipers toward their camp near a trickle of water that kept alive a few willows and aspens around grass and shrubs for the horses contentedly feeding there, two wearing hobbles. A thin thread of smoke from the abandoned fire twisted its length of blue yarn into a bluer sky. High above, a circling buzzard wheeled lazy rounds.

The two men paused before dropping off a little ledge of rocks within sight of the camp. They saw no person there.

"Where do yuh s'pose the boss is? I don't see him atall."

"Mebbe he's already took off to dump some carcasses."

"Not if I know him. That'll be our job."

"I wouldn't be surprised if he'd already went through the packs and pockets to grab what he could and cache it away afore we come back."

"If he has, we might as well figger to do him in and then look fer what he didn't git. How long you knowed the feller, anyway?"

"Long enough not to ask no questions 'bout what he did in the war and before. He don't waste no word afore he shoots er uses that pig-sticker he carries, so don't git close if you got anything to squabble over. Let's git on down now an' jist say we done the redskin in. He'll git real upset lessen he's sure no one's runnin' loose to spill what happened here."

As they approached the camp, both men kept looking for some movement that might indicate their leader's presence. They saw bodies scattered out, swept their eyes toward where they'd seen the running figure of an Indian girl fall to the ground before they pursued her companion up the hill. There was a body on the ground there, all right.

Red-beard swore in consternation. "That's him lyin' there! Looks like he's dead! The squaw's gone! Keep yer eyes open. Hit looks like Injuns coulda done it."

2

Hurriedly, well aware of impending trouble, the two approached the man sprawled on the rocky earth. Close up, they knew he was dead. Blood flooded the surface under his neck and face. Red-beard watched the nearby junipers and lava-rock benches while his partner turned the man over. Below his chin, his throat had been cut clear across. The wide-open eyes held a look of shock or surprise, but the startled outlaw beside him saw no knife near the corpse.

"Some red devil cut his gozzle!" he exclaimed. "Take a look, see if they took anything off him afore they lit out." He stood up to watch.

Red-beard knelt, ran his hands up and down. "Nothin' that I know of . . . but he shore did git his throat cut." He grimaced, rising. "You suppose some red bastard's been a-followin' us? We better pack up, head 'south."

"We got to git rid of them carcasses first. I'll keep my eyes peeled while you take what we can use off'n him. If we come out of this with our hair still in place, we'll split things even atween us. When you git through, I'll git the ponies ready."

Red-beard didn't relish the job of going through the dead man's pockets until he found several gold pieces. He transferred them into his own pockets, secured the leader's knife, belt, and tobacco pouch, his tattered clothing not worth taking from his body.

He walked back to where the first victim lay dead, sprawled in a grotesque posture, shot in the chest, and went through his pockets, finding gold pieces, a barlow knife, a watch, and some sulfur matches wrapped in oilcloth. He eased out a belt knife and pulled off the man's boots. Finding he couldn't get his feet into them, he left them for his smaller companion, who was not too happy about the way things stood at this moment. Things were hardly as the little outlaw had thought they'd be. He had never expected the boss to be killed by some unknown assailant so quickly. Troubled by this, he knew as well that he and his red-bearded partner now had to make their way alone through this unknown part of Oregon. Would Indians trail them in revenge for killing the girl? The boss's plan to kill the whole party for their money had backfired, and now he himself was dead.

As he selected ponies from the bunch that had been grazing, he worried some more. Two against how many? How had an Indian sneaked up on their usually wary leader and

3

cut his throat before he could protect himself? And hell's fire, what would they do with this horse herd? They had acquired ten besides their own to herd or lead beside the ones they rode. They would sure have to cut down that number before they left this place for good. Speed was going to be the important thing now in order to save their own scalps. The half-breed, if he got away, might upset things even more if other red devils were around. He looked around. Maybe his partner had some idea what they should do.

That evil drifter did have some ideas, but they didn't ease his own worries. He almost wished the boss was alive to help in case Indians jumped them while they were packing up. Two or three hidden up there in the lava could pick them off with comparative ease. Well, the two of them would have more to split now, anyway. He grimaced at that, then wondered, like his partner, how the boss had come to let someone get close enough to slit his throat. That bothered him more than he wanted to admit. Best thing to do now was to search the rest of the dead and get rid of their bodies, then pack up and leave the country.

He spread a small tarp on the ground and began tossing plunder onto it; knives, guns, belts, powder, and lead lay among other things of value they could trade or sell. He picked two coats, a couple of hats, a pair of new boots, and a woven hide lasso they might use later, and wrapped them in the bundle. While he roped it into a solid pack, the stocky outlaw came up leading their two horses, one pack pony tied to his own saddle.

"Whatcha got there?"

"Guns, knives, things we kin swap on the way."

"Find any money or gold?"

"Nope. I figger we better sling on the packs right away and pull out soon as we git this mess cleaned up. How many ponies'll we take along?"

"Two to ride, one to pack. That way we kin git out and go if we git chased."

"What'll we do with the rest of this stuff an' all them horses?"

"All the plunder we don't take we cache here in the rocks. Take the ponies—we kin kill some along the trail if we have to. Don't want to do no shootin' around here now."

"What about the Injun's three?"

4

"Take 'em! I'd like that spotted devil. He may have to be broke all over—he's Injun stock. Bring one pony up. We'll sling this pack on him."

They tied down one pack. They made up another from their own things to put on their own pack pony, all the while nervously eyeing the surrounding hills, where scattered junipers could hide an enemy crouching in lava and sage. The rest of the horses still fed in the little depression where water had kept green grass growing.

"Where we gonna git rid of these fellers?"

"That half-breed spoke about a deep canyon just up ahead," red-beard replied. "Said it was half a mile deep and nobody could climb down to the river fer miles ahead. S'pose we ketch up more ponies that'll pack, put saddles on 'em, and load the carcasses. We'll find a good place to throw them an' the saddles over. Then we'll cut the ponies' throats an' let the buzzards an' coyotes take over."

"Sounds all right to me. Take another look around. I'll bring in the sod-stompers' plugs."

Soon the pair of uneasy outlaws headed south to the canyon of the Deschutes River, the small herd of horses hazed along with them. After about two miles through rocky, tumbled earth, the caravan reached its edge, the gorge below them far deeper and more precipitous than they had imagined.

After following the chasm a short distance, red-beard held up his hand and halted. He tied his pony to a juniper, and going back along the line, he caught and tied each horse to a shrub or tree. His partner came up to help, over his squeamishness now at following dead men on blood-streaked ponies, but wanting desperately to be free of such damaging evidence. Dim visions of a rope swinging from a limb or cross arm had become clear. If any man in this country, civilian or miltary, saw what he and his partner were about to do, they would be shot or hung right there at the canyon's edge.

Red-beard spoke for him. "Let's git it over! We'll sling 'em down one at a time, git 'em close enough they kin keep each other company." A breeze from the gorge caught his callous cackle as he added, "Give me a hand!"

They unlashed confining ropes, took bodies from the saddles, dragged heavy hulks to the canyon rim, and heaved them into the vast gulch, along with saddles and packs.

5

The short, heavy outlaw drew a long breath. "S'pose we kin lead some of these plugs clost enough to push 'em over? Nobody'd ever find 'em."

"Why bother? Nobody's around in this blasted furnace of a hellhole, anyway. Open that big vein in their throats and let 'em wander off to die. If anybody does find 'em, they'll think they got snake-bit."

"Best idea yet. Let's sort 'em out."

"I want the Injun's three along—them's good horseflesh." Red-beard yanked down his black leather hat.

"With our three, that makes six. We'll take two from the rest fer pack er trade."

They left five ponies tied, and went along in front of them. In a moment, bright streams of blood flowed steadily down their necks. The animals didn't seem to make much of it, but took a few steps away when untied, and when the outlaws mounted and led their diminished string away, stood there weakly. Soon they would drop to their knees and settle to the ground, out of their misery, food for coyotes and buzzards.

After a few miles of travel, the men began to relax. The pudgy renegade rode up beside red-beard. "I keep wonderin' what happened he got his throat cut. He was allus pretty sharp on the look-around."

"Hell, some Injun got him, same one carried off the woman. It's got me, what took place. No shots, no noise. It shore didn't take long, neither. We wasn't away but a short spell chasin' after that boy."

"I never thought of him gettin' killed!" the other marveled. "He allus done it to somebody else."

"You damn sure the boy's dead?"

"Hell, yes. I got lead in him. 'Sides, he ain't got no reason to trail us. His girl's killed, his pardners is dead, and if he ain't dead, he'll be too weak to foller. I'm jist sorry he ain't laid out down there with the others. Don't fret about him! Jist keep yer eyes peeled for whoever kilt the boss and packed off that girl. I figger they'll be after our hair and the plunder they know we got with us."

"Yeah . . . I'm willin' to bet they been on our trail since we left. Redskins're sneaky. U.S. Army can't kill 'em off too soon to suit me."

The two riders, uneasy, kept their outfit on the move, red-beard in the lead, until they found an open place near a seep from the lava to camp for the night.

As he squatted and cooked what they had, the smaller man complained again that they had too much stock traveling with them. It looked suspicious.

"Fer Christ's sake, quit yer belly-achin'!" red-beard told him. "We'll trade some of 'em soon er sell 'em. Nobody's gonna bother us in this part of Oregon. Start thinkin' like a trader 'stead of a thief. Jist put in yer noggin an' keep it there that yer a trader an' yuh got ponies bought er traded fer. Savvy?"

"I savvy. But what'll happen if somebody spots those speckled ponies and asks what happened to the Injun owned 'em?"

"Wait'll the time comes—and I'll bet it never does. Ten chances to one we don't never meet nobody ever heerd of their outfit er that Injun. I'm goin' to forget ever'thing except that we ain't got that old boar hog along to gig us all the time. He allus was a cocklebur in the crotch of my pants, the way he give orders and cussed me out. I don't know 'bout you, but many's the time I'd like to cut his throat er shot him in the back."

"Yeah . . . that goes fer me, too. But it sure bothers me what happened to the girl an' who did the job on him."

"Injuns somewheres nearby, nothin' else but, I tell yuh! How they did it, we'll never know. Fergit it, an' let's eat."

"But s'pose they're trailin' us."

"Hell, we'll keep our eyes an' ears open and camp in the clear. I figger this way—they got the girl. If they live around here, maybe that's all they wanted. I got a hunch they're satisfied. The army's too clost for 'em to chance any more trouble with whites."

2

Riding back to Lewiston, Idaho, from the Lapwai Mission, where Walter Hill and his year-long companion, Jack Tate, the half-breed Indian boy, had gone to get Teeah, Hill won-

7

dered if he had done the right thing in encouraging Jack and Teeah to go back to the Willamette Valley to stay on the Turpins' ranch the following winter. Was he being guilty of playing God, interfering in certain people's lives because he thought his advice could avoid troubles that might lie ahead for them? After a few moments of contemplation, he shrugged off the thought and put his attention on planning the route the party might take as they journeyed west.

Mr. Turpin and his son, Roy, wanted Jack to guide them to Oregon's high desert lands through which Mr. Hill and Jack had come in the spring. The Turpins wanted to see if they could find an acreage they might homestead there, moving out of the Willamette Valley to establish a ranch in new, unsettled land.

It might be a good thing for him to leave the party before they crossed the Cascades, Mr. Hill thought, and let Jack guide the Turpins across the wide country. If everything went well, if Teeah and Jack and the Turpins trusted each other and grew compatible, he felt sure the winter and year ahead might be a rewarding time for the two young Indians, indeed might work to everyone's advantage.

But he decided not to suggest the split just yet. Maybe Turpin would think of it himself.

Rumors of Indian raids were prevalent in Lewiston. The Snakes, or Bannock, depending on who did the reporting, were raiding cattle herds south of the Blue Mountains and clear into the area known as Lake County in Oregon. A rancher south of the mining town, Day City, now in the process of changing its name to Canyon City, had claimed a loss of three hundred head to the "blasted red devils from over on the Snake."

Walter Hill kept this knowledge to himself as he mentally plotted the course on which Jack might lead the Turpin group to look for ranch sites. He himself planned to take the usual route back to The Dalles and the Hood River, then follow the Barlow Road back to Oregon City. If Carter and Smith and their sons, who had come to Lewiston with the Turpins, helping them drive cattle to market, wanted to go with him, they could make the trip as a party. Considering the amount of riffraff on the trails, and the deadly incidents he and Jack had been through together, it might not be wise for him to travel alone.

8

During their ride to Lewiston—Teeah on Jack's pack pony, Pardner—Jack and Teeah got acquainted all over again. Jack rode beside her on Booshway, who had been his father's pony, and told her of his travels and the big country he and Mr. Hill had traversed. When he related how they had killed outlaws, Teeah was not shocked; she took pride in the fact that Jack was now a warrior and could count many coups if he danced with the tribe. She had listened to her father and her uncles tell of raids in the Blackfeet country, and she knew of scalps the missionaries had never seen hidden in the lodges of her tribe.

Teeah looked forward to traveling and the new adventure with Jack. Stories told in the lodges when children were quiet and supposed to be asleep came to her mind. She too had wished she could go to the far buffalo country. Now she would travel through the land of the Cayuses, the Umatillas, and the various tribes that made up the Warm Springs country, and go to live awhile in the big river valley where the tribes did not have to migrate for their food supply. Fish could be found in its rivers; berries, acorns, and hazel nuts grew everywhere; and deer and elk lived there the year around. Jack told her that land was now settled with whites who had killed much game; the Indians worked for them and dried fish from the rivers.

Teeah did not want to go to the Indian school, but she would like to stay with the Turpins as long as Jack was there, too. To be with Jack was what she wanted. Her dread of living with white people and sharing their ways could only be tolerated if Jack shared it with her. Most of all, she wished she and Jack were to travel alone. How much fun it would be to ride into new country together, set up camp, and talk in the evenings. To hunt and fish and then move on, always seeing new country, had been the way of life for her people. It seemed natural to keep moving from place to place. Her thoughts ran ahead. If Jack took up cattle buying with Mr. Hill again, they could travel with him. Teeah liked Mr. Hill. Jack had told her how well they got along together and that Mr. Hill would like her, too. But for now, Teeah hoped the Turpins would be as nice to stay with as Jack seemed sure they would be.

Next day, the whole party grouped together south of town for final preparations. Mr. Hill would camp with Teeah and

Jack. The Turpins, Carter and his son Joe, and Smith and his son Tom would camp as they had coming up from the Willamette country. On their way to join the Turpin party, Mr. Hill quietly observed Jack and Teeah riding side by side, and he wondered how Teeah would fit in with them all. An Indian girl's presence among a group of white men and boys could cause continuing trouble. She might be considered fair game by some of them who had heard stories of "winter women" and the buying of Indian squaws of various tribes by trappers and traders.

Mr. Hill decided to size up the various personalities of this mixed party at once. If he sensed any suggestion of trouble, he would take Jack and Teeah with him and make other plans.

"Jack, I hope you and Teeah have brought along the things you'd need if by some unforeseen chance you might be separated from the Turpins," he said as they approached the meeting place.

"Mr. Hill, it wouldn't take much to keep up. We're used to living off what we find. Do you think we might have to leave the others somewhere on the trip?"

Walter Hill shook his head. "No," he reassured. "But lots of things can happen on a long trip, as this one might turn out to be. I know your father taught you to be prepared for the unexpected, and I hope you are, Jack."

When the Indian boy didn't answer, Mr. Hill's thoughts ran back to some of the unexpected things that had happened in his own life. Strange, most of his troubles had come from white men, not the Indians said to be troublemakers. It was true they had begun to raid various outlying ranches, driving off horses and cattle, and, if intercepted, shooting at their pursuers. But all Walter Hill's brushes with death had come from money-hungry misfits who perpetually dodged the sheriffs and in several cases had left mliitary service before their time was up.

Hill felt Jack and Teeah would be traveling with a fair group of citizens after he had seen and talked with them all around the campfire at the evening meal. He trusted John Turpin. With his two neighbors and their sons, the party was strong enough to discourage most booty-seekers. As long as they traveled the now much-used route to Oregon City, they would be reasonably safe. As he saw it, the Indian girl,

Teeah, was the only member who might cause friction eventually, but such were the hazards of traveling, and there was nothing much he could do about that.

The Turpin party talked a good deal about country they might want to explore for ranch sites during the coming year, the three men discussing the types of land and ranching possibilities Jack and Mr. Hill had seen as they crossed the eastern slope of the Cascade Mountains. John Turpin itched to see it all. He imagined the wide, grassy flats, a meandering stream to water hay meadows. In his mind's eye he envisioned herds of cattle grazing on open prairie away from the ranch while hay for the winter was being cut and stacked there. Walter Hill had assured him that in many places there was no real use for hay sheds. Lack of rain in the fall was an asset; when snow came, it would blanket the stacks, which would be fed out before spring thaws and showers came. Ranch buildings would consist of the house, barns for the milk stock, saddlehorses, and the plow teams in the winter. Fences could be made of rails split from straight-trunked yellow pine trees or lodgepole timber on the slopes.

As far as Indian troubles went, in much of that country they would find little to fear. The Army of the West had begun to move the tribes to various reservations, always keeping a watchful eye on young warriors who might cause trouble. Roads were already being laid out by army transports and stock-drivers. Mr. Hill had assured the party that the north-and-south route from The Dalles on the Columbia to Fort Klamath near the California border was now being used weekly and soon would be daily. An east-west road led from the Fort Klamath route across the sagebrush desert to the Boise Valley. Hundreds of cattle had already been driven over it, and before long there was certain to be a stage route established there. Yes, the country was being settled rapidly, and now was the time for Turpin to go in and pick a good ranch location. In another year or so it might be hard to find what he wanted.

By the time they reached Fort Walla Walla, John Turpin determined to see some of this new country before he returned to his ranch in the Willamette Valley.

He spoke with Hill. "You know, Walter, I think I'd like to split off purty soon, take a gander at some of the Oregon country you've told us about. Where do you think?"

11

"John, to see grasslands you could take off from right here, or you can wait until we're farther down the Columbia. If you want high flats raising up to mountains, here's where you should turn south, but you must consider the possibility of Indian trouble. Now, we won't be out of Cayuse country for some time. If you wait a day or so, go on to The Dalles, and then split, you'll move between two tribes, the Umatillas and the Warm Springs branch. So far, they havn't given much cause for alarm. There's a whale of a lot of country to settle in there, although I suspect it'll be pretty well taken up in another year or so."

"You really think it might be best to wait a few days before we separate?"

"I would. You're sure you want to take a look this fall?"

"Yeah . . . guess I'm gettin' itchy to see it."

"Then go see it and get it over with. All of you going?"

"I don't think so. I think Roy and I will take Joe and Tom with us. Jack and Teeah will be along, too, of course—that'll make six of us—a purty good bunch. Teeah says that with a little help she can cook for the outfit. I kin give her a hand while the young fellers git the stock taken care of."

"Well, Mr. Turpin, it seems like you've already figured out what it will take. Do you have any idea how far south you might travel before cutting west through the mountains?"

"There's supposed to be a cutoff going west from the place called the Bend. That trail goes up past the lava beds, winds down the west slope, and comes out on the McKenzie River."

"I think your turnoff will come before you reach the Bend. You'll find you can take a trail at a place where you cross the one to Prine City. Old Man Prine's used it to take cattle through. He's running several thousand head here and there in that country."

"I've heard of him," Turpin mused. "I hear he's quite a trader."

"Yeah," Hill replied. "Well-thought-of, but hard to deal with. He started small just like you fellows aim to. Cheap cows, cheap feed, a few good years, and you're on your way to riches."

The Turpin party couldn't wait to reach The Dalles. Impatient to see new country and look for a place where they could run a large herd of cattle, they decided to turn south at

Butter Creek. How it got that name, no one in the party knew nor cared.

Before they split up to go their separate ways, Mr. Hill found an opportunity to talk with Jack alone, Teeah busy with Mr. Turpin's help at fixing the evening meal, the other three boys having a last swim in a backwater of the river, and their fathers taking care of pack animals. Hill sensed Jack felt reluctant to leave his company but hesitated to say so.

"Jack," he began, "we've come a long way together—you've been a good pardner to me, pulled more than your weight. I expect you to continue to do the same with Mr. Turpin, but my feeling is you're not over the hump in your dealings with white people yet and, if I get the message, it would be almost impossible for you to take up with the other side. So here you are, still betwixt and between, not knowing whether to come or go. You aren't the only one who's ever been in such a fix—so don't git to feeling too sorry about it.

"One thing that will always be a big help to you is the good advice you got from your father about that, yes, and from old Chief Thunderbolt and Colonel Craig. But as I see it, you're more on your own now than at any time since your father was killed by those Sheepeaters up on the Salmon. Turpin's a good man, but that don't make him infallible. You will have to look out for yourself as well as Teeah, Jack."

"Mr. Hill, what does 'infallible' mean?"

"An infallible person is somebody who don't make mistakes. A fellow who's always sure of himself and what he does. Get what I mean?"

"I think I do. Maybe Mr. Turpin doesn't know about things that could happen and thinks everything will be all right."

"Yes, that's pretty close to it. Jack, remember when those first two crooks, Hodges and his pardner, tried to rob us? Well, Mr. Turpin and the boys would have been fair meat for their pot. There's another thing I want to mention—you'll have Teeah along. A single girl or woman traveling alone among three or more men is almost certain to cause trouble. I have noticed that you and Teeah don't touch each other very much even when you're alone. I have watched the boys looking at you and Teeah, trying to figure out if you're more than just friends. Do you know what I mean?"

"Yeah, I think I do. They wonder if we sleep together."

"That's about it. I know Mr. Turpin will keep an eye on Roy and the other two, but he can't be around all the time. And you'll meet up with other boys and men who'll try to force their way on her. That's when you'll be in a tough spot. If they push too hard and you try to interfere, they'll resent it because you're half Indian, too. So, Jack, that's going to add to your responsibilities. I had thought of not leaving the party but decided it's time you were going off on your own, learning more about the way things are apt to be for you all your life. You've had a pretty good preparation. Just figure you're always in hostile country and be ready."

"Paw told me something like that. I see what you mean, Mr. Hill. Paw didn't think those Sheepeaters were anywhere around when they came up and killed him. And Memaloose didn't know Badger was hiding with the rifle, either."

"You have the idea. Of course, you can't keep track of everything, but you can keep alert yourself and watch out for Teeah. Remember that if you stay alive you can help others, but if you're killed or put out of action, you can do nothing. Jack, you have survived and you've learned by doing so. It was you saved our lives when I got careless with Hodges. I have no doubt they would have killed us both that day. I expect you to come out of any mix-up alive, unless someone's able to nail you first."

Jack fell silent, thinking that Mr. Hill had some idea that trouble for all of them lay ahead. The big adventure of leading the party to a place where the Turpins might establish a ranch began to take on complications Jack hadn't considered.

"You think we and the Turpins might run into men like Hodges or the ones who tried to hold us up down near Fort Klamath?" he asked at last.

"There's always that chance, Jack. And you're apt to find that even friends are willing to take advantage of you. In my dealings with people I've found that once you have money, goods, cattle, or horses, someone always gets greedy and tries to get part of what you own. There're so many changes going on that I can't keep up with all of it. All kinds of people are moving into and coming through this western country. Where a year ago I saw ten cattle buyers there are now fifty, and where one or two families looked for places to start a ranch or farm there are now ten or twenty."

Mr. Hill looked toward the fire where Teeah worked and

wondered for a moment if he had talked too much about Jack's future problems. Maybe he was too pessimistic about the boy's future. He couldn't play God to Jack all his life; still, he saw problems ahead for them both that he didn't care to even think about. A half-breed and a young, good-looking full-blooded Indian girl going into strange country with one white man and three half-grown boys . . .

Roy Turpin, with Joe and Tom, ran up from the river where they had enjoyed a swim. All three youths were now reliable and would become steady men, good solid citizens who would help stabilize the state. Still, though Oregon might not have the troubles that the southern states experienced, if war came these young fellows' lives remained uncertain. Trouble seemed everywhere if a person looked ahead, Mr. Hill sighed.

"Well, Jack, maybe I've talked too much, but I couldn't leave without my own warning. Like your father said, keep your knife sharp and your rifle ready. Don't trust too much to luck. I'll look for you at the Turpin ranch in about two months. In the meantime, I'll be picking up cattle over in the valley on the way down to the junction."

"We should be there before then, Mr. Hill. It all depends where and how far Mr. Turpin wants to go. I don't think he has much idea of what he wants just now, do you?"

"No, and I believe that the more he sees, the less he will know. It's too big a country for someone who's been a dirt farmer, too many places he might settle. Don't worry about it, Jack. Just ride along and look out for Teeah and yourself. If Turpin can't find a place to throw down his bed, that's his hard luck. You can always take someone else in to look for a ranch."

"Maybe that's what I'll be doing myself in the next few years. I want to find a place where Teeah and I can settle down and raise a few cows and horses someday."

Next morning, Mr. Turpin and his five young riders gathered their mounts and pack ponies for departure. Roy Turpin rubbed Shep's head between his hands and scratched his ears before he put foot in the stirrup. Carter whistled the dog to him as he and Smith and Mr. Hill started west down the river road, raising their hands in farewell as the others turned south.

15

3

In hot weather as the trail left the Umatilla river valley and climbed over the benchlands, Turpin's party sweated, and the ponies fluttered their nostrils occasionally to clear them of dust. There were no mosquitoes to irritate them this far from the river, and at night it cooled down rapidly. Occasional riders the party met assured Mr. Turpin that the grasslands here were already spoken for. Turpin could not envision such vast areas of benchland ever producing anything except grazing for cattle and horses. Used to the tree-lined creeks and rivers of the Willamette Valley, he was not intrigued by the idea of a farm and home place where the wind blew as constantly as here.

Teeah grew accustomed to traveling with the crew. Occasionally she rode with the Turpins and let Jack roam ahead searching for a better way, but also as actual cover for his trying to spot possible trouble. He had become used to being alert for the unusual in his travels with Mr. Hill and his father when he was younger. When Jack and Teeah rode together, they could talk and discuss things that concerned them alone, and Jack passed on to her the gist of Mr. Hill's advice and warning.

"Teeah, Mr. Hill said we should always be on the lookout for trouble. You know I have the little gun—nobody else knows about it. I wish I could give it to you, but I can't, because I'll be the one any troublemaker would try to git first. But kin you carry that Green River skinning knife where people couldn't see it? You got to keep it in a sheath or it'll cut right through yer clothing or hide. I honed it like my Paw showed me, and it'll cut hair or whiskers like nothin'. If you ever have to use it, do like that old woman you told me about said, the one who killed the brave that stole her. Do it quick and do it right!" Jack's hand came across in a flat, chopping motion.

"I will, Jack," Teeah told him. "Do you think we might get held up?"

16

"There's always that chance. Mr. Hill wasn't too sure it was a good idea to split up the party, but Mr. Turpin wanted to see the country, thinkin' he might find a place to settle. I don't think it'll be Indians we have trouble with on this trip. Where we're going they're pretty well settled down, and they're watched. But we want to be prepared for anything."

"Mr. Turpin and the others don't seem to think we'll have any trouble at all," Teeah demurred.

"Neither did Mr. Hill when Hodges and his men showed up. They had the drop on Mr. Hill before he knew what was going on."

They rode along in silence, Teeah thinking of a time when just she and Jack could ride into new country, places they could stop and camp, high above plains and benchlands where pines and tamaracks grew, cold waters rushed and gurgled, trout in their clear pools. She imagined their camp at the edge of some meadow where elk bugled in the early mornings and mists arose like gray shadows. She and Jack could kill deer and elk, work together to dry and smoke the meat. She could tan and soften hides while Jack made snowshoes for winter travel in the high country.

Jack dreamed his dreams too. He wanted horses and cattle, a stout log house where they could live, and corrals in which to start their herds. No thoughts of children entered his mind, nor of the protection they might need from people who resented a pair of Indians' possession of land and cattle. Jack had lived with white people in the Willamette Valley and he wanted the same things they enjoyed. Now all he owned was old Booshway, Pardner, and Speck, the packhorse that carried his few personal possessions. Oh, Mr. Hill was keeping some money for him, but that meant nothing at the moment. Jack had so little experience with money that having some somewhere was to him like knowing rain might come to the desert someday, but you couldn't count on it at any given time.

Three days after leaving Mr. Hill and his party, company appeared from behind. Roy noticed them first, having stopped to look back after they climbed to a benchtop on the plateau. Three men leading a pack pony, themselves mounted, came into sight on the back trail. Roy watched for a moment to make sure, then rode to rejoin his father.

"Pa, there's some people on the trail back of us."

17

"Yeah? You sure?"

"I counted three riders and one packhorse, but they're so far away I couldn't tell much about 'em."

"Well, they'll ketch up if it's us they want to see. When they do, you and the boys be careful about what you say until we sort 'em out."

"Jack and Teeah ought to know, hadn't they?"

"No sweat about that. We'll jist ride along and see what happens, not borry trouble. Maybe it's good company we got coming. We could use some help in case them Warm Springs Indians decide to add to their horse herd."

The Turpins caught up with Jack and Teeah at a creek with a good grazing meadow near. They found that Jack had killed a deer and had it skinned, the meat already hanging in the shade to cool out. Teeah worked on the hide, cutting and scraping off bits of flesh and fat, beside a small fire that burned off to one side, sending a thin, scraggly column of blue smoke into the air. Horses nickered back and forth as the riders drew near.

Mr. Turpin swung down from his horse and grinned at Teeah. "Fresh meat for supper, it looks like. Good! I'm hungry. You going to fry the liver tonight?"

Teeah looked up, nodded, and smiled. She didn't like to talk much, ashamed of her broken English except when with Jack or Mr. Hill. She was learning fast, but sometimes got her words mixed up; when listeners laughed at her confusion, it embarrassed her. Now she was relieved when Turpin spoke to Jack.

"Boy, we got three fellers trailin' us. They'll ketch up pretty quick. They been on our trail for mebbe four, five miles. Roy saw 'em after we climbed the last bench. We'll have to size 'em up."

Jack nodded acknowledgment and thought: Now's when I wish Mr. Hill was along. He can sort strangers out fast.

To the half-breed it seemed unusual that travelers followed their trail. Meeting people was different. Men from the Willamette Valley or farther south used this route as a cutoff to Fort Walla Walla but not to head for the valley or for Fort Klamath—there were easier ways to reach there. True, they could be on the search for land, like the Turpins, but that didn't make a lot of sense either. Jack tried not to show his concern.

18

He became more suspicious at once when the travelers rode into camp. The apparent leader, a great hulk of man stooped and bent over the army saddle on his long-legged black horse, required more than a casual glance. Bearded and dirty, a wide flat hat drooping over heavy eyebrows to shade narrow, lidded eyes, he aroused a viewer's uneasiness. Blood ran from his black, rangy animal's flanks from spur marks or some cutting instrument, but the beast bore no brand. Jack's attention turned back to the rider as he spoke.

"Well, folks, we sorta figgered we was trailin' somebody but never give it a thought thar mought be a cook in the bunch. Kinda missed squaw cookin' since last winter. This'n looks purty good fer warmin' soogans, too. Whar you fellers headed?"

Turpin looked straight into the man's face. "Going across country to the McKenzie turnoff. That girl you see is in my care. She's a Nez Percé from the Lapwai Mission, going to make her home with us. The Indian boy, Jack Tate, is our guide. My name is John Turpin, this here's my son Roy, and over there by the fire is Joe Carter and Tom Smith, sons of my neighbors."

"Well, ain't that somep'n. I'm called Old Stubbs. This red-beard feller's Ort Galley an' t'other is Ace Diller a-ridin' that glass-eyed paint. We're driftin' on the same trail you fellers are. Mought be good fer us to kinda herd along together. I heered them red bastards up ahead're out itchin' fer hair an' ponies."

"If you're in any hurry, we won't hold you up," Turpin replied. "We aim to travel slow, size up the country."

"Naw, we ain't runnin' no race. The trail's jist a place to go through er stop an' sweat. We might camp down the crick a ways. I see somebody got lucky an' come up with some meat. We hain't seed a thing clost enough to butcher. Even our hawg meat is drippin' grease."

Mr. Turpin thought quickly. Might as well be generous.

"Get your camp made and I'll send a chunk over to help out until you shoot one. We're getting into deer country now."

"Wal, I must say that's moughty good of you-all. Ort, we'll move down crick a spell, git set fer the night," Stubbs said to the red-bearded rider behind him.

The three moved downstream. Jack caught a backward

19

look from the other rider, a short, heavyset man Stubbs had called Ace. The half-breed's eyes sought Mr. Turpin. If the rancher felt uneasy about the newcomers, he didn't show it.

Of all the people in the Turpin camp, Teeah felt most uneasy. Her Indian woman's instinct told her these men would try to possess her. She glanced across at Jack and saw that he sensed danger, too. Teeah's elbow brushed the slight hardness beneath her left arm where Jack's razor-sharp knife rested. Having the weapon gave her a certain reassurance, and knowing Jack felt the same way about the strangers helped to give her confidence as she thought about a possible confrontation.

Roy was chosen as the one to take a quarter of venison down to the strangers' camp. His father called him to one side. "Keep yer eyes and ears open, and don't talk too much. When you come back, wait till we're alone to tell me what you think."

Roy Turpin found Stubbs half-lying, half-sitting, his back against the butt of a big yellow pine. He chewed a wad of tobacco and, as Roy came up with the venison, spat a brown stream of juice and saliva at a scurrying ant.

"Well, fellers, here comes one of the pups with meat fer you hungry hounds," he announced. "Hand it to the grub-burners, kid, then tell me somep'n 'bout what goes on in yer outfit."

The man named Ace squatted by the fire. He took the meat. "Looks good," he said. "You kill it?"

Roy stared down at the stocky shoulders. "No, Jack brought it in. He'd gone ahead looking for one."

"Jack's the Indian kid?"

"Yeah, he's half white. His father was a trader, Bill Tate."

The man with the scraggly red beard had come to listen. "The hell he was! I've heerd Old Stubbs talk of Bill Tate," he said how.

"Yes, Jack's been over this trail before. He knows some of the country we're goin' to look at."

"Well, ain't that somep'n! Better go see Old Stubbs, a-settin' there waitin' fer you." Ace's grin was sly. "Cross him an' he riles easy-like," he concluded.

Stubbs, still chewing tobacco, pulled his old greasy black hat over the bushy eyebrows. "Well, young feller, you through yer chawin' with my cooks?"

"I guess so. Ace asked me a few questions about where we were going."

"Yuh shore took yer sweet time gittin' back to see me."

"I'm sorry, Mr. Stubbs. I didn't think you were in any hurry. Is it important?"

"Kid, anything I ask fer is damned important, an' don't fergit it. How soon you fellers gittin' out in the mornin'?"

"We usually leave soon after daylight, get a good start before sunup."

Roy saw Stubbs's bearded lips twist in a lazy grimace. "Well, tell yer daddy if we ain't up, we'll see to ketch him later. Mought as well hang behind so we kin s'prise any trouble. Don't figger tham two redskins yuh got with yuh is spies fer some scalp-crazy Injuns, do ye?"

"No chance of that, Mr. Stubbs!" Roy's tone was firm. "We've known Jack for almost a year now, and he's traveled a lot with us. Teeah's his friend. She'll stay with us in the valley for another year."

"Well, if that's the way she is, then that'll be the way she goes. Me, I don't trust none of them dog-eaters. It's bad enough to stand the smell of a squaw yuh got to cook for yuh and sleep with." He guffawed. "Go on back an' tell yer old man what I jist said."

As Roy walked the short distance back to his father's camp, he felt a twinge of worry about the three men camped close to them at nightfall. And Old Stubbs had said he'd follow and catch up with them on the trail tomorrow. His father wouldn't like that, Roy thought. But the trail had to be open to anyone who wanted to use it. He saw his father walking slowly to meet him.

"Well, son, what happened down there? I could see you talkin' with Stubbs."

"Paw, I'm scared of that bunch. I believe they mean to follow us no matter where we go. Stubbs said to tell you that if we left early they'd catch up to us later. Nobody, not one of 'em, thanked me for the meat. The little guy, Ace, said Stubbs got real mad if he was crossed, and Stubbs told me anything he said was real important and for me not to forget it. I don't like bein' so close to them, Pa."

"Well, I'll talk it over with Jack," Turpin replied. "One thing we can do is take turns on a night watch. We mustn't

21

let on we're doin' that, though. We'll act as normal as we can—maybe they were just bluffing you."

"Not Stubbs. He's a mean man. The other two do all the work. Ort, the red-bearded one, said he'd heard of Jack's father, that Stubbs knew him."

Turpin nodded. "Don't fret about it, son. Things'll turn out for the best. We'll ride along tomorrow and be prepared for anything that might come up. We outnumber them two to one. That ought to be good enough odds."

Over at the Stubbs camp, Ace did the cooking. He sliced some steaks off the deer haunch, and began to fry them in a skillet. The coffeepot boiled up; when the grounds settled, Ort poured a cupful and carred it to Stubbs.

"Well, chief, what do yuh think of our chances?"

"I don't know about you fellers, but I think I'll have somebody else to cook my grub in another day er so, somebody to warm my bed, too."

"You figger it that close, do yuh?"

"Why not? They're all ripe fer the pickin'. Only reason fer not doin' the job here is we're still too close to the fort an' we don't know fer sure if some more they know're follerin' er if they're about to meet up with somebody. Let's let 'em git closer to Injun country so we kin let the redskins get the blame."

"I'll go along with that." Ort laughed. "Set quiet, I'll bring yuh a plate of grub. Ace cut lots of steak—we kin fill up tonight."

"Tell Ace we'll sleep late, let that bunch get going head of us far enough so we kin make the plans."

Stubbs chuckled to himself as he slobbered over the meat, grinding chunks between his teeth, occasionally wiping greasy saliva from his whiskers with his sleeve, happy to have an opportunity for a tussle with real live meat. He thought of how he'd take care of that big flat-footed sod-stomper. It might be fun just to get him wrapped in his arms and bend him over backward until he snapped his trunk. When he caught that young squaw, he'd teach her some tricks he knew. Ort and Ace could wait for their fun with her. He'd let them plunder the packs.

Over in Turpin's camp, things were not the same as they had been before Stubbs and his crew came into sight. Even their good hot meal could not disperse the tension. Jack felt

22

Mr. Turpin and the boys stayed too close together, huddled like sheep he'd seen farmers bunch for shearing. He and Mr. Hill always stayed separated from each other just a bit: even when they slept, so that both could not be covered by one man's gun. He sat apart, then saw Mr. Turpin glance in his direction, curious as to why Jack avoided the company by the fire. Teeah, too, had split away. She sat some distance from Jack. The two had instinctively separated.

During the night, there was nothing to startle them. Mr. Turpin, Joe, and Jack changed places in turn to sit to one side and keep silent watch until morning. While Jack was awake, alone with his thoughts, Teeah, silent as the owl that drifts through the trees looking for sleeping birds, came over to him and sat close. Neither spoke, only brushed hands and listened to the night sounds. Then, silently as a shadow, she moved back to her place under the trees away from the fire, but before she left she took Jack's hand and moved it to her side to feel the knife concealed under her doeskin jacket.

On the trail, the next day passed without incident. They saw mountains far in the distance and Jack said they would probably reach the north-south military road by sometime the following day. He decided that when they arrived there, he would suggest to Mr. Turpin that they turn south and follow that road until they shook off Stubbs's outfit.

So far on the trip, Turpin had not found just the land he sought, although there were many places he might have chosen to stop and settle. Just what the rancher had in mind he somehow could not express to Jack. So the day passed and nightfall found them camping by another small stream. Stubbs and his men had not shown up; nevertheless, the campsite was chosen with great care. They had just eaten their evening meal when Jack saw Booshway lift his head and look back up the trail. Stubbs and his companions must be coming.

Jack and Teeah sat off to one side, Jack's rifle close at hand, loaded and ready. Mr. Turpin did not seem worried. His gun stood leaning against a tree beside him, Roy and his rifle not far away. The other two boys, busy near the fire, washed up dishes. Packs near them supported two rifles.

As Stubbs rode up, his roving eyes noted everything. He decided not to push his luck that night.

Next morning, Turpin's group saw the sun shining on two

white peaks far to the west. They knew a trail passed between them and into the Willamette Valley, but before the travelers came to it they would have to reach the military road. It seemed to Jack they should get there around noon. He and Turpin scanned the country ahead. Its rising terrain indicated a watercourse which would be the Deschutes River. From crudely drawn maps they had seen and from travelers' conversations they knew the road would be on the near side of the river gorge and that they could not cross the river chasm for many miles—it was too steep, too deep, for any human's descent to the water. They would follow the road south, and perhaps, meeting other travelers now and then, discourage Stubbs from an attempt at robbery and murder.

Before they reached the military road, they saw dust rising, either from a passing stagecoach or an army escort riding rapidly north. The sight renewed the Turpin party's confidence that they would be fairly safe from attack if they reached and stayed on this traveled road. Surely Stubbs and his crew wouldn't be so foolish as to commit a crime with other travelers and army escorts so likely. They wound down from the sage and juniper benchlands, feeling more hopeful.

The army road, rough, rocky, and dusty, crawled across the landscape like a confused worm, twisting and winding to avoid lava rock and sudden deep ravines left by the receding floods of ancient times. But it was a real road that had seen considerable travel of late. The party rode close and grouped together to plan where they might camp that night and to talk of whom they might first meet on the new trail.

It was not to be friendly folk. To their surprise and dismay, they found Stubbs and his two cohorts riding into the road from the east just ahead of them.

4

"Wal, I'll be blasted fer a saint if it ain't Turpin an' his litter of pups!" Stubbs shouted. "We done cut across lookin' fer redskin signs, an' jist as luck had it, we come in 'bout where you did." His voice boomed as the three rode close. "Bein' as

24

we're together agin, we mought's well continue the same. That way we'd have us a leetle more fire power iffen we meet up with some of them thievin' Malhoors er Bannockys. Real throat-cutters, they is, horse thieves mostly. They'll kill fer fun er feathers. Worst of all the tribes hereabout, I say."

"Well, Mr. Stubbs," Turpin replied, "I didn't realize those tribes ranged over here so far. I thought the Warm Springs branch controlled this country."

"An' didja, now? Turpin, yuh got lots to learn 'bout this part of old Orygun. She's a big country, squirmin' with vermin. Soon as the army gits them redskins killed off, it'll be better fer us white folks. I hain't goin' to settle in these parts till the last one's shot and fed to the buzzards."

"I expect that won't be for some time, Mr. Stubbs."

"Aw, it'll come. But old Whitman and that mealymouthed Spalding upset things right when they tried to talk religion into those red devils. Now folks're comin' in to settle and they'll raise a bunch of brats. They shouldn't never've come to this country. It's already sp'iled for tradin' an' trappin', and now the game's done gone."

Everyone rode south in silence for a spell; then Ace drifted back alongside of Jack and looked over the half-breed's outfit carefully before he asked, "I hear yer paw was old Bill Tate."

"Yes, he was a trader around Fort Hall."

"Heerd he got kilt up on the Salmon. Who done it?"

"I saw two Sheepeaters shoot him."

"The hell yuh say! Where was you at the time?"

"Across the river. They didn't know I was there."

"Must've been rough on you."

"Yeah, I had to make my own way out of there. Where you and Stubbs headed?"

"Just moseyin' south, maybe to Californy. You shot meat for tonight's supper yet?"

"There's enough left over to do us. When that's gone, I'll get more."

Ace gigged his mount and moved up closer to Stubbs.

Jack knew Ace had deliberately dropped back to see how he was armed and to size up the rest of the Turpin riders, see where their rifles were and just how they might be prepared for trouble. If something broke loose right now, Stubbs and his men would meet lead. Too many guns here loaded and ready. If Stubbs decided to jump them, Jack thought it would be later.

There was no graze for the ponies close to the roadway. Hundreds of horses and cattle had passed that way during the summer and left nothing edible along the route. If they camped, it would have to be off to one side where they could find water and some browse. Stubbs brought up the subject, saying to Mr. Turpin that he had not been over this part of the trail and had no idea of a good place to camp. Then he suggested they send one of his crew and one of Turpin's boys ahead to locate water and feed off the road at a place where they could camp for the night. Finally, Ort and Joe Carter offered to go.

Jack watched Mr. Turpin during the conversation and saw that he did not seem particularly concerned about splitting up the party, his fears of Mr. Stubbs evidently lessened now. But Jack knew that if Stubbs was planning something, this could be the beginning. He dropped back to the rear, where Teeah rode with the pack stock.

Ort and Joe soon met three bearded riders, their two pack ponies following behind them. The picks and shovels atop the canvas-wrapped packs indicated they were miners or prospectors headed for the Idaho diggings to seek their fortunes. The leader held up his hand in greeting, and exchange of information began.

"There's a camp spot up ahead another ten or twelve miles," the rider offered. "Yuh break over this hump, you kin see behind us. As yuh go down, a crick comes in from yer left. Hit ain't much, but as the valley flattens, there's willers an' some feed, too, but most of hit is fed down clost by stock comin' from the south. I'd say turn when yuh hit the crick and foller it back up a ways where there's some medder fer browse. We camped there last night. The only trouble we had was from a few skeeters."

Ort took up the questioning. "You seen many travelers on the trail?"

"Not many. A few fellers goin' our way, mostly with stock an' lookin' fer places to run more. A stage runs by here oncet a day. Hit passed us goin' north early this mornin'. Next one'll come by 'bout dark. Allus drivin' hell-fer-leather, tryin' to keep ahead of the dust, hit seems like."

"Since we know where to camp now, we mought a's well

26

ride along back together to our outfit," Ort said. "It's comin' this way."

After they met and talked with Mr. Turpin and sized up the two parties, the miners went on their way north to the river and fort where the road turned east. The leader turned in his saddle and remarked almost casually, "Boys, yuh better take a last look at that crew—there's a bunch of sheep there headed fer shearin', effen I'm not mistaken."

"Yer too optimistic, Bobb," another rider told him. "What that greasy, squinch-eyed wolf called Stubbs is goin' to do is cut their throats, drink their blood, an' take ever'thing they got. Some sorry bunch of homesteaders won't never find out what happened to Pappy and the boys." He shook his head. "How they ever teamed up with that bunch of cutthroats, we'll never know." The three went on their way.

The two parties found the little stream and camping place just as the miners said. At a wide area with graze for the horses, Stubbs proposed, "You and yer pups take this place, Turpin. There's feed right across the crick, an' a good spot to shanty up right here next to the lava wall. Me'n my crew'll go on up the crick a ways."

"Well, that's a good of you, Stubbs. We'll leave fairly early in the mornin' so's not to disturb you." Turpin smiled.

"Hell, we been figgerin' we jist might git up 'fore the sage-hens do in the mornin' and light out. Ever'body's in a lot better shape here on this road. No need, as I see it, to be edgy anymore. Me'n the boys aim to take out fer the Californy country."

Jack did not hear this part of the conversation, but learned of it later from Mr. Turpin. Silent, Jack decided that, if anything, the three were going ahead to waylay them at a more desirable place. Perhaps meeting the miners had had something to do with their decision to split away. He said nothing, but took the ponies across the creek, hobbling Booshway and Pardner. Speck wouldn't stray far from them. Finished, he climbed up the rocky sidehill to a place where he could see the Stubbs camp. If they had it in mind to slip back and bushwhack the Turpins, this would be the ideal place. Mentally Jack planned where he and Teeah would sleep and be on guard. He felt uneasy about this camp spot. Something about Stubbs's saying the parties would split up and go their

27

separate ways didn't make sense to him. With the lay of the land well in mind, he went back to camp.

Everyone in the party seemed more cheerful tonight. But Jack's fears gripped him and he followed Mr. Turpin as he walked to get water from the stream, at first undecided what to say, almost afraid Turpin would make fun of him.

"Mr. Turpin, have you thought of kind of staying spread out tonight?"

"No, Jack, I hadn't thought of doing that. What's on your mind, boy?"

"I don't trust Stubbs. He's got something in mind. That's why he talked of splitting up. Mr. Turpin, if they decided to jump us, there couldn't be a better place than right here."

"What do yuh think we should do?"

"For one thing, keep guard tonight. Don't bunch up at any time until after they leave us in the morning. We outnumber them now—they couldn't kill all of us the first round, and Stubbs won't take any chance of gittin' killed himself if he kin avoid it."

"Yeah. So far, so good . . . then what?"

"We'll have to wait and see, never forgetting he's sure to make some move to jump us."

"Jack, do you really believe that?" Turpin was skeptical. "I think Stubbs has given up any plan he might've had to rob us. Being near the road and so close to other people has discouraged him, boy."

"No. You're wrong! I don't trust him at all. We have too many things he wants—guns, ponies, grub. They know you have money with you, and they all want to get hold of Teeah." Jack's voice remained steady.

"Well, I guess I sensed that, too. You got any more suggestions?"

"You go ahead and make camp. Make sure all guns are loaded. Keep spread out as much as possible. While you're eating, I'll slip back up the hill like I'm lookin' for deer and watch their camp. If everything looks all right, I'll come in at dark."

Jack found a vantage point where he could overlook Stubbs's camp and not be seen, but there was no way he could approach close enough to hear what was being said there. He could see the three were in no hurry to settle down for the night meal. They squatted and talked. It looked to

28

Jack as though Stubbs was laying out some plan or giving orders. Questions were asked occasionally by Ort and Ace. Finally Ace set to making a fire while Ort carried water up from the creek. Stubbs had settled himself against a lava rock, his greasy old hat over his eyes.

Jack stayed hidden until he saw the three spread saddle blankets and prepare to lie down for the night, then made his way back to his own camp and asked Teeah for a bite to eat. While he ate, he told Mr. Turpin and the Indian girl what he had seen and what he thought Stubbs might do.

"They're bedded down for the night," he related. "From the way they acted, I don't believe they'll do anything until tomorrow or maybe even later on. But I don't trust Stubbs. Even if they leave early, we should be prepared for them to try to kill and rob us. Let's sleep spread out, and tomorrow night do the same. I'll stay up the trail where they'd have to pass if they come at us during the night. Don't look for me in the morning. I'll stay where I can watch the camp until I'm sure they're leaving."

In falling darkness, Jack soon left to settle down and watch the trail to Stubbs's camp.

While Jack watched from the rocky hillside earlier, Stubbs had laid out his plan for the morning.

"I'm t'ard of waitin' fer good grub an' plunder," he began. "Old Turpin an' his bunch of half-growed pups's right fer pickin', I tell yuh. We'll git up early, leave here, and git to their camp while they're eatin' er packin' their plunder. We ride in, nice an' easy, spread out jist a mite, all guns loaded an' the pistols primed. I'll take keer of Turpin. Ace, you an' Ort pick off the pups, one at a time. If we work it right, there ain't goin' to be guns in or near their hands, but ours'll be loaded and cocked on the saddles crost our knees. We got to git three with our first shots.

"Now, if we're lucky, they all go down, but I've seen some as don't. That's whar we use knives er the leetle guns. Remember their guns, wherever they are, is apt to be loaded and primed too. After you fire yers, git one of theirs an' use it. Now, I'll go first. You boys watch me. My sign for ac-tion'll be when I reach up and pull my hat off'n my head like I'm makin' a bow to old Turpin. Then I'll blast him—I want to hear yer guns right quick after that."

The two listeners nodded assent. Stubbs rolled his chew

29

around his mouth and splattered a rock with a liquid spurt. "Leave the Injuns to me unless you have to kill 'em to save yer own hides," he continued. "We'll keep the squaw fer a time, but I want the boy to play with to pay off what his daddy done to me oncet!"

"What'll we do with the carcasses, Stubbs?" Ort asked.

"Load 'em up, take 'em down to the canyon crost the road, and sling 'em overboard. Nobody'll ever climb down to where the buzzards'll be workin'. We'll sort out their plunder and move camp to where we kin hole up an' have some fun fer a day or so with our new cook, and that Injun pup fer a plaything."

Morning dimness changed to soft rosy light as the hills took on the rising sun's glow. The coyotes had finished their morning song when Ort gathered the horses and brought them to camp. By full light they drank their coffee and talked over plans made the night before.

"Now, we'll jist give them fellers a leetle more chanct to git ready to leave," Stubbs said. "I'll go ahead far enough so I kin see what goes on. When yuh see me start up, you fellers foller along like you'd been late doin' yer chores, but don't git too clost to me. Make shore yer guns is pointed in the right direction even if yuh have to swing yer pony, easy-like. When yer clost enough, all yuh'll have to do is pull the trigger and be ready to use yer leetle gun or yer knife. Got it?"

"Hell, yes! Ain't we been through this afore, Stubbs? You take keer of yer enda things an' don't worry 'bout us. C'mon, let's git it over!"

"Now, Ace, yuh got a lot to learn. Yuh cain't hurry things. Just take it easy an' do just as I say."

From the hill, Jack saw Stubbs's preparations to leave. He slipped from his vantage point, found his own camp was up and doing, Teeah with Mr. Turpin at the fire, the boys rolling up the beds, shivering a little in the coolness of dawn. Wisps of mist rose among the willows along the creek.

"They're packed up. They'll be along in a few minutes," Jack told Turpin in a low voice. "I believe they're on their way to get ahead of us. While you're getting something to eat, I'll bring the ponies to camp."

"You think they intend to ride ahead of us?"

"It looks like it . . . If they do, they'll be going through

30

here pretty quick. Then we can eat, and leave later. I won't feel easy until they're gone and we're out in open country." He smiled at Teeah, crouched by the fire, laid his rifle off to one side near her blanket, and quickly crossed the creek, heading in the direction of the feeding horses. By the time he reached the farthest pony, the Stubbs gang had arrived at the camp. Booshway and Pardner, still hobbled, greeted him from the edge of the lava rising at one side. Ready to touch them, Jack heard the first shot. Before he could turn, two more shots followed. He leaped up the rock wall and saw the camp all confusion.

Men on the ground grappled with others. Jack saw Teeah running down the trail headed for the lava wall at the far side. At camp, Stubbs aimed his pistol at the fleeing girl. The smoke of the shot came before the sound, and Jack saw Teeah pitch forward to the ground. Hardly believing it, he heard someone scream, then Stubbs squalled, pointing toward Jack where he stood above camp.

"Git that red bastard on the rocks!"

There was no chance to get a horse or gun or do anything but run for cover. Words spoken to him by his father years ago echoed in Jack's mind. "Save yer hide, boy! You kin allus help others if yer alive. If yer dead, yer dead, an' you cain't do nothin'!" He scrambled up the hill, looking for some way to escape.

Stubbs had stopped at the turn in the trail, gloating over the scene before him, the camp, his prize, getting ready to eat and leave. He saw Jack head across the creek for the horse herd, Teeah and John Turpin at the fire, young Turpin going to the creek for a bucket of water.

When he rode in, rifle across his lap ready to fire, and approached Turpin, he noticed the Indian girl walking down the trail beyond camp. From the corner of his eye, he saw Ace and Ort coming close behind him.

"Wal, Mr. Turpin, I see yuh're about ready to eat breakfast. Figger on leavin' purty quick?"

"Yes. We'll be on the trail in an hour or less, Stubbs. I see you're gettin' an early start."

"Yeah . . . an' this is jist the beginnin'!" With those words, Stubbs tossed his hat to the ground and pointed his rifle at Turpin's chest. Before his victim could move other

31

than widen his eyes in astonishment, the gun roared and powder smoke covered Turpin's face. The rancher lurched forward but did not fall. He reached for Stubbs, but the outlaw gigged his pony out of his way as two shots echoed behind them. Ort shot Tom Smith in the chest. He fell, clutching the ground and gagging. Ace's shot had killed Joe Carter. The two turned to see what Stubbs was doing, and saw him raise his pistol and point it at the fleeing girl. At his shot, she fell.

Stubbs yelled and pointed to Jack scrambling up the hillside. The two swung their ponies toward the creek. Roy Turpin, shocked, unbelieving until Stubbs shouted, ran to his rifle lying near the fallen boys, but before he reached it Stubbs leaped from the saddle and grappled him to the ground. Roy was no match for the great hulk who held and stabbed him until the struggle ended.

Teeah fell and lay there unconscious for a few moments until her own scream of pain and terror brought her to life. She touched her head and found blood on her hand. Fully alive and alert, she lay quiet, looking toward camp. She saw Stubbs load his rifle, saw him turn and come her way. Teeah reached under her jacket and slid out the razor-sharp skinning knife. Lying motionless, she recalled what the old Indian woman had told other squaws during a talk-time in the lodge.

She had been captured and taken by a small band of Crows raiding for ponies, plunder, and women. She had not fought, but waited her chance, managed to steal a knife, and hid it under the buffalo robe she and her captor used for a bed. She told how she had been cooperative and how when he knelt above her, unsuspecting, she rose slightly and with one slash across his throat stifled his scream and released her from bondage. The old women in the lodge cackled and laughed at her story. It had been a trick well played! Now Teeah waited, playing she was dead.

Stubbs, curious about the girl he had probably killed, decided to take a look at her. He wanted to see her up close, see what he had missed by killing her instead of capturing her. He walked to where she lay, blood all over the back of her head and hair. He pushed her with his foot. She made no movement. He laid down his rifle and crouched over her like a great bear, turned her to see her face. His eyes widened just as Turpin's had when he saw Stubbs's rifle aimed at his heart.

Before the outlaw could move or dodge to the side, Jack's Green River skinning knife sliced through his black beard and deep across his throat clear to the neckbone.

5

Ort took charge as he and Ace raced their ponies through the willows and across the meadow. "Go up the creek and climb the wall," he urged. "I'll climb up arter the red bastard here. Shoot to kill, Ace!"

Jack saw their swift approach. Sure they would have to trail him on foot, he scrambled up the rocky slope, one thing uppermost in his mind—to stay alive!

Instead of reloading his own rifle after he shot Joe Carter, Ace had grabbed up Joe's and Tom's rifles and handed one of them to Ort, keeping the other in hand as they mounted to chase Jack, then running up the hill in plain sight. Now, farther up the creek at the base of the bluff, Ace leaped from his pony and began climbing. He knew there was a little draw just left of where Jack had been headed, and he suspected the boy might go there. With himself on this side, and Ort riding around the hill, they might head him off, git an open shot.

Scrambling over rocks, Ace swung to his right. If Jack tried to double back, he might cross an opening between the junipers. Winded from the climb, he stopped to draw breath and wait. At the dull boom of a rifle, Ace tensed for action, but he heard no yell of triumph and success.

A movement up the sidehill! The Indian was slipping from tree to tree, looking back toward the sound of the shot. Ace steadied himself. When Jack crossed an opening in the trees, he fired. The Indian collapsed in a heap, his body out of the outlaw's direct sight. Ace looked for movement. When he saw none, he reloaded his rifle and set out again.

He would have to make a circle up the hill and come around the deep cleft that separated him from his victim at this point. If he went directly across, he would have to climb down the cleft, then take on the difficult scramble up the other face.

Suddenly Ace decided: 'I ain't goin' to chance gittin' ambushed if that kid's still alive. He had a gun. Hell's fire!' he thought. Why, he could kill me with a rock goin' up that cliff! To hell with it! I'll just say I put a hole in him and let it go at that.

He walked down to his pony and met Ort coming around the hill.

"Did yuh git him, Ace?"

"Plugged him good. You shore musta scattered rocks in his hide when yuh fired, the way he was comin'. Runnin' like a scared jackrabbit, he was."

"You sure he's dead? Redskins kin be real tricky, yuh know."

"He's deader'n the ones we left down there on the flat. Let's go see how old Stubbs made out. Hain't heard a sound since he shot the squaw. He's prob'ly got her stripped by now, an' I'm damn sure he's went through all the rest of their pockets."

The two outlaws rode down toward the campground.

As Jack climbed the lava ridge, he planned how to dodge the two men on his trail. If he could only get far enough away before they could begin shooting at him, he would have a fair chance to escape completely. He went left at the head of the little brushy draw and surprised a mule deer bedded there. It bounded up the hill. When Ort Galley saw the deer run up the rocky slope, he looked for the cause of the flight, saw Jack dodging up the hill, and fired a snap shot, hoping to wing the Indian and also alert Ace.

Rock splinters scattered close to the running boy, now almost at the ridgetop. He altered his course and flashed through some junipers on the edge of an outcropping lava ledge. Ace's slight movement below him as the outlaw raised his rifle in the rays of the rising sun caught Jack's eye and he threw himself in a sprawling dive behind the ledge just before the gun's boom reached his ears. The lead bullet fragmented the rock edge and caromed off into air.

Jack rolled farther down, rose a little, and bent over. Protected by the lava ridge, he began his run to safety. Before long he circled back and crouched motionless under the

34

friendly shelter of juniper limbs at a spot where he could watch the trail leading down the creek to the road. There he waited. Sooner or later, the outlaws would have to leave.

To Jack's knowledge, all in his party but himself had been killed . . . even Teeah. He had seen Stubbs fire, seen the running girl fall. A painful spasm of regret shook the Indian boy, but he thrust it away. There were three men either on his trail or gathering their plunder down there.

Patiently Jack squatted, waiting, while the sun climbed higher. Evidently no one had followed him after the last shot. They must think him dead. He remained quiet, occasionally wiping tears from his eyes at the sight of buzzards gathering in the sky.

Finally he saw Ort riding the trail, followed by a string of pack animals, Booshway being led, a light pack on his saddle, then Pardner with a full pack, and Speck, Jack's pack pony. Behind them came the Turpin horses, a body laid over each saddle, arms and legs tied down. He counted five. More pack animals followed, with Ace bringing up the rear to haze them along.

Jack looked for Stubbs but didn't see him. Quickly he counted, then strained to see if Teeah's body lay on one of the ponies. All the bodies were men! Could he believe that? Stubbs must be one of them! How had he been killed? What had happened to Teeah?

When the string of ponies and riders passed out of sight, Jack scrambled down from his vantage point and dog-trotted up the trail to camp. He passed where Teeah had fallen, saw the pool of blood, and squatted to read what messages happenings there had left. Several long strands of black hair he knew had come from Teeah's head. Shorter black curly hair that might have come from Stubbs's beard. Boot marks at the spot showing someone had moved the bodies and loaded Stubbs on a horse. But where was Teeah? His eyes swept the rocky soil, but no sign made itself known to him.

Jack went to the campsite. The outlaws had tried to brush over the signs of struggle and blood with alder and willow branches. In his mind, the Indian boy pieced together where things had been before the attack. The killers had taken almost everything, but he found his own woven lariat hidden near where he had slept. He wrapped it around his waist, suddenly realizing he was hungry. When he left, Teeah and Mr.

Turpin had been getting the morning meal. What had been done with it? He looked up and around. A magpie fluttered down from a juniper into rocks next to the lava wall. Jack walked to the spot to see what the bird had found.

From what the thieves had dumped for birds and scavenger animals Jack salvaged fried meat and chunks of bread and ate. The hurry of impatience prodded him, and he made a last survey of the camp. Satisfied the outlaws had packed off everything of value, Jack set out to trail them. Unencumbered by mount and packhorse, he could take to the ridges and look far enough ahead to keep sight of Ort and Ace.

When the procession of men and animals reached the army road, Jack was surprised to see the leader, probably Ort, cross over it and head out through juniper and lava rocks due west. Jack kept pace through broken country and had no trouble ducking and dodging close enough to see the five ponies' grim burdens, and spotted his three, Speck and Pardner with their packs, Booshway saddled, his lead rope tied to Pardner's tail.

Jack decided Ort and Ace had problems with so many horses and so much equipment to account for. As he followed along in the heat of the high desert, the half-breed weighed his chances of acquiring some of what they had taken. He had with him only his knife, the little derringer, a small bag of powder and shot, and the lariat. To obtain anything else, he would have to keep out of sight until they dropped their guard.

Sometimes running, sometimes stealthy among tree thickets, Jack kept the caravan in sight, frozen in grieving disbelief as he squatted in the anonymity of lava outcroppings and watched the doomed bodies of his friends flung over the edge of the Deschutes river gorge. But he did not fail to notice that some packs and equipment had gone with them.

After the outlaws left the canyon edge, traveling south on the military road once more, Jack found his way down to where they had disposed of the bodies and loot. Five ponies lay dying there before his eyes. He looked down into the gorge, but the cliff was too steep and sheer for him to descend and look for a route into its depths, and there was no time for that now, anyway.

He marked the very place by cutting and breaking many limbs of a juniper he could reach below him on the canyon side. Now the struggling, slow-growing tree would never send

36

forth enough new branches to cover its scars. The tortured form would mark this tragic spot until it too died and was uprooted, to finally disintegrate and merge into the everlasting lava desert.

6

Jack stood long at the place where Ort and his partner had disposed of the bodies and possessions of his former companions. Now the shock of what had happened really hit him and he wanted to sink to the earth, bury his head in his arms, and cry. In shock, he began to wander around in circles, trying to think. It had been bad to lose the Turpins and their friends, his three prized horses, too, but to have seen Teeah fired upon and then be able to find no trace of her body—that was the final blow. Again and again the questions arose. What had happened to Teeah? Was she still alive?

Eventually his thoughts got around to Stubbs. Who or what had killed him? The Indian boy felt a fleeting satisfaction that the outlaw no longer lived.

At last, almost unthinking, he set off on the trail of the thieves and their plunder. As he traveled, his thoughts settled down to basic things. He alone knew what had happened to the Turpin party, but if the thieves were ever caught, who would believe an Indian? No white man in this part of Oregon would, and if Indians had taken Teeah away, they would be suspicious of his story because of his white blood. No, if he did anything about what had happened, he would have to do it alone, and keep his mouth shut until there came a right time to open it.

He had his knife and the derringer. Yes . . . and his lariat. The few pieces of meat and hard bread he had found near the doomed camp would feed him sparingly for a day or so. Water he could find or go without until he came to it. Jack made up his mind to trail Ort and his partner until they grew careless, then do whatever he must to recover what remained of the stolen goods. He determined that if and when he got a chance at them, Ort and Ace would not live to trail him.

37

Before long, he spotted the outlaws and trailed along out of sight, watching Ace haze a string of ponies. When they found a place to stop for the night, Jack ate some of the meat and bread he had salvaged. He had found water during the afternoon, and now he worked his way close enough to their camp so he could monitor their every move and still not be seen.

The two men hobbled all the ponies, now nibbling sparse grass on the flat. Saddles and equipment piled near the fire made a small barricade and windbreak. Jack watched. Ace seemed alert and suspicious. He constantly looked around, stopping to stare at close-growing junipers and scanning the rock benches east of camp. Jack decided that if he were east of them when the sun rose he would be better able to observe their actions, while the sun would be in their eyes if they looked his way.

The late-summer moon rose early, flooding the landscape with its light. There was no chance to steal horses or guns without being seen and getting shot. Jack played the waiting game, finding a place where he could sleep in comparative comfort. Accustomed to the desert night, he did not worry about snakes or scorpions.

Below him, Ace and Ort were not as comfortable. They both wondered unceasingly about Teeah's disappearance and Stubbs's death, always ending up believing that Indians had killed him and taken the dead girl away for burial.

Ace took first watch. He sat with a rifle across his legs, another loaded and within reach, listening to the night sounds. Every sage rat or scurrying mouse in search of food startled him. An owl, noiselessly gliding by, cast a slight shadow in the moonlight as it swept across an open space. Instinctively Ace raised his gun, then lowered it, his hands shaking. Finally he woke Ort to stand guard, but still he couldn't relax. His mental image of old Stubbs, throat slashed through, made him shudder and reach up to feel his own scrawny neck.

Next morning, Jack watched the two men get up and make a fire. While Ace cooked breakfast, Ort brought up the ponies and tied them close for saddling and packing. Ace had made coffee. A pan of bannock baked in a reflector near the fire, and he fried steak in another skillet. They ate, and drank their coffee while saddling the horses. From the accumulated food and equipment, Ace had cooked more than they managed to eat, and now he scraped it into one pan, carried it off the campground, and dumped it. No dishwashing for him! He fitted pans and kettle together; they were ready for the pack.

Booshway laid back his ears when saddled. He didn't like his new masters, but Ort wasn't about to take the time to smarten him up. Everything on, he led the way, and Ace hazed the loose stock into line behind the led ones. They kept the outfit off the road and to the left of it about four hundred yards, taking no chances of meeting anyone just yet.

Once the outlaws had gotten well away, Jack went to the camp and found enough food for a scanty breakfast. They had left nothing else of value.

The day passed. The thieves grew more relaxed about watching for Indians who might be trailing them. The animals moved along, but Ort was having trouble finding a way through the rocks and junipers so as to avoid the stage route. Junipers along this portion of the army road grew from ten to twenty feet high, indicating either better soil or low-lying moisture from winter snows, and twice they stopped at a sheltered vantage point to try to determine what was causing dust to rise behind them. At last they saw the stage, drawn by six running horses, careening over the rocky roadbed, two men on the seat, one driving, both with feet braced against the dashboard. The first stage of the day, this one hurrying south toward California. Later in the day, when the sun had swung well west, a second dust cloud appeared from the south, then the stage, a duplicate of the first, horses slowing on the grade, then picking up to a run as they topped it and found easier going on their way to The Dalles on the Columbia River.

Two hours later, the outlaws' caravan came to a change in the terrain. The hill they had been climbing leveled off, then sloped to the south, and from an open place they looked down on grass meadows, a tree-and-willow-lined stream winding through, many cattle grazing there. They saw no smoke to mark a habitation. The two riders sat their mounts, discussing what next to do, camp where they were or boldly enter the road now and follow it.

"I say let's find a spot to camp outta this jumble of rocks an' brush." Ace looked around them. "If we're goin' to git bushwhacked by Injuns, this here's a good place."

39

"Hell's fire, Ace, git over the jiggers! Nobody, not even a greasy bunch of gut-eaters, is goin' to trail us this close to the road. Naw, our troubles from them's about over. I say we need to meet people, do some tradin'."

"This clost to where we did them fellers in? You talk like you sure enough figger nobody'll come lookin' fer 'em! Nope, I say let's git clear away from this road, down where it'll take 'em a year to git on our trail. If we keep goin' south a ways, then swing east t'ward the Harney Valley country, nobody's goin' to trail us."

"What makes you figger it that way, Ace?"

"It's late summer. We'll git rain purty quick. Then winter'll set in. Nobody I ever heard of is goin' to trail horse thieves through these parts when the blizzards hit."

Ort took up the reasoning. "Them sod-stompers ain't due in the valley fer some time yet. Old Turpin let us know that. His kid told me he figgered it'd be two weeks afore they got home. We kin git to the Harney country in a week, an' another week'll put us down in Californy or Nevada territory."

"Makes a leetle sense," Ace mused. "Maybe we oughta scout ahead fer a place to camp right now. You wanta take a look while I stick with the outfit?"

"Naw, it war yer idea," Ort replied. "Look the country over afore yuh come back. I might even take a leetle snooze while yer gone. That way I kin take the night watch an' give you a chanct fer a good sleep."

Jack watched Ace ride away, headed for the flats and the stream. Curious, the Indian made sure the rider was well away from camp before he circled like a wary coyote at a bait before approaching from the east. Ort had tied up the ponies and made sure they couldn't get loose. Leaving them switching their tails at flies, he took his rifle and walked off to sit in the shade and watch both back trail and ponies at the same time.

Jack remembered some of his old man's advice about living in hostile country. "Ever' time yuh kin split a bunch of yer enemies, yer chances git better. Iffen yuh git the leader er chief, it shore discourages the rest. Allus remember that to save yer own hair yuh got to git the other feller's first."

With Ort out of the way, it would be easier to take care of Ace. Jack thought this might be his only chance.

The cool shade, the pungent scent of juniper sap in the hot sun, and the feeling of being fairly safe from pursuit had its effect on Ort Galley. Within minutes he lay sound asleep and snoring, his head dropped down, his hair over his face, oblivious of any sound or movement. Ort never awoke from that nap. A heavy rock put him out for good; then a swift knife made sure he would never waken.

Ace Diller, happy to be away from camp, thought that if he had a little grub and some of that plunder he would just keep on riding south and to hell with Ort and the burdensome herd of ponies. It was pleasant even though hot on the grassy meadow where scattered groups of cattle stared in amazement at the lone rider. Ace found a good campsite by the little stream, drank, and splashed water over his face and head. Maybe they could lay over a little while and relax at this spot. Satisfied it was the best they might find tonight, he turned his pony and headed back to Ort at a fast trot.

Jack had dragged Ort's body back into the junipers and searched it, taking the outlaw's knife and some gold pieces. Leaving the body, he returned quickly to the horses and found his own rifle packed in with the others in the packs. He inspected Ort's rifle, found it loaded and primed, ready to fire, then trotted down in the direction Ace had ridden and found a place to conceal himself. It was Ace's turn.

There was no hesitation when the front sight of the half-breed's weapon centered Ace Diller's chest. Smoke from the black powder did not obscure the sudden look of surprise and shock he saw on the outlaw's face when he fired. In a moment, Ace fell from the startled pony, who ran forward to where the other ponies were tied. Another gun, one more knife, and some pieces of gold were laid aside while Jack dragged the body away from the spot and stripped it, taking clothes, hat, and boots a distance away to cover with rocks. The buzzards would now have easy access to Ace. He deserved this fitting reward for past deeds, Jack scorned as he looked down at the naked form.

He went back to perform the same tasks on Ort. Then he walked straight to Booshway, rubbed his ears, and talked to him, making sure the old pony knew him and letting him know that he would take care of him as they once more traveled together. When Jack rubbed Pardner's chin and patted his neck, he nuzzled the boy's shoulder.

41

Jack had his ponies and his outfit back, but in addition he had inherited troubles. Any Indian or half-breed, or even a lone white man for that matter, attempting to lead and haze seven ponies, some with packs, some free of saddles, would be eyed with certain suspicion. The first thought of anyone he met would be: "Here comes another horse thief. Wonder where he picked up all those ponies? Ain't a brand on 'em. And what's on them ponies packin' the freight? The army oughta check on this feller. He's prob'ly runnin' guns and whiskey to the Modocs or Piutes."

How to overcome this situation was Jack's big problem, how to keep what he had once fairly possesed and keep his freedom. He would tackle one thing at a time. First the ponies would have to be watered and fed and the packs cached somewhere so that if held up, he could return someday, somehow, and recover things of value. Jack looked into the distance. He had observed Ace come from the flat, maybe from a place he had chosen as the campsite for the night's stop. Checking the saddle on Booshway, and tying his lariat to it once more, he put on the pony's bridle, untied him, mounted, and rode to the distant stream. Pardner and Speck nickered a protest as Jack rode away, but the rest of the ponies stood quietly, switching flies.

Thinking of the necessity to trim his herd, Jack trotted down the slope, watching intently for sign of smoke or human habitation. All those grazing and resting cattle belonged to someone close enough to care for them. Down the creek, mud was still damp from the last stage crossing. Poles, logs, and broken rope lying about showed that in the spring, with water up and frost just leaving, there had been troubles with bogged wagons and stagecoaches. Beyond the ford, a dim road led off to the southeast, but wagon and buggy tracks showed its recent use.

Satisfied that he was not alone, Jack turned upstream and rode for a half-mile before deciding on his camp for the night. Water here, and good feed for the ponies. Now to take care of the stock and dump the packs. He rode back, and moved the string of ponies around the edge of the lava bench until he found a likely-looking gully under an overhang of rock. Porcupines and pack rats had used the place, and the rank odor lingered, but there was room enough under it for everything he needed to dispose of. He dumped the packs, took the ponies to the meadow camp, watered and hobbled them, before he returned to the gully.

In one pack he found the cooking outfit and some grub. Bedrolls, extra clothing, and boots were tied in another with four pistols, two cans of powder, four buckskin bags of round balls, and four boxes of caps tied around with a buckskin string. A third pack held four rifles and the shotgun that had belonged to Mr. Turpin. He saw extra moccasins, Teeah's beaded jacket and buckskin bag with her comb, brush, and the little bells Jack's father had given her years before, and he cried as he touched things once dear to her. She was gone . . . and he had no idea what had happened to her body.

Back at the meadow camp he waited until dark to make his small fire, then prepared coffee and quickly fried meat. He dipped dry bread in the pan grease to make it more palatable. When he finished and had scrubbed the fire out in the sand, Jack lay with his head on his saddle and listened to night sounds while he planned for the coming days.

Down on the meadow at dawn, he gathered the ponies and led them up to the edge of the junipers. He tied them and looked them over for any brand or ear mark. He found none. The five branded animals had been disposed of by Ort and Ace on the trail by the canyon edge. Now Jack eared down each pony's head and with his knife made a slit on the left ear of each before he turned it loose to head toward the meadow. He kept only Booshway, Pardner, and Speck. The others could run free until picked up by some rancher or a traveler.

He rode Booshway to the cache, leading the other two, and sorted out two small packs, one for Pardner with grub and the camp equipment, the other for Speck—his held an extra rifle and the shotgun. He wrapped a good pistol in his jacket and tied it behind his saddle, then wrapped the rest of the plunder and shoved it under the ledge before he carried lava slabs there to block up the outward face. Stepping back, he looked to make sure a passing rider could not see the hidden cache. His footprints in the sandy places he dragged over with a juniper limb until there was no visible trace left, and to mark the spot, he again chose a juniper tree, cutting one

43

limb partway through to dangle, hang on, and yellow in the sun.

With Pardner and Speck trailing Booshway, he rode into the meadow, crossed the stream, and began the gradual descent to the distant military road that led to Fort Klamath. If stopped and questiond as to his destination, his answer would be that he was carrying a message of importance to Sergeant Dan Hogan at the fort. If asked to describe the sergeant, he could do that. If asked where he came from, he would mention Fort Walla Walla. In Oregon, Washington, or Idaho, if a man mentioned knowing the military, and had a message for an officer, it not only gave him safe passage but also gained him a certain respect.

The end of the Civil War had seen greater movement of army troops to the West in order to answer civilian pleas for help against marauding Indians. Any Indian riding well-equipped on his way to Fort Klamath to see an officer could only be a friendly one, perhaps his message information as to where the next raid might take place.

7

Jack did not meet anyone who might test his carefully thought-out explanation.

Jubal Street's camp lay in a bend of the Crooked River canyon on the trail to Prine City, a cluster of small houses and shelters named after the cattleman Mr. Prine. Jack had decided to take the river trail rather than follow the army road across the benchlands. As he rounded the bend, Booshway's head went up, his ears pricked at the sight of horses under the cottonwoods. At the sound of the ponies' welcoming nicker, a woman working at a fire in front of a lean-to tent straightened and turned. Jack saw that she was Indian.

She must have made a slight, indistinguishable sound, for a man dressed in buckskins at once appeared from the tent. He stood straight and tall, a rifle cradled in his arms, and as Jack and his ponies approached, Jack's hand raised in the sign of peace, the man raised his own hand in acknowledgment.

"Well, stranger, yer too late fer breakfast and jest in time fer dinner. Want to light and see what the woman kin fix up, or are yuh in too big of a hurry?"

"No, just traveling through to see the country." Jack's tone was easy. "They call me Jack. I'm old Bill Tate's boy."

"The hell you say! I knowed old Bill. I heerd he had a boy, too. What happened to yer paw, anyway?"

"The Sheepeaters killed him up on the Salmon five or six years ago."

"Well . . . that's too bad! Bill warn't such a bad feller. Tie yer ponies and set a spell, son. This here's my woman, Sarah. Her Injun name's like 'Star of the Morning,' er 'Morning Star.' Guess they give her that 'cause she's allus up to see it." Laughing, the man leaned his rifle against a nearby tree and walked to where Jack was dismounting. He held out his hand.

"I'm Jubal Street. Yer paw allus called me old Jube. Glad to meet his boy. Iffen yuh turn out the man yer pappy was, you'll make it in spite of the blasted army and the gov'ment officials."

They squatted and talked there under the trees, while the woman worked off by herself, seemingly uninterested in the stranger. But Jack knew that the Indian way was to notice everything about any newcomer. Morning Star would remain silent until her man asked her something.

Jubal Street had heard of Mr. Hill. After they talked awhile, Jack decided to tell Street of the killings. The old trapper took it all in, then sat and smoked, thinking of Jack's dilemma.

The Bannocks and Snakes were raiding from the east as far west as the Ochocos, and from the west the Warm Springs Indians harassed the settlers' cattle and horse herds. Harney and Lake counties experienced raids by Modocs and Piutes. With the war in the South over, people tired of being harassed by soldiers had begun settling the West. The army would soon move all Indians to reservations. Street himself must settle somewhere so Sarah would have a place to live. He knew Jack would be questioned and might have a difficult time explaining how he had managed to survive those killings and end up the sole survivor, all the ponies and stolen plunder in his possession. A half-breed would be looked on by most whites as an outcast. The three slain outlaws had been white men, regardless of what they had done. Who would believe Jack's story of the complete disappearance of the Indian girl, Teeah? Jubal Street knew Jack was in a real fix.

The former trapper turned trader, about to become a settler, a substantial citizen of some community, would make a deal with this half-breed boy and take him along to help. Then he would git back the horses left loose on the flat meadows and Street would slap his brand on them. He had no brand now, but when money and property were concerned, he could somehow come up with one.

"Jack, how'd you like to work for me?" he asked. "Yuh ain't got no other plans right now, have yuh?"

"No—except to stay out of jail and not be hung for a horse thief."

Street drew on his pipe. "Well, I see the deal this way. Yer free, them ponies're loose with no owner and no brands. Sure as hell somebody'll pick 'em up. Let's ride back and git 'em. I'll slap my brand on 'em and bring 'em here. Sarah kin watch the camp and the two ponies you leave here. We'll jist take a bite behind the saddles fer bait on the trail. Kin yuh ketch 'em up 'thout much trouble?"

"Yeah, they'll be salt-hungry. I'll ride up to 'em on Booshway, and once they taste salt, they'll be easy to ketch."

"Good. Know a place handy there where we kin burn the iron on? I don't aim to git caught out on the flats with strange ponies, a fire, an' a runnin' iron. They hang fellers fer that."

Street felt enthused about the ponies. They could discuss the cached plunder the boy had told him about later. He called to the woman at the fire that they would eat when she brought it. While she dished stew into bowls, Street went to his canvas warbag and scrummaged, coming up with cinch rings, a short slender rod, a hammer, and a pair of tongs. He poked the rings and rod in the fire to heat.

With stew, hot and good, Sarah gave them cornbread, and Jack watched Jubal dump a piece into the bowl and slurp it down, mulling it around in his mouth to savor the flavor of the mixture before he wiped off the clinging crumbs and drops from his beard with the back of his big hand. No sooner was his mouth emptied than up would come the bowl and his mouth once more filled with stew-covered cornbread. Jack watched in fascination. Jubal Street enjoyed his meal.

How old Sarah was, Jack had no idea. As he ate bowlfuls

of stew and more cornbread, he watched her and Street. The woman made sure the bowls and the tin cups did not remain empty of stew or tea for a minute, moving quietly and gracefully to the men with kettle or pot before Jack was aware any dish or cup needed a refill. At first he had thought of Sarah as a young woman, slender, and with a rosy smooth face. Her hair glistened black in long braids, with blue and red yarn woven in. At the end of each braid dangled the black-tipped white tail of the ermine, a winter-coated weasel.

Today she wore a beaded and fringed doeskin jacket, once white. It hung below her waist, covering the upper part of her light doeskin skirt. On her feet were ankle-length moccasins, her brown legs showing smooth and unscarred between foot-gear and skirt.

Her face and eyes interested Jack. He tried not to seem too bold. but it was hard to keep from watching her. Across Jubal's head, as he squatted eating his food and talking, she looked at Jack and smiled, her expression so like Teeah's that tears came to his eyes. He brushed them away with his arm before Jubal noticed. But Sarah saw and wondered.

The two men had no trouble rounding up the horses Jack had left loose on the meadow. Watered and fed, their bellies full, when Jack rode up on Booshway they came to see what it was Booshway licked from Jack's palm. Once they had tasted salt, they were easily roped together, and Jack led the whole string back out of the meadow to where Jubal had found a place to build a small fire and heat the branding iron. In no time at all each pony bore the letters JS on the left hip in addition to the slit in his ear. Old Jube had set himself up as a horse trader.

As they traveled back to Sarah and the camp, Jack couldn't keep from wondering whether he should try to travel over the mountains to tell Mr. Hill and the rest of the Turpin family what had happened. Old Jube hadn't given that much thought, but now he decided that would be up to the Indian boy. It was no affair of his, but he and his woman were in business for themselves now, and if Jack wanted to leave, well and good. Talking, he concluded that of course if Jack stuck with him they'd make a pretty good team. They could swap the ponies and the plunder Jack had cached, and Jack could start a small spread of his own.

Familiar with Booshway and Jack, the band of ponies was not difficult to handle. Old Jube knew the trail; after the moon came up it was easy traveling. Sarah heard Pardner nicker from where he was picketed, and stirred up the fire. Long association with Jubal Street had taught her that food and hot tea or coffee kept him in an easy mood after a long day's travel. With her short throwing stick she had killed several young sage chickens, and now they were in the pot with odds and ends of bulbs and a few potatoes.

As they rode into camp, Jubal turned to Jack. "Will they stick together or should we tie 'em up er hobble 'em fer the night?"

"Hobble the black. He belonged to Old Stubbs. I don't trust him."

"How about the glass-eye?"

"He's used to being with the black. The others'll stay around Booshway and Pardner. You think there's any chance of horse thieves being near here?"

"Hain't heerd of such. White settlers been purty rough on that action. That's why I want my sign on 'em. Iffen I was you, I'd put a mark on them of yourn. They're good stock, and some feller's might git the itch to glom onto 'em. First one marks 'em claims 'em in this country."

It was one thing that Jack did not want to do. His father hadn't branded Booshway or Pardner—why should he? But here was old Jube saying that unless an owner marked his stock they would belong to the first man who managed to do so. As Jack turned this problem over in his mind, he considered how he could prove to some stranger his ownership of those three horses of better-than-average value. He rode in a strange country where almost no one would be familiar with or favorable to his parentage and background.

"Jube, what mark you think I should put on 'em?" he asked at last.

"Hell, I don't know what you'd want. I jist used the front letters of my name, JS fer Jubal Street. You kin think of some mark that's fittin'."

"Like what?"

"Wal, I've seed some peculiar marks made on critters' hides. A feller might like the number fifty-four, the year he come west, er twenty-seven, signifyin' how old he was when he got his start. One feller I knowed drawed an' old boot for

48

his brand. There's plenty ways to mark up a critter, but I wouldn't spread a big burn on such purty stock. Fact is, we could make a leetle mark up on the neck where it wouldn't show up too plain, and then in case some feller tried to pull a fast one by claimin' yer stock, you'd sure have a better holt on 'em."

Jack rode along, beginning to feel that while he had Old Jube to help him and be a witness to his ownership, it might be well to brand his ponies. Jube's woman could also be a witness. When he met Mr. Hill again, he too could swear the three horses belonged to Jack Tate.

If he used his own initials, other men might claim them as theirs. A figure of some animal? A bear. No, too hard to draw with the hot iron. Something easy to draw that would always remain the same. Little Badger . . . Teeah . . . old Chief Thunderbolt. Could he and old Jube make a mark like a striking thunderbolt, lightning coming from above?

In camp, eating while Sarah watched to see their cups and bowls were always full, Jack waited, having already learned not to hurry Jube unless it was necessary. When Jube filled his pipe and r'ared back to smoke and contemplate the day's work ahead, he spoke. "Jube, could you make an iron that would burn a mark like a streak of lightning?"

Street looked across at the Indian boy. "Don't see why not."

"I was thinking if I used letters, like you do, some feller might say they was his'n. I want something that only I know the meaning of."

Old Jube puffed away, blew a slow ball of smoke into the morning air, then looked long at the ponies grazing along the riverbank. "What made you think of lightning, boy?"

Jack's thoughts turned to that faraway day when he had come to old Thunder's lodge. The chief later called him son. Jack wanted something definite to keep that relationship firm in his life. To use the chief's symbol to mark the ponies would establish such a relationship if he ever got questioned. Jack saw Sarah busy gathering things together in preparation for moving on. Evidently she knew her man would soon be ready to travel.

"When I was lot smaller," he replied slowly, "my father was killed by Sheepeaters up on the Salmon. I got away and

49

stayed a long while with Chief Thunderbolt. He took me into his tribe and called me his son. He knows these ponies. If I ever had to prove they were mine, he and Mr. Hill and Mr. Craig would say they were. I thought the Chief's name symbol might be a good mark for my horses."

Old Jube puffed away, thinking that he would like to have those ponies for his own herd. He considered how the letters JT could be worked into a different brand over his own JS. If Jack used the lightning strike, he knew he might as well forget such a plan, and now he thought: Oh, hell, let him keep 'em. I'll have plenty of my own.

"Where would yuh put yer iron?"

"Up on the neck, close to the mane, like you said. Hard to see."

"That's easy."

"I think the sooner I get it done, the better," Jack decided. "I want to make sure that you and Sarah know the ponies are mine before I leave for the valley to meet Mr. Hill."

"Well, boy, let's git busy makin' marks in the dirt."

The two squatted in the sand, drawing straight marks and jagged marks. They wanted a half-circle that could be called a cloud, with three straight lines below it set at angles like a crooked lightning strike, with two short straight lines on the end as a strike might split above the ground; but their first attempt looked like a striking snake with open mouth.

"Hell, Jack," Jubal laughed. "Some feller'd claim that was his snake brand! We gotta round out the half-circle an' angle the lines more so you kin argy the story of the old chief. This should be an easy one to burn. Yuh got a half a cinch ring fer the cloud and a short straight one fer the lightnin'. Which pony yuh want to brand first?"

Jack went to get Speck while Jube found irons to put in the fire. Soon the smell of burning horsehair drifted downriver with the breeze, and before the camp packed up, Jack looked several times at his own mark on his own horse herd, pleased with his decision. It was his brand, visible to anyone who cared to look.

But his other problem kept haunting him. He knew that he should be on his way to the Willamette Valley to tell the Turpin family and Joe and Tom's parents of the tragedy befallen Mr. Turpin and the boys. He had recovered their money and

50

had it well hidden, but he knew the loss of money, goods, and horses would be inconsequential to them compared to the deaths of beloved family members and friends.

8

At Fort Walla Walla, one of the many strangers on their way to Portland asked about a man named Stubbs, but had no luck finding anyone that knew of him until he got into conversation with some miners just arrived from the west. When he asked whether they might have met Stubbs as they came east, one bearded miner inquired what the man in question looked like. After the forthcoming description, the miner pulled on his whiskers and said, "Now, I never heerd his name. Fact is, the feller that looked like the one you described jist set his horse an' glowered. He had a flat black hat that sorta matched his whiskers. Big heavyset feller with a belly that laid over the front of his saddle. Friend of yourn, maybe?"

"No, I'm jist takin' a message to him from his folks back home. Where'd you see this man?"

"Well, it war 'bout three, four days back on the trail. Right after we left the gorge of the crooked river. He war travelin' with a party of men an' boys."

"Any of 'em give their names, say where they was headin'?"

The miner reached for his glass of whiskey, now nearly empty, but the stranger slid it to the bartender. "Fill this up for my friend here," he said.

"Wal, now, I recollect one feller said he was from the valley, name of Turbin er somethin' like that. There was three boys an' two Injuns with him. The man name of Stubbs, if that's the one, had two purty rough-lookin' sidekicks along. The Turbin feller said he was lookin' fer a place here to come to and settle."

"Could you describe the whole bunch to me? I'd like to know about what they looked like, and what horses they was ridin', so I'll know 'em if I catch up to 'em."

51

The other two miners joined in when the stranger, who said he was Bardo Stebbins from Ohio, ordered the bartender to fill their glasses. When they got through drinking and talking, Stebbins had gained some ideas for his search. In the herd of horses, there were four that would be remembered. The two Indians rode spotted ponies, and one of Stubbs's friends rode a glass-eyed paint. There was one black, the rest bays. Armed with this knowledge, Bardo Stebbins set out on the trail of Old Stubbs, whose real name was Olden Stebbins, and who was Bardo's brother.

As he traveled the route his brother had taken to join the Turpin party, he found more travelers that knew of Turpin and his group than those who'd met Stubbs. More than one person recalled seeing the Indians and their spotted ponies in Turpin's group. Bardo also learned that Turpin had worked for a prominent trader and cattle buyer by the name of Walter Hill. Sure of catching up with them now, he was bewildered when he finally reached the turnoff to the Willamette Valley through the lava beds without having heard one more word about the party.

He stopped in a little settlement to consider what information he had gathered. The last people to have seen the group were the three miners he had met in Fort Walla Walla. That had to mean that both parties, Turpin's and Stubbs's, had turned off the trail somewhere along the crooked river, and that they had to have turned east, because there was no crossing of the gorge at any point for miles.

Stebbins considered the trail they would most likely take. Knowing his brother and how he operated, he was certain that the only reason Stubbs had joined the Turpin party was to somehow acquire their possessions. Olden had never been noted for open and fair dealing. Mean, sly, and tricky, he liked to bully the weak, take advantage of the innocent, and degrade women. He had stolen from the army. He had robbed and burned farms and homes, blaming it on the Southern raiders, and since the war was over, had made his way west to live off the country and its people. Since escaping from an army jail himself, Bardo was anxious to join his older brother.

If they went east, he reasoned, they might have taken the crude road across country to the growing settlement of Prine City. If they had gone south as far as he was now, they could

52

turn directly east to the town. Bardo determined to go there and inquire. With this plan in mind, he left his horse at a livery stable and caught a stage, able to travel faster than by using his own mount.

Prine City, a morbid collection of rude houses, shanties, and tents, marked the beginning and end of civilization for many rough miles of travel. Stebbins found a room in a crude hotel near the livery stable and after cleaning up and eating dinner made the rounds of the saloons. He recognized no one.

At the livery stable, he asked about travelers going through with a bunch of horses, three spotted Indian ponies, one paint with glass eyes, the rest bays and blacks. There would be two young Indians along, a boy and a girl, who took care of the stock and helped with the cooking.

No one had seen such an outfit. Back at the rooming house, Stebbins, weary from travel, went to bed thinking what his next move should be, and woke in the night wondering again what could have happened to the two parties. A group that large traveling together had to have been seen sometime or other. He decided to wait over in Prine City another day and ask more questions. Then he drowsed off, assuring himself that probably his brother and his two partners had done the job they set out to do and were now covering their tracks.

Talk the next day added to his only slight knowledge of the enormity of Oregon territory. Sure, he could go east up the creek called Ochoco after the old chief of the tribe, follow over the mountains to the John Day River, and come out at Day City. Or he could swing southeast and follow the trail along the crooked river and wind up in prairie and desert country, and from there take the army road across Oregon and come out at the Snake River crossing.

That could be the way his party went, but the odds were they hadn't ever reached Prine City. The liveryman told him of a cross-country route that missed the crooked river route on the way back to the gorge country. It was overland— maybe his folks had followed that. If they had, Bardo could backtrack and he might meet them coming in or find them camped someplace. Chances were if any one of them was looking for a place to squat, they'd find it in that area, not down here.

53

Stebbins had money. He invested in a horse and outfit, knowing by the time he reached the place where he'd left his own horse he could recover most of the price for this one by selling it to that livery stable. With some grub and a crude map he set out on the trail back to the area where his brother and the other bunch had last been seen and identified.

At the camp farther up the river where there was good feed for all the horses, Jack worried constantly about going to the valley where he had arranged to meet Mr. Hill at the Turpin ranch. Finally he could keep still about it no longer, and told Old Jube and Sarah.

"Wal, boy, yuh still got a problem," Street ruminated. "Here yuh are with yer own stock which yuh kin claim an' kin prove it. But you're still an' Injun kid to most white folks. The big question'll come sooner or later—what you're doin' runnin' loose with this kind of stock when the gov'ment fellers're puttin' the rest of yer tribe on reservations.

"It's like Sarah here. They been arter her, but I'm strong enough to keep her under my wing. As I see the signs, yuh might have real trouble gittin' to the valley 'thout losin' yer ponies and plunder. And on this side of the mountains I'm willin' to bet a plug of tobaccy 'gainst yer spit that there's more thieves than honest fellers you'll come up against if you make sich a sashay."

Sarah stood watching the two talk together. She knew what Jack was feeling, and that it seemed to him he was caught in a trap, no way of getting free. She knew that if it wasn't for her man she too would be sent to a reservation. With old Jube, she could travel from place to place like in the old days when her tribe moved with the seasons and with the game. If she had to settle in one place, she'd feel like a wild pony when first put on a picket line, front feet tied with rawhide hobbles, wanting to go and run with the wind, but confined to one small spot vainly to paw the ground.

"Then you think I shouldn't go to the valley?"

"Naw . . . I didn't say that. I jist wanted to let yuh know yer chances. Yuh see, iffen yuh do make it through to the valley, if anything's happened to yer pardner Hill that he didn't show up to back up yer story, you wouldn't stand one chance in hell of havin' them folks there believe yer story. Ever'thing you told me 'bout what took place can be changed 'round against yuh. Like yer story of how you was after the ponies when the killin's took place. Some feller might argy you was in cahoots with Stubbs an' signaled fer 'em to come in, an' then when ever'body in camp was dead, you took up with the gang, saw one of his pardners kill Stubbs, an' when yuh got yer chance, yuh bushwhacked 'em both.

"Now, all this took place a fur piece from where you're tellin' the story. Ever'one listenin' wonders what yuh did with the plunder. Yuh tell 'em you'll take 'em to the place you hid it. But winter's comin' on, an' all winter they break yer story into little pieces. They know the killin' took place near a reservation an' that Indians could've helped kill their folks, an' now they have the ponies, the plunder, and their money. There'll be no way you can prove different at the time."

Jack was silent, sitting head down, eyes almost closed. Sarah moved quietly to where she could see his face, and Jube continued.

"Now, supposin' the Turpin tribe and some neighbors believed yer story an' come over in the spring. All they'd see would be the spot where you say the killin' took place, all growed up with grass now an' no marks. Yuh go to where they slung the fellers over the cliff into the canyon. Hit would take more rope than one pony could pack to let a feller down over that rock wall to where the bones'll be scattered, so nobody's goin' down there. Yuh take 'em to where the plunder is—yuh never showed me where yuh put it. If it's there an' they git it, they'll say where's the livestock? You say the two fellers kilt Turpin's branded ponies, but by then they're gettin' tired of this wild-goose chase. If yuh insist on bringin' 'em to me, hell, even if they do find me, my mark's on all the ponies but yourn, so they're mine."

Jack raised his head. Morning Star saw a look of absolute defeat in his eyes. He had never considered all those possibilities. The massacre of his friends, the death and loss of Teeah, had been shocking enough; somehow he had lived through it, beginning to take a new attitude and consider prospects for the future, but what old Jube had just told him sank him to even lower depths.

Sarah wondered what Jubal would say next. She saw him tap tobacco into the old pipe he had traded for years ago, his thinking pipe. When he filled and lighted it, he puffed away, leaning back in comfort before he spoke. Jack's head sank

55

lower. Sarah thought he might have tears in his eyes and was trying to cover his emotion.

Settled, Jube began to talk once more. "Now, this is how the sign reads to me. Iffen you try to make the trip, all it'll git yuh is trouble. Iffen I was to go with you, we could make it with no sweat. But that'd leave Sarah with the ponies, an' her bein' a squaw, she'd be hit up by the first white feller seed her. There's a short supply of females in this country, 'specially good-lookin' squaws. They're allus open season fer randy fellers lookin' fer a woman in the blankets. So that's out.

"Jack, s'pose you stay here with Sarah, ride herd on the leetle hideout I got over on the river while I take off over the mountains an' give out the word what took place. You kin tell me where to look fer the Turpins an' write somethin' to give yer pardner, old man Hill. If he wants to come over here, git the plunder, an' clear yuh, fine an' dandy. Sarah, you kin put in a word around these parts fer Jack. He kin be somebody I hired to help yuh look after the place."

When Jube paused to relight his pipe, Jack spoke up. "When kin you go?"

"Soon as we git figgered out what all you an' Sarah gotta do to make out through the winter. We got a leetle money to buy grub with. I allus figger on trappin' an' doin' some wolfin' fer the cattlemen. You kin do the same iffen yer handy at it. Ever do any wolfin'?"

"No, but I know somethin' about trapping small stuff."

"Well, Sarah kin show you more. She kin handle all the hides, work on the deer an' elk skins fer clothes too. You'll make out if you're keerful."

"How far is it to the place where we'd winter?"

"Takes two days with no trouble. Yuh got to git there so Sarah kin see old Bullhead Bailey about stayin' on part of the range he claims. She'll tell him you'll keep the wolves thinned out so the ponies kin pasture, an' he'll let you kill a beef in case yuh need it. But make sure yuh keep the hide to show him."

"When would you expect to be back? Couldn't you make it back before snow closes the trails?"

"You know much as I do 'bout that. Iffen I'm lucky and meet up with Hill an' he's willin' to come, we might make it

56

right soon, but if I don't show up this fall, look fer me next spring when the passes're open."

While Jack wrote a short message to Mr. Hill about what had happened on the trip, Sarah helped sort out Jube's outfit. Sarah seldom spoke to Jack, but he knew it was the Indian way, and did not feel ignored, and he wondered about the coming winter and sharing a camp with her, hoping Jube could make it to the valley and back before spring. By this time Mr. Hill should be near Junction City and the Turpin farm. If Jube pushed his ponies, he could be at that place in a week's time. At the most, Jack thought, he should be back here in not more than three weeks unless something unusual happened, and then he would not have to spend the whole winter alone with Sarah.

Jubal Street seemed anxious to get going, but he did not hurry his careful packing preparations, having lived too long now to let eagerness to get on the trail override his judgment in selecting essential gear. Finally, his pony packed, his own mount ready, he looked at Sarah and said, "You an' the boy take keer of yerselves. I figger to be back when I git here."

Morning Star watched him ride out of sight. When she turned to Jack and spoke as he slowly gathered things together for their own departure. "Jack, you an' me git along good. No troubles. Now we move to cabin on Bailey range. You ride for cows, watch ponies. I stay in camp, make you new clothes."

"Thanks, Sarah. You'll have to tell me what to do and where to go until I learn about things." He straightened and looked up into the yellowing cottonwoods. "I hope Jubal makes it over to Turpin's place and finds Mr. Hill. I'm sure Mr. Hill will come back with him and help me git the things that belong to my friends."

They moved camp that day ten miles upriver to a bend where in the loop where high water had overflowed there was good grass and a camping place. A few cattle rested in the shade of cottonwoods, and more browsed on the bench above, where bunch grass showed thick and tall. After they set up camp and Sarah was busy at the fire, Jack saw a rider coming off the hill, his pony sidestepping down the steep bank. He motioned to Sarah. She straightened up for a long look at the newcomer.

57

"Don't know him, Jack. You Jube's boy. Say we go help Bailey upriver, trap wolves, watch cows for him."

The rider, tall and slim on his blue roan pony, held up his right hand in the sign of peace or welcome. The stranger looked at the grazing ponies; they lifted their heads, and some began to sidle toward him. Jack knew the rider had not overlooked even one small detail of everything connected with themselves and the camp. He asked a question.

"You two come from around here?"

"I Sarah," the Indian woman replied. "Me old Jube's woman. Go to Bailey's to wolf and watch cows."

"Jube the old feller that trades, comes from over on the Day?"

Sarah nodded her head. "We come work for Bailey, watch cows. Stay up on Jube's claim, South Fork."

"Where's old Jube?"

"He go to git trade stuff. Mebbe soon back, mebbe not. Gits winter things. You know Bailey?"

"Yeah, I know the hardheaded old bastard," the stranger said, not looking at her. He had been sizing up Jack, squatted at one side. "Who's this feller?"

"Jube's boy. He come with ponies for Jube. He mission boy."

"The hell you say! What's yer name, boy?"

"My name is Jack."

"What mission you come from?"

"Mr. Lee's, in the valley. Up at Lapwai with the Spaldings, too."

"You talk purty good fer an Injun. You a half-breed?"

"Half Nez Percé."

"Where'd yuh pick up the ponies? Them spotted two ain't from around here."

"They come from Thunder's band up on the Salmon. Paw traded fer 'em long time ago."

"Ever run 'em?"

"Paw used to. I did once or twice."

"Win anything?"

"Sometimes. Sometimes no."

"Yeah, that's the way she goes, all right. Where you been campin'?"

"Downriver ten or twelve miles, in the bend where the big flat is."

58

"You mean where that steeple rock's on the north?"

"That's the place."

"See any cows down that way? I'm a-ridin' fer old man Prine. They brought over a new bunch from the valley a while back. They stick purty close to the river, but he also had some rangtangs what head fer the hills."

"We saw some scattered along. One short-horned red bull with a bunch of cows an' calves. A few yearlings, too."

Sarah had put on the coffeepot. Now it boiled up. She set it to one side, and picked up a battered tin cup from among nearby pots and kettles, filled it, and walked to the rider, whose pony began to roll his eyes and back away. A spurred heel in his flank steadied him while the man reached his hand for the cup. As he took it, he cracked a little smile. "I kin sure use that. Been a long time since I had anything smelled as good—and that was a whiskey jug."

"You want to eat? We cook now."

"Naw, I got a long way t' go. Made a bigger circle than I figgered."

"I tell Jube your name when he come back?"

"Wilson—Lee Wilson. I work fer Prine. You know Prine?"

"No . . . Jube, he know Prine. I know Bailey."

"Well, here's yer cup, Sarah. Stay away from town. You're too good-lookin' a squaw to show yer shape to all the drunks hang around there. So long, Jack. You want to run that spotted pony sometime, I'll pick up somethin' to match him."

Wilson wheeled his pony, raised his hand in farewell, and urged the roan into a trot up the river trail toward Prine City.

With Sarah leading the way, a pack pony behind her, the others loose and trailing, the two made their way upriver toward Jube's cabin and small corral, a camp used now and then, Sarah told Jack, when they came to hunt or help stockmen with cattle, or to thin out wolf litters. The place where they would make their permanent home lay more than a hundred miles farther east on the John Day forks.

Up the river, they met one of Bailey's riders. Sarah said to tell his boss she and Jube's boy were moving up to Elk Hollow for the winter, that Jube had gone over to the valley for supplies and trade goods. The rider, known only by the name

59

of Rusty, told them Bailey had left the range to locate more cattle but had left word at headquarters that old Jube and his outfit would look after this part of the country for a while.

9

Lee Wilson met a stranger headed downriver. The fellow said he was looking for his friend's brother who'd left Fort Walla Walla sometime back and nobody had heard from him since. When questioned further, the stranger identified himself as Bardo Stebbins and said the man he was interested in was a big fellow named Stubbs, who had joined a party led by a rancher called Turbin or some such name. In the bunch were three or four older boys, all whites, and two Indians about their age, a boy and girl. Yes, there were two other white men but they might have been with Stubbs or had joined the group on their own. The Turbin party had one red-and-white-speckled Indian pack pony, the other a brown, kind of thin-necked common horse. The two Indians rode black-and-white-spotted horses, good ones, and the rest of the horses were bays. The only other horse in the herd that took the eye of anyone who saw the party was the big black Stubbs rode. Five of the Turbin ponies were branded on the left hip. They'd noticed at least two with a mark that looked like a letter T lying slantways.

"Did the fellers say how many ponies in the bunch?" Wilson asked idly.

Bardo hesitated as if thinking of the conversation. "Near as they could call it back. twelve or thirteen. counting the pack ponies. The makeup of the party was what really took their eye. You seen a bunch like that lately?"

"Well, a while back I run across two Indians with a bunch of horses goin' upriver. They had three spotted ones and a big rangy high-headed black in their herd, all marked, though."

"Two Injuns with spotted ponies?" Bardo was alert.

"A young feller an' an older squaw. I know 'em. The woman belongs to a white trader, Jube Street. He traps,

60

trades, an' moves around the country. They was goin' to look after old man Bailey's cows up in the Ochocos this winter. Not the two you're lookin' fer, I reckon."

"The ponies might be. Yeah, the young feller, too. Where might I run onto 'em?"

"Upriver beyond Prine City twenty-five or thirty miles, you turn up a crick to a place called Elk Hollow. They're headed there. Told me to tell Bailey they'd do some wolfin' fer him this winter. I think you're barkin' up the wrong tree if you figger them's the people you're lookin' fer."

"It's worth a try. It's the first lead I've had for weeks, an' you're the first rider I've met that's seen spotted ponies and two Injuns."

"Well, I shore hope you find yer friend, but I ain't seen no sign of any party that size up this way."

"I want to check on their ponies. A bunch that big don't just take off and fly away. Horses leave tracks, an' people leave some sign where they've gone to, unless they're killed or holed up someplace."

"Yuh figger the Injuns kilt 'em all an' stole the ponies?" Wilson marveled in mock alarm.

"It's been done before." Bardo nodded. "Fact is, it's bein' done all the time from what the army an' people I've met say."

Bardo Stebbins returned upriver toward Prine City, and Lee Wilson went his way in search of cattle, thinking to himself: That feller's apt to stick his nozzle in a hornet's nest if he tangles with old Jube. If his woman an' that boy did steal them ponies, they ain't about to give 'em up to the first feller comes ridin' in. Well, it's his nose he'll git skinned.

Unaware that a curious stranger was on their track, Jack helped Sarah establish their camp and went about learning the area where Bailey's cattle and few horses ranged. Bailey had not intended the horses to take to the hills, but his herder had been careless, and lack of time and help to round them up had hampered their capture. Bailey, a tough old cattleman, counted every hide to make sure nobody put an iron or knife mark different from his own on it.

Bullhead Bailey, a strong, hardheaded man in a land that needed strong men, had come into this country with only his pack outfit. He rode all through it to locate a place to start his cattle spread, and talked with a band of Ochoco Indians, at first suspicious and aloof. With shrewd trading gifts that included guns, powder, and sheet lead, he learned from them where in this region he could run cattle summer and winter.

To hold this range, he made friends with the tribe, and when other white men began to encroach, they warned him well in advance where the newcomers were squatting. Those who insisted on staying ran into streaks of bad luck, their cattle mysteriously run off or moved from place to place. Many just vanished.

Old Jube moved about the region before Bailey moved in. On their first meeting, each man recognized the other's strength but neither felt like testing it. As long as Jubal Street wanted to hole up in Elk Hollow with his squaw, Bailey didn't object, and gradually a mutual respect arose between them. After Street trapped or shot wolves, killed and skinned bear and cougar that harassed the herds, and kept passing Indians from slaughtering too much beef, Bailey saw that Jube had become a distinct asset on his range. He furnished the two a beef if he saw they needed it, and had riders take in supplies now and then.

Now, when he returned and Rusty told him that Sarah and Jube's boy had moved up to Elk Hollow to maybe spend the winter, Bailey went to see for himself. He had never heard of old Jube having a boy, or even rumors of such a thing. He rode into their little camp in late afternoon, only to find them both away.

Bailey put his pony in the little corral close to a log shed where Jube kept hay and a sack or two of grain. He stripped off saddle and bridle, hung the sweat-soaked blanket on the pole corral, and let his mount roll in the dust. As he passed the shed, he looked in at the contents, saw a packsaddle, extra ropes, and a canvas-wrapped pack tied with elkhide strings.

The cabin door swung inward as he pulled the latch string. One thing Bailey had learned about Jube's woman—she kept a clean cabin and a clean camp. The rough, oilcloth-covered table next to the little window had been set for two people, but the small stove was cold, no fire there for hours. Bailey opened the firebox, put in a few splinters of pine pitch, laid dry tamarack sticks on top, and struck a match. He looked for coffee, found it, filled the pot with water, and dumped in a handful of ground beans. A copper teakettle sat to one side; Bailey pushed it closer to the heat. Next he went outside to see if any meat might be hanging handy, and found a canvas-wrapped bundle under the eaves. A haunch of venison! He cut steaks enough for a meal, wrapped and hung the bundle back. Debating about whether to fry or boil the potatoes he located, he finally washed and rubbed them with his hands to clean grit and dust from the skins before he put them in a pot over the fire. He looked for hardtack or bread, found two loaves of hard-crusted sourdough, and set one on the table.

On a shelf stood a cup of bacon grease for the skillet; he put in a dab to melt. Making sure the potatoes were cooking and that the coffee had boiled, he pulled back the pot before he stepped outside again. Off up the meadow where the timber crowded in, he saw two riders coming at a trot, the first pony a fair-sized animal of the type the Nez Percé tribe used to race, mostly white with black spots. The other pony had reddish-brown spots. Both riders were Indians. Jube's boy and Jube's woman.

Bailey went inside and poured himself a cup of coffee. Holding it in his hand, he walked out to meet the riders. "Put up yer pony, Sarah, and I'll put on the steak, unless you want to take over the chore."

"No, Bailey. You cook." She slid down. "This boy Jack. Jube's boy. He come stay and help Jube."

"Well, Jack, if you're goin' to stay with old Jube and Sarah, you come to a good place. We got winter comin' on, wolves to thin down. There's grizzly workin' up near the lava cliffs. Git the ponies taken care of—me an' Sarah'll have grub on the table in no time."

"Thanks, Mr. Bailey. Sarah, I'll take care of Booshway and Pardner. You go on in and help."

As he heard Jack speak, Bullhead Bailey thought: That boy don't talk like no Indian. He's a half-breed that's spent a lot of time in mission school with white people, and he ain't from around here. Somethin's goin' on.

There was little talk as they ate. Afterward Sarah told Bailey how Jubal had gone to the valley for supplies and to meet with Walter Hill, a cattle buyer who knew Jack. Jubal was due back before the snow hit the passes unless he was held up some way or other, and if he was, she and Jack would stay in the hollow this winter. Jubal had made a deal for some ponies for trading stock, and they were running here on Bailey's grass until they could move them over to the John Day.

Bailey decided to let the two see his suspicion. "Sarah, a feller—stranger to this country—come through Prine City a spell back lookin' for two Indians, a boy and a girl with a bunch of men and horses. Said three head was spotted. He claimed he was lookin' fer a feller by the name of Stubbs an' said the whole shebang had plumb disappeared. I never paid it no mind until I see them two ponies single-footin' down the trail. You ain't got another spotted one in the bunch along with a glass-eyed paint and a big rawboned black, have yuh?"

It was Jack who answered. "Happens we have. The spotted ones have my brand and the others have Jubal's. They all belong to us."

"Well an' good, Jack. You keep yer stock an' look out fer mine, an' I'll do the same fer you an' old Jube. If some feller comes in and starts somethin', take care of him. Do it right an' don't bother me. But keep yer nose clean an' yer gun primed and loaded. If that feller rode this far west, he ain't goin' to quit until he comes up with somethin', good or bad."

As they walked out to the corral, Bailey looked at the dimming light in the western sky. "Goin' to be frost on the medder by mornin'. You'll hear the bull elk whistlin' an' gruntin' afore then. Knock one over fer me, a fat cow if you kin. Let it hang a night or two, then haul it down to the cabin. I kin send you back some hog meat. Later on, I'll have some sowbelly smoked fer you an' Sarah. If she gits a few hides worked up, I kin use a new jacket an' some mitts. Have her line 'em with rabbit fur—I look fer a cold winter."

"We'll do that, Mr. Bailey. I can get an elk most anytime. Tomorrow, maybe." Jack's tone shifted. "You think that feller might show up looking for the ponies that disappeared?"

Bailey looked over the corral as he reached for his saddle. "If the stock's yers and old Jube's, you kin figger on trouble. That hombre's got somethin' pushin' him to ride this far, an' I got a feelin' it ain't jist the ponies. You better keep in mind that if Jubal ain't here, you an' Sarah are jist a couple of thievin' Injuns to him, an' if he kills you for stealin' his stock, nothin'll be done about it. Right now, damned near ever' white settler in this part of Oregon is blamin' redskins fer whatever goes wrong."

Bailey slung the saddle on, reached under the pony's belly, caught the cinch, and pulled it up. He made the tie, rocked the saddle to settle it, and looked over at Jack. "Buster, I happen to know Walter Hill. If you traveled with him an' he put up with you, that's good enough fer me. Stay alive! If you're forced to pertect Sarah, yer stock an' mine, do it! So long. I'll be lookin' fer some meat in the next few days."

As Bailey loped his pony toward his ranch headquarters, Jack thought of the message behind his last words. Did he actually mean that if this stranger rode in and claimed the stock, Jack and Sarah should kill him if necessary? Bailey said to stay alive, but he had also said to keep him out of any trouble, that he didn't want to know what happened. Jack knew that if the stranger killed him and Sarah, white settlers here would be on the white man's side. He went back to the cabin, but he said nothing to Sarah about his thoughts.

Since the murderous killings in the canyon near the gorge, Jack was ever suspicious, reluctant to be caught off guard. During their travel here, he had always made his bed some distance from the fire where Sarah lay. He slept lightly, often awoke and listened to night sounds. As soon as they arrived at old Jube's cabin, Jack looked for a place to bed down away from it. The nights were not too cold yet; sleeping out under a blanket with a canvas over him was not disagreeable. Always thinking he might be slipped up on unawares, he changed his sleeping place every night, usually after dusk, so as to be unseen by any hidden observer.

Never a night passed that he did not think of Teeah and wonder what had happened to her body. Had Ort and Ace found a hole in which to deposit it? Silently grieving, he hoped so. The picture of buzzards or coyotes circling, coming finally to completely destroy her flesh and scatter the bones, was so awful to contemplate that he forced himself to think of Mr. Hill. Where was Hill now? Would old Jube find him at the Turpin farm? How could they tell the Turpin girls. their mother, and the neighbors what had happened on the trail? Would Mr. Hill and Jube decide to bring Carter and Smith back with them to investigate, and try to get the things thrown over the cliff into the gorge?

Thoughts running through Jack's brain always led to what his own future might hold. Must he confront the stranger looking for the ponies and kill him? Mr. Bailey had almost told him to do that. It seemed to Jack that no matter where he traveled, he had trouble with someone. Even when he and Mr. Hill were together on the trail, they had had to kill to keep from being killed and robbed. Where could he live without being threatened?

Maybe with Sarah and Jube on the John Day. But always living and trading with Jube didn't sound good to him. What Jack really wanted was to move here and there in the hills and higher mountains. He would drift off to sleep remembering life with his Paw, old Bill Tate, their trips on the Clearwater, the Lochsa, and Selways, even the Salmon where Sheepeater Indians had killed his Paw. He had liked living with Thunder and his tribe after that. Was Little Badger still with Chief Thunder, or had he joined Coyote's band?

Each morning Jack awoke clearheaded. Before he made any move in the blanket bed, he listened for a few moments, then quietly raised his head to look around in the dim light for anything unusual, his rifle always handy under the canvas to keep moisture from dampening the powder. Under his head he kept the little two-shot derringer, just within reach the short-handled throwing ax with which he was careful to practice a few throws each day. Sarah had seen him do it. It reminded her of days when she was young, traveling with the tribe, and had seen the boys and young men practice their skills with knife, bow and arrow, and the throwing ax.

The morning after Bailey had been there, she and Jack took two pack ponies up the dim trail to where young bull elk squealed in anticipation of the rut. The cold nights, frost now in the upper meadows, and yellowing leaves on the willows and cottonwoods marked the beginning of fall. Bailey wanted a fat young cow, and Sarah wanted an elk calf. She needed the soft hides to make up shirts and gloves. Heavy bull hides took too much time and hard work for her now. That could come later after they had gotten their meat supply and steady cold lay over the land.

10

Bardo Stebbins backtracked to Prine City, stayed there overnight, and sought information about Bailey and his cattle range. People who knew Bullhead Bailey seemed reluctant to say much about him, but at the livery barn the hostler told him where the log cabins and corrals that comprised the Bailey headquarters were and that his range lay wherever his cattle and loose horses fed, roughly on the east bank of the river twenty or thirty miles south of town. Elk Hollow? Well, he could find that place up a little creek that entered the South Fork five miles beyond the Bullhead Bailey ranch, the hollow itself nine or ten miles farther.

"What sort of feller is Bailey?" Stebbins probed. "How come they call him Bullhead?"

"Well, he's bullheaded!" the hostler replied. "When he moved in here years back, some feller told him that, so he made his iron like a bull's head. When you see that brand on a critter, you know it belongs to Bullhead Bailey, and effen you're half smart you won't change it, even if yuh think yuh kin. Bailey's rougher than tough. And another leetle thing—the Injuns up in that country look after Bailey's stock, don't ever fergit that."

"I've heard Injuns farther east're killin' cattle and runnin' off stock. Why not over here?"

"Them around here's purty much barn-broke and civilized. Old Bailey an' a few like him seen to that, but don't stir 'em up effen yuh run into a bunch. They kin be mean!"

"Where I come from we tamed 'em permanent-like." Stebbins sneered. "I never had no trouble with 'em I couldn't handle. I'll head up that way, talk with Bullhead. Maybe he knows where the two I told you 'bout're hangin' out. If they've got my brother's ponies, I'll bring 'em back, all right. See yuh in a few days."

After Stebbins left, the barn boss spoke to the hostler. "Frank, want to bet we don't see that jaybo agin?"

"Give me odds an' I'll take yuh on."

"Two bits agin a bottle of whiskey?"

"Yeah, that's good enough."

"He hired the outfit and the pony fer more'n a week and put up a coupla twenties agin the bill. If he don't show in two weeks, you buy the whiskey."

Frank slid his hand under his ragged cap and scratched his head. The boss was older and smarter—but why wouldn't the stranger come back? Oh, well, two bits was a day's wages, but a bottle of whiskey would give him several good drinks.

"If he comes back termorra night or the next one, you git the bottle," he agreed. "Good stuff this time, not that slop they pour out in the First Stop Saloon."

Bailey was pushing a little bunch of cattle off the open bench above the river when he saw a rider approaching from the direction of Prine City. A stranger. Bailey took a quick guess: He's on the trail of the ponies. Him and his rented livery-barn outfit better not spook these critters, or by God he'll eat dirt!

Stebbins watched ahead and above him and saw the cattle come over the hill, then the rider crowding them upriver. He held back, knowing half-wild range cattle would scatter like leaves in the fall wind at the sight of a strange rider coming at them. Bailey worked his way down, now well behind the bunch hightailing it for the bottom of the bench to the trail along the river. His pony slid and plunged, scattering sand and rocks as he came down to flatter ground, both horse and rider looking as though they had already put in a full day's work, although sun time said not much past midday.

Bailey kept his spurs close to his mount's flanks as he crowded the cattle hard so they wouldn't break for the river or hills. Stebbins followed along, and caught the cowman and his heaving, sweat-covered pony half a mile farther on, Bailey now putting up poles across a trail that led east up a narrow canyon. Stebbins halted and looked on, but Bailey finished his work before he turned to Stebbins.

"What the hell do you want?" was his opening question. Sweating, his bearded face red from sun and exertion above the brown hair that covered mouth and cheeks, he looked mean and tough. Gray-blue eyes glittered in the sun as he faced Stebbins. He wore a buckskin shirt, grease- and water-stained, a rip in one sleeve, some of its fringe gone. When his left hand pushed up his ragged hat to wipe off the sweat, Stebbins saw Bailey's forehead, white in contrast with his red face and brown beard.

"You Bullhead Bailey?" Bardo asked.

"They call me that. What's it to you?"

"I'm on the trail of some stock stolen from a friend of mine. He left Fort Walla Walla with a party on their way up the crooked river and never showed up again, last seen where the army road leaves the Deschutes gorge. A fellow works fer Prine—Wilson, he said his name was—saw two Injuns around here, a squaw an' a young buck, with some ponies looked like some in my friend's outfit. I heard they're squatted up at Elk Hollow."

"Yeah, I know 'em. What's the stock look like?"

Stebbins gave him the three miners' description of the ponies and of people in the missing party.

Bailey and his pony cooled off and got their wind back; as he listened, some pieces began to fit together. Jack and Sarah hadn't told him everything. Well, better let this feller sniff around—no use to try to head him off now.

"I kin tell yuh where they was t'other day. Might as well mosey on up to my place with me, it's right on the way. I'll take down these other rails first."

Bailey pulled poles from the gateway he and his riders had made across the upriver trail and laid them to one side. The two rode through. Stebbins decided the cattle had been driven into the side gulch where Bailey had a cattle trap to hold them.

When they reached the Bullhead Ranch headquarters, Bailey didn't follow his usual custom of inviting a visitor in to eat or have coffee. Instead, he waved a gloved hand at the trail continuing upriver and said, "Yuh go on up that trail till yuh come to 'nother branch goin' uphill to yer left. Yuh can't miss it—I had the boys put up rails across the main trail to keep the critters from goin' that way. Jist foller up the hill, drop into the crick a mile or so above the canyon. The hollow's five or six miles beyond."

"Well, thanks, Bailey. One more thing—can I go on over the hill and come into the road that crosses to John Day country? If I can, it'll save going back to Prine City."

"Yeah, you kin. It's an old Injun trail clear on through. If you're trail-and-mountain-raised, you'll make it through easy.

Iffen you don't show up back here, I'll figger you went out that way, huh?"

"Not really. I just wanted to get the lay of the land in case the horse thieves took off an' I'd have to trail 'em."

"Well, now . . . horse thieves, did you say? Them's strong words in this country. But if they sure enough stole that stock, I'll furnish the rope an' help hang 'em. See you prove it first, though, mister!"

"If they're my friend's ponies, I'll prove it, all right." Stebbins' tone was grim as he urged his pony forward.

Bailey didn't even watch him go. He turned his own pony into the corral and unsaddled him, then went to the main cabin, where he set a coffeepot on the stove, pushed kindling and wood into the firebox, and lit it. When the next riders came in off the hill, they could grab a bite and all change ponies before going out once more. Old man Prine was gathering a herd of fat stuff to trail out, and Bailey wanted to throw in a hundred steers to go with them. He needed the cash to pick up more stockers for the range over in the valley next year.

The trail uphill from the river climbed steeply until it reached the benchlands, then leveled off to the streamside. Cattle had made it dusty with use; only along the creek's bank did the rider see trees and brush.

Stebbins had a poor regard for Indians, believing them only to be tolerated if necessary, gotten rid of if possible, and he had not formed as yet any idea of what his approach to the ponies' possessors would be.

He saw a small log cabin at the edge of the meadow under tall yellow pine trees, a thin trail of blue smoke coming from the stovepipe above its roof, a log shelter and pole corral nearby. His pony nickered and was answered by one there. Among the several ponies in the enclosure, he saw spotted ones, and as he rode closer, the animals now in better view, Stebbins picked out a big rangy black, a paint, and two small-spotted black-and-whites standing with a red-freckled pony in the far corner. Thinking the larger spotted gelding exceptional, Stebbins decided it would be a chief's pony in most Indian tribes. Were these the ones the miners had told him about?

Stebbins tied his pony to a post near the corral and walked toward the cabin. When he called out, the door

70

opened and an Indian woman came out and held up her right hand palm toward him in a sign of peace. Stebbins did the same.

"You speak American?"

The woman shook her head. "Me Jube's woman. He gone."

"Are those your ponies?"

"Jube he gone—no here."

"Listen, old woman, those ponies . . . horses." He pointed. "See 'em—in the corral! Where'd Jube get those ponies?"

"Jube he gone. He no here. Me Jube's woman."

Hot, tired, hungry, and impatient, Stebbins felt on the verge of violence, but he caught himself, turned away from her, and went to the corral. The black, yes, and the glass-eyed paint. The three spotted ones the Indians had ridden. Two brown ponies, one with a stripe down its nose. He went back to the cabin, sure of his evidence, enough to hang these people as horse thieves.

Sarah stood there beside the door.

"Where . . . is . . . Jube?" he said slowly and forcefully. "When will he be back?"

"Me Jube's woman. He no here." She shrugged her shoulders. Her black eyes showed no sign of understanding. Stebbins felt growing anger, sure she knew the answers to his questions and could talk American if she chose. He looked at her and saw she was not past the point of desirability. Her hair hung in long black braids. She looked clean and attractive in her buckskin shirt and doeskin skirt, colored yarn in the fringe. Stebbins moved toward her, sure that all Indian women and girls desired white men as bed partners.

Sarah did not flinch or back away. As he approached, she said once more, "Me Jube's woman." Then, "He kill you, white man."

"He come, maybe I kill him, squaw. Now, you be nice to me and maybe I'll be nice to you. We'll go into the cabin— you cook me some dinner. Maybe you can remember where you and Jube got those ponies that belong to my brother."

"Those Jube's ponies."

"Well, Jube's woman, come on, dig up some grub fer me. Then we talk about the ponies. Maybe you be my blanket squaw, huh?"

"No blanket squaw! Jube kill you quick."

71

"The hell with that! Git busy afore I kick yer fat rump!"

Sarah realized that to appease this stranger might forestall violence, but that sooner or later he would force himself on her. She turned to the doorway. The remainder of a deer haunch lay in the cabin. Could she spread out enough time preparing steaks for a meal to allow for Jack's return? But how could she alert him to this new danger? Jack, usually on the alert like some hunted animal, would note the stranger's pony and be cautious, but he might come into the cabin without waiting to see who it was. Somehow she must leave a sign for him outside to indicate special danger.

When Jube and Sarah had fashioned the cabin, they left a fairly wide overhang of the shake roof's eaves under which they hung various articles, wet clothing, and head coverings. The two pegs nearest the doorway were now unused. As Sarah went in the door ahead of Stebbins, she decided how she would warn the Indian boy.

Stebbins' eyes became accustomed to the gloom, and he looked around carefully but saw nothing to arouse any suspicion of danger. Confident of his own ability to handle the squaw, he hardly noticed when she picked up a curved skinning knife and began to cut the meat. Placing several slices to one side, she wrapped the rest in its canvas and tied a knot in the string around the leg bone, leaving a loop. Then she opened the door and hung the haunch on one of the pegs.

In the meantime, Stebbins sat down, watching the doorway. When Sarah turned back from hanging the meat outside, he was gratified to see her fill the small stove with dry wood and light a fire. Calmly she looked at the coffeepot, put in water and coffee she took from a glass jar. At the table, she rubbed the red-and-white-checked oilcloth with a damp rag; then, frowning, apparently not satisfied, she gathered it up, took it to the door, and hung it on an empty peg opposite the one where the meat now hung.

Inside again, she found another piece of oilcloth and placed it on the table. She picked up a kettle near the stove and inspected its contents, stirring with a wooden spoon before she placed the pot over the firebox, then put an iron skillet to heat, meanwhile silent.

Stebbins, resting, began to relax. He looked around the cabin, saw that the bed near at hand had been used by only one person. There was nothing to indicate a man's recent presence here. Evidently old Jube and the boy too were long gone someplace or other. Well, he had found the ponies and some rare entertainment as well. He opened his tobacco pouch. When he had lit his pipe and puffed, he gave a sigh of contentment as he blew smoke toward the open door.

"What's your name, my pretty?"

"Sarah. Me Jube's woman. Me no blanket woman!"

"Now, that's somethin'! He marry you?"

"Me Jube's woman. He come back, he kill you."

"Sarah, that don't bother me none."

She did not answer, but placed a tin plate, cup, and spoon on the table along with a loaf of sourdough bread. She stirred the pot, then moved back. Bacon grease from the cup smeared the skillet, and she dropped two steaks on the sizzling iron. The fragrance of cooking meat filled the room.

"Yuh know, Sarah, if you're nice to me, maybe I'll give yuh a present afore I leave." He reached in his vest pocket. A gilded chain, dangling a bauble glittering with imitation jewels, hung from his fingertip. He thought he saw a look of distinct interest in the woman's eyes, and he was sure he saw them widen in surprise.

But Sarah had just heard, for the second time, a valley quail's warning call back of the cabin. In a moment came the excited chatter of a chipmunk. Jack had seen her sign by the door and was near at hand! She no longer feared this man sitting at his insolent ease in her cabin.

She turned the steak, then moved the kettle from stove to table and took off the lid. Fragrant odors of vegetables, meat, and herbs escaped with the steam. She motioned Stebbins to the table, picked up his plate, and put a steak on it.

Stebbins gobbled the stew voraciously, wiping liquid and juicy pieces from his beard with the back of his hand before he speared a piece of steak to push into his gaping mouth. Sopping bread, he pondered his next move. The squaw needed a lesson. He'd teach her to answer his questions! Maybe she needed batting around. In Indian camps he had visited, he had once seen a half-drunk buck "lodgepole" his woman to make her accede to his wishes. Such a beating might help this squaw forget her high-and-mighty ways. Who'd she think she was—a white woman?

Sure there was no other person around, Stebbins pushed

73

back the crude chair and stood erect, stretching his arms. The woman with her back to the stove sensed his mood.

"Sarah, you goin' to tell me where those ponies come from?"

Again she acted as though she didn't understand. "Jube not here. He gone."

"The hell with that noise! Listen, squaw, tell me about those ponies, and be nice to me—I give you this purty necklace. If you don't, I'll take a stick an' beat you like any dog!"

Out of patience, Stebbins moved to grab her. As he stepped forward, Sarah drew back against the stove, cringing as if to ward off a blow, raising her left arm to cover her face.

As Stebbins bent to encircle her, his right arm passing below her uplifted hand, she reached back for the coffeepot, and when his bearded face came close, hot scalding liquid hit his eyes and nose and soaked his beard. He jerked erect, and Sarah squirmed from his grasp. Quick as she was, the man whirled and lunged to grasp her skirt as she reached the doorway. Both off balance, they struggled and fell down the cabin step, Sarah trying to get free, Stebbins in furious pain, unable to see through his burning eyelids, but holding her fast with one hand.

As he lay partly over the Indian woman, trying to wipe his eyes clear, a heavy club of pine pitchwood thumped his head. His body went limp and his struggles ceased. Sarah looked up into Jack's face.

The half-breed pulled Stebbins away and turned him onto his back, unconscious but still alive.

11

Sarah stood up, her face impassive. "Not dead! We kill him quick," she urged. "Jack, pull him back of cabin. Not bleed here."

The two grasped the man's arms and slid him over the pine-needled ground. With her curved skinning knife, Sarah made one strong, slashing stroke across his throat, making

74

certain now that her attacker would not live to tell what had happened.

She looked to where the livery-stable horse stood tied to the post, then wiped off the knife on a pine-grass clump; an expression that passed for a smile crossed her face. "Git pony, Jack. We take bad man to Happy Hunting Grounds."

Jack had no question. He went to untie and fetch the horse, and while he was gone, Sarah looked through Stebbins' pockets, laying aside his tobacco pouch while she dug deep into his coarsely woven jeans. A pocketknife, some five-, ten-, and twenty-dollar gold pieces. She rolled him over. In his left-rear patch pocket she found a leather wallet of tanned elkhide, dark with grease and wear. Banknotes, of which she had no knowledge. She placed the wallet with the other plunder and explored the right-rear pocket. A small pouch, heavy with material Sarah knew to be gold dust and fine nuggets, folded and wrinkled around it a bright red-and-blue silk scarf. She tucked that into her skirt belt.

Jack came back with the pony, and they removed the saddlebags for inspection. Some more gold, a little jerky, and fire-making materials in one. The other contained a rolled-up piece of oiled silk for rainwear, a warm cap of muskrat fur, rabbit-lined buckskin gloves, and a Colt revolver similar to the one Mr. Hill had bought on the trip from Jacksonville to Fort Klamath, and bullets, cloth-wrapped, to go with it.

Sarah looked at Jack. "We keep all this," she grunted.

"Sarah, we must take away everything that could be claimed as his. He looks like Old Stubbs, and I'll bet he's kin to that man. The pony and riggin' looks like livery-barn stock. Where can we hide 'em?"

"Git pony. We ride, I show you. Be long ways, Jack—we go quick."

Jack saddled Stebbins' pony. He and Sarah wrapped the body in an old canvas, tied it at both ends, then heaved and tugged it to balance over the livery pony's saddle. Sarah fastened it down. Jack went at a quick walk for their own ponies. By the time he returned, Sarah had packed food which she now placed in her saddlebag before she climbed easily onto the stocky, short-legged pony she called hers, and with Jack leading Stebbins' borrowed mount, started through the pine timber headed southwest.

The fall sun was low when Sarah stopped above a rocky bluff at the head of a steep, narrow gorge.

"Bears down there," she said. "No man come here, find bad man. Bears eat pony."

Jack nodded his head and dismounted. He was all for throwing Stebbins over at once, but Sarah stopped him. Clothes—worn, dirty, bloody, or patched—had value in this country far from stores and supplies. They stripped the corpse, then rolled it off the cliff. Stebbins slid away, dropped over a ledge. Only the sound of rolling rocks marked his descent to the depths.

The livery pony was now stripped of all rigging, then led to the edge. Tired though he was, the beast seemed reluctant, sensing danger. Jack had Stebbins' revolver in his hand, and when Sarah nodded, he cocked the weapon, pointed it at the animal's head below the ear, and pulled the trigger. The pony fell onto the slope, hind legs kicked out in muscular reaction that pushed its body over to join the late Bardo Stebbins.

"Snow come soon," Sarah almost whispered. "Bears come, find pony and man. We hide saddle and other things until John Day, huh?"

Jack was already packing clothes and the man's boots into the sack Sarah had brought. The bridle and army saddle were tied on behind his pony.

As they retraced their route, the morbid thoughts he could not shake off for long crowded Jack's mind. All the trouble he had seen since leaving Mr. Hill on the Columbia River! Would others follow Stebbins? He had thought the deaths of Stubbs and his two henchmen would be the end of violence. How had this man known where to find him and the ponies? The rider, Lee Wilson! Then Bailey must know! Maybe that was why Bailey had told him so emphatically to take care of anyone who bothered them, but keep him out of it.

Next morning Jack and Sarah left the hollow early, their two ponies loaded with elk meat, to ride to Bailey's cookhouse, a long, low building with a thick shake roof Bailey had covered with dirt as insulation. The place served as kitchen, storeroom, and sometimes as a bunkhouse, its long table usually laden with food for hungry men.

The cook, an old bedeviled character, drank anything that might take his mind off his imagined troubles; he had been

76

partly crippled in a long-ago bear-garden brawl but now claimed it had happened as he rode a particularly wild outlaw pony. Bailey put up with his foolishness because Old Brew could mix up palatable food and look after the place when all the others were away.

Cooks were scarce in this country. All able-bodied men out to make their fortunes, if temporarily out of a job or money, might take on cooking for a short time but would fly the coop at the first opportunity. Bailey's crippled cook had once been named Adolph Brewer, but after he escaped his father's hard-scrabble farm he called himself Brew. Now, crippled and bent as he was, he chose to be called Old Brew, in an effort to solicit sympathy for his condition.

Bailey had left with his steers. When Sarah and Jack arrived at the cookhouse, Old Brew met them at the door. His usual sour look and words were enough to discourage most Indians, but Sarah knew him.

"What in hell you two redskins doin' around a white man's diggin's?"

"We come with elk meat. Bailey said bring some."

"It ain't gonna be any good. You fellers live on spoiled meat and rotten fish. Well, what yuh waitin' fer?"

"Is Bailey here?"

"Naw. Old Hardhead's out chousin' cows. I run this place whilst he's gone. Git that meat off those sorry-lookin' ponies you prob'ly stole an' I'll open the meathouse. Don't pull no scalpin' knife on me or I'll kick yer butts outta here."

Jack kept quiet and let Sarah do any necessary talking. Old Brew growled on about being overworked, what he would do with the meat, and why Bullhead let lazy Injuns camp on his land. When they unwrapped the elk haunches, Brew saw that the meat was clean of blood, dirt, and hair. After the quarters had been hung on hooks, he began to complain about feeding every bum that came through the country.

"I s'pose you two're starved to death fer grease an' lard," he groused. "Hell's bells, here's a slab of sowbelly to go with yer beans and grease the skillet. Don't tell Bullhead I give it to yuh, hear? Sarah, I got a sack of beans—an' how yuh fixed fer dried prunes? Jest so happens there's some extry I could throw in."

Wordlessly Sarah took the supplies he passed over to her.

"My feet git awful cold in the night. I wake up an' can't

77

sleep," Brew droned on. "S'pose yuh kin make me some moc-casins lined with fur an' high enough to cover my shinbones? Bring 'em next trip yuh make down this way. How yuh fixed fer sweetnin'? Got a jug of 'lasses I kin let yuh have." He handed it to Jack and looked closely at him for the first time. "Bailey says you're old Jube's boy. That right? Well, Jack, you're with a good man an' a good woman. Never thought much of Injuns till Sarah here give me some of her medicine fer an earache."

Sarah went close to the whiskered old man and gently pulled his earlobe. "No more hurt, Brew? Ear feel good?"

"Finer'n silk," he replied, and gave her a sly glance. "Say, old Bailey said a feller come through here t'other day on the track of horse thieves. He stop up at yer place?"

"No see 'um, Brew. We been gone on hunt. No see tracks in trail."

"Prob'ly got lost. Looked like a city dude. Borried pony. Want some grub afore yuh go back?"

Old Brew set out food he knew Sarah and Jack wouldn't have at their camp in the hollow. Bailey had gotten eggs and vegetables along with some ham from a settler down the trail. He let the man run some cattle along the river.

Sarah and Jack feasted on vegetable stew with slices of ham in it, baked beans hot from the oven, and bread the old cook had baked. Then he set out a bowl of stewed peaches and a pot of coffee, and while they ate, filled a flour sack with odds and ends of food for them, talking as he moved around his kitchen.

"So that feller never come by yer place? The dude talked to Bailey—fact is, he rode in with Bailey. I figgered Bull-head'd ask him in to eat, but he didn't. What the hell? When the old man comes in, I asked him what the dude want, an' Bailey answered, real short-like, 'Says he's on the trail of some horse thieves.' I says to Bailey, 'You think so?' Then Bailey says, 'He's the thief an' he's on the dodge. That's why I never had him come in here to eat.' "

Jack did not know Sarah's thoughts. She had told him the man had come to the place plying her with questions about where Jube had gotten the ponies. Jack felt sure the stranger could be related to Old Stubbs because there was such a strong resemblance between them. Now Brew was confirming his suspicions that the man had seen Bailey, been at the

78

ranch headquarters. Had Lee Wilson told the stranger, maybe Bailey too, that Jube had stolen the ponies? Jack saw nothing he could do now to protect himself and Street from being called horse thieves until Jube showed up with Mr. Hill.

After the meal, Sarah and the half-breed loaded what Brew had sacked up for them and returned to the cabin in the hollow. The problem of the ponies they had acquired began to present itself to Jack in no uncertain terms. They could not be kept corraled because there was no hay to feed them. What little remained in the shed Sarah and Jube had cut with a scythe and dried in the meadow earlier for use in the winter when snow was deep, grass and other browse no longer available. If turned loose without hobbles, they would stray, and join up with others loose on the range. Good ponies were valuable as the only means of travel other than on foot. To raft or boat the wild rivers that brawled their way through the deep canyons was more dangerous and laborious than following the trails.

Elk continued to squeal and grunt in the hills. Tamaracks towered golden yellow in the sun. Winter was at hand. Soon the passes over the Cascades would be frosted white, later impassable.

A week after Sarah and Jack made their trip to Bailey's spread, they had another visitor, a bearded, rough-looking rider who rode into the hollow and yahooed. Sarah had already seen him down the trail. When she opened the door, the rider said, "Sarah . . . is Jack around?"

"I know you?"

"I ride fer Bullhead Bailey. He sent me up to tell you an' Jack to bring yer ponies down to headquarters."

"Why Bailey want ponies?"

"Fer Pete's sake, Sarah, some feller rode in sayin' yer man Jube is down on the river where he left you a while back, an' he wants the string down there purty soon. Bailey says to git movin'."

"You go with us?"

"I figger on it. Where's Jack?"

"With ponies. You wait. Come in, have coffee. We git Jack on flat up there." She waved her hand toward the southern rim. As the rider climbed down from his pony, Sarah asked, "What Bailey call you, huh?"

"Usually the old bastard jest yells 'Jump to it!' " The rider

79

laughed. "I go by the handle of Bent. How long you known Bailey?"

"Long time. Bailey met Jube. Bailey and Jube hunt an' git cows. Bailey good man."

"Well, he's a rough rascal. I wouldn't cross that old boar hog fer nothin'!"

Sarah thought as she talked. If she took only what she needed for the trip, she and Bent might work the ponies down the trail while Jack cut across to the cabin to get his own plunder. She knew he would not want Bent or anyone else to see where he had hidden his belongings. What he took must be up to him. In the meadow, Sarah removed her pony's hobbles. While Bent drank coffee and ate a bowl of the stew she always had ready, she saddled it and tied her own necessities on behind. Then she and Bent gathered the string and set out for the flat.

Jack saw them coming and wondered, fearful that this man had come seeking the other stranger. He rode to meet them.

"Jack, this Bailey's man. Wants to talk."

Bent explained. "Old Bailey sent me to fetch you an' Sarah an' the ponies down where Jube's camped on the river. He sent word with Wilson."

Sarah rode close to the boy. "Go to camp, get things you need. You catch up to me an' Bent. My things on saddle." She pointed.

As Jack loped Booshway back to the cabin, he thought he would take everything except the Colt the stranger had carried. Let Sarah and Jubal have that. What was done with the ponies would be up to Mr. Hill and Jube. Quickly he carried his blankets and the tarp to the cabin, took some of his gold and the Turpin revolver, and wrapped it all in his coat and a small canvas, then tied it on behind the saddle—a large bundle, but he thought it would ride out the trip.

At the ranch, Bailey had the corral gate open; the ponies trotted in. He looked up at Sarah on her pony. "Well, Sarah, yer man's waitin' down on the river. He said the nights was gittin' too cold for him to sleep alone. I said I'd fetch him a winter woman."

She smiled. "I go, Bailey. You want me bring you winter woman?"

"Hell, yes! A young one, nice and round and soft. One that kin cook, mind yuh! Old Brew burns too many beans an'

80

he's homely as an old mule that's rolled in the mud and got stuck full of cockleburs. 'Sides that, he snores at night."

"We go to meet Jube, Bailey?"

"Yeah. He's downriver. Old man Hill's there with a few other fellers waitin' fer Jack to show 'em the place where a killin' took place. Maybe that's why that dude Stebbins was on yer trail. I s'pect he's over the mountains to John Day by now."

Jack heard the name. "You must be right about that, Mr. Bailey," he put in. "No one stopped at our camp."

"Yeah, chances are we won't see him around these parts no more. Now, if you're ready to light out, I'll ride along with you till we git past the town, but yuh better grab a bite to eat first. Old Brew's got some hot grub—I kin stand some chuck myself. Git down, Sarah, an' come in."

Inside, Bailey leaned forward across the table. "I figger I better go along with you," he told the two hungry riders. "That skunk Stebbins let out the word he was on the trail of two Injuns with some spotted ponies an' a glass-eyed paint. If you go through Prine City alone, you might have to do some fast talkin'. Jack, could be a posse's on yer trail, 'cause you're s'posed to have kilt this dude's friend or brother."

They passed Prine City without incident, and after a mile or two, Bailey turned back. Sarah rode alongside him and reached out her gloved hand.

"Bailey, you good man. I make you warm mittens."

"Better git busy, 'cause there'll be skim ice on the bucket in the mornin'. Tell old Jube I hope ever'thing works out fer him, you too, young feller, and tell old man Hill I think he beat me on that last cow deal. He'll grin like a fox."

At the bend in the river, they found Jube and Mr. Hill. Carter and Smith, the fathers of the two murdered boys, stood by sober-faced.

12

Mr. Hill greeted Jack and Sarah, and took charge. Jubal Street had already repeated to Hill and the two farmers Jack's story of the killings and how he had then hidden some of the Turpins' possessions and escaped with the ponies, but the group gathered there were impatient to hear more about the tragedy. It was too late in the day now to go on to the meadow where Jack and Jubal had rounded up and branded the horses. They sat around the fire and drank coffee while Sarah and Jube rousted some food.

With Mr. Hill beside him, Jack felt at ease, and began his story, going over the trip from the time the group had left Mr. Hill and the other two men. He told of the three men who caught up with them and of his suspicions, recalling his attempt to warn Mr. Turpin, and how he had tried to stand guard. He spoke of Turpin's feeling that all would be well when they reached the army road, and of meeting the three miners there. Jack pictured their camping place in the canyon that night, and noted his listeners' expression of shock as he described the morning attack, but when he came to Teeah's death, tears filled his eyes and his voice choked off. He got up and walked around the fire, then sat down again close to Mr. Hill before he went on to tell of watching Ace and Ort at their grisly task, how he followed and saw them throw the bodies over the lip of the gorge, then kill the five branded ponies. The hard tone a proven warrior might have used came into his voice as he related how he killed Ort and Ace and told the men he would show them where he had hidden the plunder he had taken.

Questions were asked and answered, suppositions made. Mr. Hill asked how the ponies had gotten slit ears and the brands they now wore. Jack replied that he and Jube knew anyone found with unbranded stock was apt to be considered a horse thief. An Indian, he said, would be shot or hung without question. At this, Jube nodded, agreeing.

It was decided that they would leave to go to the scene of

the killings in the morning and from there follow the outlaws' trail.

At the canyon camp, they went over the details once more. Others had been there since, but Jack led the men to the place where Teeah had fallen, killed by a bullet from Stubbs's gun. He bent to the ground, searching, and arose with one long black hair in his fingers.

"I don't know where she is," he said. "She was gone when I came—I never saw her on the ponies."

Walter Hill put his arm around Jack's shoulders, his own eyes misting. "Jack, don't give up. Maybe we'll find her yet. These things never are settled immediately. Suppose you people were watched by other Indians as you traveled, especially when you left Umatilla lands and entered the Warm Springs Indians' territory. Could it be possible they saw what took place here and carried Teeah's body away so white men couldn't defile it?"

"I thought of that and I know it could happen." Jack looked up at the rocky slope where he had stood that morning. "But for some reason I think Ort or Ace did something with her. I looked for sign, but I could find nothing. Stubbs died right where Teeah was lying. I thought Ort and Ace came back and killed him after he chased her and got careless, then . . . I don't know."

To get Jack's mind off Teeah, Mr. Hill said gently, "Mr. Smith and Mr. Carter want to be able to go home and tell people where their folks' bodies are. Mrs. Turpin couldn't come. She lost Mr. Turpin and Roy—you're the only person knows. Take us to the gorge and let's see if we can get to what's left of them."

As they rode, they often found the ponies' trail, still visible in the sand and soil; there had been no rain or wind to disturb it. The broken juniper branches had begun to fade and dry, and like broken arms pointed the way to where the bodies had been thrown over the edge.

As they stood above the abyss, discussion arose on what to do. They could not see down very far. Finally Smith spoke up.

"Boys, I ain't goin' home an' say I looked over the edge and seen nothin' but a piece of the river at the bottom. Folks wouldn't believe the story. I got to git where I kin see what's left of the bodies or their clothes—something to tell me where my boy is."

"How do you think we can do that?" Carter asked, eager.

"How much rope we got with us?"

"I brought a couple hundred feet," Carter replied. "If that ain't enough, we kin use our throw ropes. You want us to let you over the edge?"

"Yes. Once I'm over the lip and overhang I might see where stuff landed or hung up."

They laid out the new, uncut portion of their rope, first from the edge back and around the bottom of the trunk of a juniper. Jack said he would go down first, but they argued over that.

"Fellers, Jack has first rights," Jube settled it. "He war there, he lost somethin' too. Jack, I'll lay clost to the edge so we kin hear each other. When you see somethin', sing out. I'll tie a bowline in this piece of hemp, an' you keep it up under yer arms tight, 'cause it's a long rough way to the bottom."

Jack stepped into the loop. Carter and Smith held the rope, ready to play it out around the trunk at the rock-anchored juniper. Mr. Hill and Jubal crawled close and lay flat on the brink as Jack edged backward into the depths of the forbidding gorge. Almost out of sight, he said, "I can't feel anything with my feet now. Let me down slow."

The two farmers let the rope slip around the trunk while Jubal and Mr. Hill waited for Jack's voice. The line slowly slipped over the edge, and cut a little furrow in the soil until it reached bare lava. Fifty, seventy, a hundred feet were paid out before the half-breed's faint call came. "Stop!"

Moments passed with no word from the depths; then another shout drifted to them, echoes across the canyon repeating it. "Up . . . up . . . up!" The men, Mr. Hill now hauling on the rope from his side of the tree, began to reclaim the line.

Finally Jube turned his head. "Easy, now, he's at the edge. Hill, grab my legs while I scootch over an' git his hands."

Jack came up, short of breath, content to lie still and close his eyes. The men gathered close.

"I saw where the things lit. Some are still there. Over the edge there ain't nothin to lean against or touch. The rope kept turnin' me, but I got down far enough to touch a rock, and I pushed out. Past that, I could see three bodies, but I don't think there's enough rope here to get down where they are. You can look for yourself . . ." His voice trailed off.

"Boys, let me go next. I weigh no more'n Jack—take care you don't jerk me loose."

Mr. Smith got into the loop. Jack took two of their felt hats and twisted them around the rope under Smith's shoulders.

"That's where it cuts in when you hang. Don't look down. When I did, I almost got sick. Look right at the wall until you git to the rock. Brace yerself there an' look down."

"Thanks, boy, I'm glad you told me. Now, grab onto that rope, 'cause I'm goin' down!"

Smith stayed down longer than Jack had. When they finally pulled him back, he lay with his eyes closed until Jube brought a small flask of whiskey and made him take a drink. He gave a sigh of relief, then took another swallow or two, got to his feet unsteadily, and walked to the slight shade of the tortured juniper.

"Boys, they're all five there. My God, I saw what I'm sure was my boy an' Turpin. Your boy . . . Carter . . . he could be layin' close to mine. There was a big man off to one side—probably Stubbs. The Turpin boy—if it was him—lays in a rock slide. I seen everyone but the girl." Smith and those around him fell silent. "Want to take a look, Carter?"

The farmer shuddered. "No, I'll take your word and Jack's. There's no possible way we could reach their bodies?"

"Not unless we fly."

"Then I say let them be! Let's go on to the other job now."

Within a few steps they found evidence of the dead ponies. Coyotes and buzzards had been at them, but Carter and Smith had no doubt they had once belonged to the Turpin party. Near the rock where Ort sat in his last sleep and at the turn in the meadow trail where Ace had died, Jack pointed out more grisly evidence of the deaths of these two men unknown to his present companions, and as the group paused for a few moments in a sort of horrified inertia, the Indian boy saw in their faces a reflection of his own fearful, questioning state of mind.

Finally they traced the trail to where he had concealed the rifles and money under the rocky ledge, but when Jack led them to the exact spot, things there didn't look quite the same to him. He dismounted for a closer look. What he saw as he peered under the overhang shocked him. Guns, saddles, and all the rest were gone!

He stood still a moment, then squatted and looked close around him for the tracks of whoever had discovered the hiding place and taken the plunder, while Mr. Hill and the others sat their ponies. They saw the look on Jack's face when he crawled from under the ledge, and they feared the worst before he spoke.

"It's gone! Everything I hid is gone!"

"Who do you think could have taken it, Jack?" Mr. Hill asked.

"I don't know . . . I can't find any tracks or sign."

Jube climbed off his pony and walked to the Indian boy. "Jack, let's you an' me circle the place. That stuff sure didn't dig itself out an' fly off, hit had to be carried. If there was as much in there as you say, hit took more'n jest one er two, an' they had to leave tracks."

They walked an ever-larger periphery, but came at last to the conclusion that those before them had been smart enough to step only on the lava rock, alert enough to brush out any chance tracks they made. Finally Mr. Hill again took charge.

"Jack, did you leave the gold and money there, too?"

"All except what I had with me. I wanted to leave everything the others owned until you came. I'm sorry, Mr. Hill—I thought I had it hidden so no one could find it."

"Jack, it looks to me like Injuns follered you and spotted where you done the job. They didn't try to kill you because they had what they wanted. Besides, you were a redskin, too. Now, as far as the ponies go, I think they missed 'em there in the medder. They probably come across the river on foot and crawled up the side on an old secret trail."

Jube took out his pipe and tobacco and began to smoke.

Smith looked at Jack. "Boy, I believe everything you've told us," he said, "and I'm sorry the things you hid got stolen. Hell, that'd be nothin' . . . if only my boy and the others hadn't been killed. It's lucky for us you're alive. If they'd killed you, not one of us would have ever known what happened to the party. But for your sake, I wish we knew what happened to your friend, the Indian girl." He stood silent, unable to say more.

They moved on to the meadow. Jubal showed them where he and Jack had built the fire and heated the crude branding

86

iron. The story had been concluded, words verified, but two questions remained unanswered. Where was Teeah? Who had taken the gold?

At the temporary camp, Sarah had a meal going. The men settled down for a smoke and to consider what should be done next. It seemed of no use to search further. Smith and Carter must go back to the valley within the next few days. They had come through some snow on the way over, and soon it would lie heavy enough to stop all winter traffic. Mr. Hill, unsure in his own mind as they discussed the situation, finally brought Jack into it by asking him his plans.

"I want to stay with Jubal and Sarah for now," was the half-breed's reply. "I want to learn this country—maybe I'll come back to the gorge next summer and try to find out more about what happened to Teeah and who took the gold. If I ever find it, I want to take it to Mrs. Turpin and the rest. You and they can have the other ponies—we put brands on 'em just so nobody could say they didn't belong to me."

"No, Jack, I think you and old Jube should keep all of them. Jube had a long hard trip just to git us, an', Jack, we know you done your best in stayin' alive an' killin' those two skunks. Wouldn't you say as much, Carter?"

"Yes, I would. Keep 'em, sell 'em, or swap 'em."

Smith nodded his head in firm agreement as his neighbor spoke.

Later, Hill told Jack he had taken a liking to Jubal and Sarah. Jack had chosen rightly. Better not go to the valley now—he would be questioned endlessly about the massacre and why he alone had stayed alive.

"Come next spring and summer," Hill concluded, "I intend to be back over in this country with cattle or to buy some, and I'll get in touch with you if you're still around. I want to remind you, Jack, that you can expect people will say you helped some Indians to kill the Turpin party and steal their ponies, their possessions, and their gold. You have already been called a horse thief, and they say Jubal Street's in with you. They'll figger that the Indians' share was the gold and plunder."

Hill's forthright statement of the rumored accusations made Jack wince. "Mr. Hill, you know I wouldn't have done any of that!"

"I do, Jack—but others don't. Try to work it out. Someone must have trailed you and stolen the gold and plunder, and if that's true, there's hope they might have picked up Teeah, too."

Jack nodded, wanting to think that Teeah might be alive. Could it be as Mr. Hill said—that strange Indians had helped her escape and killed Old Stubbs? He began to hope once more.

13

The group split up after their meal, Mr. Hill and Carter and Smith to go west over the summit and back to the valley, Jack to join Jube and Sarah for the trip to Elk Hollow.

Jubal Street knew Bailey would think the meeting at the river with Hill and the others had been important, dealing perhaps with rumors that Jube and the two Indians were horse thieves. On the way Jubal sold two of the ponies to the livery stables in Prine City. Their new owner demanded a bill of sale for the animals, the first time Jube had ever been asked for one. At first he grew hostile, thinking the man doubted that he was the lawful owner of the ponies, but when a rough bill of sale was written out, both he and Jack signed it, though Jube still seethed as they left the place at having to sign such a paper.

"Jack, that skinflint of a barn-sweeper set me thinkin'," he finally said. "By grannies, I'm goin' to deal the ponies we got left to old Bullhead Bailey. I ain't never been called a horse thief yet, but it got purty darn close to it back there."

"I didn't like that much, either. But doesn't Mr. Bailey have enough stock of his own?"

"Hell, no! Did you ever see any of yer people had enough ponies? The cow men're jist the same!"

Bailey was at his diggings, as he called his headquarters buildings, when the three rode into the Bullhead Ranch. "So you fellers're back," he greeted. "Git yer business handled?"

"Yep," was Jube's laconic reply. "Got any grub in yer dugout we kin use afore we head to the hills?"

"Well, Jube, if it warn't fer Sarah an' Jack, I'd say you git yer own. Run that sorry-lookin' bunch of livestock into an empty corral and come on in. I want to set an' chin awhile. Sarah, if old Jube didn't need yuh to skin critters an' chew on hides, I'd hire yuh fer a cook. Old Brew's gettin' worse ever' day, I tell yuh!"

Sarah laughed at Bailey's oft-repeated complaint. "Bailey, I find woman for you yet," she assured him as the three entered the cookhouse.

Jack sat back and listened there at the table while Jube worked on Bullhead Bailey.

"Yuh know, Bailey, we stopped at that shed an' clutter of corrals Ike Cafferty calls a livery barn an' sold him two ponies. He acted like I stole 'em, an' had me sign a paper he called a bill of sale. He wanted to know what happened to the feller who borried his pony an' went on the trail of Jack an' the woman."

"An' what'd you say to that?" Bailey's eyes were shrewd.

"I says to him, 'Friend, you're barkin' up the wrong tree. That boar coon'd been over in the valley tellin' some people their daddy an' friends was massacreed by white jailbirds an' I heerd when I come back that you'd lent him a pony 'cause he was on the trail of hoss thieves. Mister,' I told him, 'that feller was the brother of a killer by the name of Stubbs, who led his pards in them murders.' " Jube looked Bailey square in the eye. "Then I told Cafferty that this feller had stopped by your place on the way over the hill to the John Day country. He never stopped at the Elk Hollow cabin, that I know, so he must've kep' on goin'."

Sarah took a swallow of coffee and shifted in her chair, but Jack sat motionless.

"What was Ike's answer to that?" Bailey said.

"Aw, he jist spit on the floor. 'Guess I lost my pony fer sure,' he says. 'Lucky I had him leave me some money.' "

"What're you gonna do with the rest of them cayuses?"

"Swap 'em or sell 'em to you. They're already used to eatin' yer grass."

"What makes yuh think I'm goin' to need more grass-eaters? What I need is more cows!"

"Bullhead, you're slow to figger. Hell's fire, you kin run five hunderd to double that up in the head of Elk Crick alone, but you'll need ponies to herd 'em. Iffen you're goin' to stock this range, yuh better git at it 'fore someone with more gumption moves in."

"Well, what do yuh want fer the three of 'em?"

"I'll be doin' yuh a favor by pickin' out three cows with their calves come next spring as a trade."

"The hell you will! Those cows'll winter here—be worth more money next spring!"

"Well, you need ponies worse'n you need cows. I should git two cows fer one broke pony—I'm lettin' yuh off easy. What's more, I'll lend yuh a good rider to help yuh through the winter."

"Yer lettin' me have Sarah? I'll take that deal!"

"Nope, not Sarah. You kin have Jack. He kin stay in the hollow while me an' Sarah drift over to the John Day an' git ready fer the stock Jack'll drive over next spring."

"If Jack sticks, I'll go fer it."

"Jack'll stick. Iffen he don't, we'll hang him fer a hoss thief." Jubal guffawed. "You gotta pay him, though, an' he don't come cheap."

Bailey turned to the half-breed. "Jack, you heard the deal. Stay in the hollow, work on varmints, an' watch the cattle. I'll throw in grub, grain fer yer ponies, an' twenty bucks a month."

"Mr. Bailey, that suits me." Jack was impassive.

Bailey laughed. "Oh, Jube's a slick old buck," he said. "I've tried to trade him outta Sarah, but no soap. She won't leave him fer fear he'd starve to death."

Jubal Street and Bullhead shook on their deal. Jack felt better. He would be alone at Elk Hollow to work and plan. He might even have a chance to visit the gorge, try again to find out what could have happened to the gold. He might even visit the Warm Springs Indian reservation and ask about Teeah.

Jack kept Booshway and Pardner with him, but Jubal put a pack on Speck to carry his few possessions to the John Day cabin. Before he left, he made a map for Jack of the country comprising Bullhead's possible winter cattle range. As he drew the crude outline on the brown paper, he talked.

"Now, you're in the upper end of where stock'll be slow driftin' down. It'll be up to you to ride out an' push 'em down to better feed. I've seen snow come a little easy, kind of like goose feathers, then git thicker an' heavier an' keep on till you'd think it had to run out sometime, but it'd jist start to blow an' git colder. Nothin' movin', all the deer an' elk holed up in jack-pine jungles in the hollers where the wind can't hit 'em. An' that's what kills old Bullhead's cattle unless they drift down farther along the river. The wind'll whip some snow off'n slopes, an' when she quits, there's feed.

"Along the breaks there's mahogany, bitterbrush, sage, an' all sorts of stuff fer the critters. I call it gut-waddin'. Bailey's brought in a lot of valley cattle. I see 'em rangin' purty high. Sarah said you an' her had seen 'em clear up to the bear dens. That's right here on this picture I'm drawin'." He tapped the paper with his pencil stub. "Work the cows south, slabbin' the slopes till yuh come to the second bench above the river. It's the best winter feed old Bailey has. Once you git his cows in there, you'll see. But right there's where yer wolf an' varmint troubles'll be. Old Bullhead's hell fer gittin' rid of ever'thin' works on his cows, but 'specially wolves. You git some of 'em afore they git wise, that's how you'll make yer mark with Bailey. I got four good Newhouse traps, had a blacksmith in the valley make 'em while I waited fer old man Hill. I'll show yuh how to make the sets an' leave yuh some stink bait. It ain't gener'ly known how to catch smart old timber wolves."

Jack watched as the ragged, bushy-faced trapper squatted in the dirt and drew pictures of how to make blind sets with nothing in them to draw the wolves, "trail sets" where the animals used to following game trails might step and be trapped.

"Now, with the old fellers this won't work too good. You'll catch a pup or two, maybe brush wolves, but the old loafers're the devil's own—they got most of his brains. It ain't no use to try to catch 'em at the kill—they like fresh warm meat and hot blood. Here's where you use the stink bait. It'll pull 'em off the trail. But don't use this till you've tried other tricks. Here's how I do it."

Old Jube walked to a nearby tree. "Find their pissin' place on a bit of sage or a rock or tree. Snow'll show you tracks to it. Put a leetle smidgen on a straw and touch the trap—less'n a drop'll do. Then back off. I like to set my traps out where they circle."

The old man went on to tell Jack more tricks. When the

wolves grew suspicious by using false settings—a bit of metal or small tatter of buckskin or woolen cloth—he could veer the wolves in the direction of the well-hidden, unscented traps. He knew Jack was smart and that he had learned much from his father and his Indian friends, but they were not trappers. Jubal had learned that skill the hard way, by trial and error.

"Iffen it were me, I'd try shootin' one or two of the old ones first. The pups're big now. Soon as snow comes, their paw an' maw'll be out teachin' 'em how to kill, an' they know cows an' yearlin's're easier than elk or deer. If you're on yer toes, yuh'll know the bunch of critters they're after. They don't kill all to oncet. One of the old ones'll cripple a cow so she can't travel too good an' then lead the pups in to play with her till she tires out. That's where yer rifle'll come in."

Jubal lit his pipe and smoked awhile. Jack waited while the smell of tobacco smoke drifted his way. The old chief was thinking, going back to old times.

"Don't be in no hurry to shoot," Jubal went on. "The old ones'll be watchin' the young 'uns gittin' horn-hooked and kicked, dodgin' here an' there. Pick an old dog first. If you're lucky an' git both parents, yuh might git the rest of that pack afore they git wise. They usually light out to new territory after you kill or trap a few, an' the ones that live over the first year of trappin' an' shootin' git way too smart fer most trappers. That's when a feller like me kin come in an' pick 'em off with tricks ain't been tried yet."

14

After the old trapper and his Indian woman left for the John Day River country, Jack spent much of his time riding, changing ponies every day, letting one graze and rest while the other worked. His meals, lots of simple hot food, kept him satisfied. A coal-oil lamp and a lantern made light in the cabin while he cooked, then skinned the fur-bearing animals he had trapped: badger, fox, and along the creeks mink and an occasional otter. Sarah would tan the skins for use in making clothing and mittens. Two days after a heavy snow, he killed his first big wolf.

He had learned in his Indian upbringing never to approach a valley or gorge by riding up to look in. He always dismounted and climbed slowly to peek over the brink, never exposing his whole body or his head. He often moved through snow and got wet to the skin as it melted, but in his scouting he learned the territory. One early morning, light just hitting into a little basin where a bunch of cattle browsed, he saw the wolf. Slowly sneaking from bush to bush, it approached the nearest yearling feeding on a leafy shrub, all unconcerned.

Jack's rifle was primed and ready, and he knew he had not been seen. When the beast drew close enough for a sure shot, Jack fired.

In the old male's bladder he found enough scent for a batch to use in another wolf's territory miles away. His war on the wolves had begun. It would last until winter left and warm winds took snow from the slopes where grass would green, once uncovered. Out of the pack that worked on the south benchlands, Jack got all but the old bitch and one pup before they left for far places.

To the north, where Bent had a line camp, a small pack harassed cattle that ranged near the river. Bailey rode up to see how Jack was doing. When he looked at the hides stretched on boards to dry, he rubbed his scarred, weathered hands together with pleasure.

"Boy, you're shore doin' us some good!" he said. "Better'n I expected. Old Jube must've put you wise to some of his tricks. Looks like yuh cleaned out most of the litter. By God, there's one of the old ones, too!"

"The old bitch and one of the pups were too smart for me," Jack explained. "I think they've left this country. I haven't seen tracks for weeks."

"That so? Well, you kin bet they'll be back, an' when they come, they'll be real smart killers."

"Jube said he has a trick or two they might not be able to figger out."

"Mebbe so, but he'll have to have the devil's own luck. Now, Jack, I got an idee you can help me out over where Bent's ridin'. He's havin' trouble with the ornery devils in the breaks. Pack up yer traps an' drift over there. Try to git the old ones. The bitch'll be heavy with pups afore long. If you kin figger where she dens up, you might git her afore she has the litter. That'd save me at least ten head of stock this spring. Wolves cost me from ten to twenty head every year. I never had no count till the last two years—jist thought it was winter kill. I had the boys check. It's been those gray bastards teachin' their young 'uns to kill."

Jack made the rounds and picked up his traps. With Pardner packed, he drifted downriver and up into the rocky breaks where scattered cattle fed on steep hillsides, bunch grass thick, browse brush in the pockets. Bent told Jack what he knew about the wolves' habits, and with a brass telescope Bailey had lent him he could watch their travel from a distance. The country where the wolves were located was so steep and rough that he decided to make camp nearby and work on foot.

It was March. Spring was at hand, some days warm and sunny with gentle winds sweeping across the greening open places. Then came days of slanting, misting rain turning to snow, bitter wind and sleet to sting a man's face. Watching the wolves from hidden vantage points, Jack knew from the way they acted that he must be close to where they denned. He gradually worked closer, noticing the direction from which they came into view.

He had several chances for long shots but passed up the opportunity. After ten days of watching and waiting, Jack thought he could ambush the pair he kept seeing. Generally the two old ones kept far enough apart so they could approach their quarry, move in from either side, or flush it to the waiting mate.

If he wanted to shoot them both, the big problem would be reloading his rifle. As he lay in the sun or squatted huddled in the rain, back up against a rock wall out of the wind, he tried to plan out his attack.

When he finally located the den on a south slope at the base of a rocky overhang, Jack knew the time to finish his task was at hand. He watched from a distance to observe their actions as they approached the den after they had fed. They would stop on an outcrop of rock to survey the area, and once all seemed clear, the bitch would crawl to the den and go in to inspect it. Satisfied, she would come out, wag her tail, and lie down and wait for her mate to join her. He too sniffed the den, rubbed noses with the bitch, then found a place where he could lie and soak up the sun, staying quiet until the urge to travel and hunt came once more.

Knowing the wolves were always out before dawn to make their hunt, Jack decided to approach on a route that would put him within rifle shot of the rock outcrop while they were away. When they returned, he would have to do everything at the same time. There would be no second chance.

By gray light, Jack moved down to his chosen spot and found a place where he could lie concealed, only the golden eagle that often swept up and down over the canyon to see him. A little coney might squeak at him and alert the wolves to danger, but they might think it only a weasel or hawk the tiny animal saw.

The pair of wolves came to the rock, sat, and watched the canyon and slopes below, Jack saw the female reach over to lick the dog's face, cleaning blood or flecks of flesh from his muzzle and neck. Then she made her way off the rock and down to the den entrance, stopped, looked around, then wiggled into the hole out of sight.

Jack sighted his rifle on the dog wolf, now looking down into the valley where shadows still lay along the river. At his shot, the animal leaped into space, and landed rolling and twisting on the rocky slope below. Quickly Jack reloaded and watched for the bitch. But she did not immediately appear. Finally she edged slowly out, sniffing the air. Suspicious and alert, she looked for her mate on the rock. As she stood, statuelike in the sun, Jack fired. Before Jack could reload, she was dead.

He thought at once that he could save scent from both animals and make sets to catch last year's litter, certain to come looking before long. He did not skin the wolves there, but carried them one at a time to where he could ride in on Booshway, leading Pardner, and take his prize to Bent's cabin. This done, he returned with Pardner, bringing the wolf traps. He had watched the comings and goings of the parents enough to know well the trails their offspring would use.

He made trail sets and two blind sets spread well away from where he had shot the pair. Their skinned bodies would later be used to attract other wolves to circle and investigate, perhaps step into deadly, foot-clamping steel jaws.

Jack felt an Indian's respect for these killers of deer and

elk, now the killers of ranchers' cattle. They were wise, crafty, and bold. He had always lived among them without fear, but now his job was to rid the range of all that he could kill or trap. He decided that once he had this bunch of young ones, he would leave Bailey's range and drive Jubal's cattle to the John Day country.

He caught four young wolves in the next few days. Bent was at the cabin when he rode in, his traps pulled for good.

"Figger yuh got 'em all, Jack?"

"Not all, but I got the ones doin' the damage. I might stay on for a month and get nothing. I'll go on up to the hollow now and stick around there until the calves're big enough to travel with their mothers. If Mr. Bailey comes through, tell him where I'll be."

Bent's look was quizzical. "Afore yuh leave, I'm goin' to say I reckon you as a good feller, Jack, but I better put you wise to what's driftin' around. The boys've heard talk in town about you an' the killin's up near the gorge, an' somebody put out the word you was the one smart enough to stay alive, git the gold an' the ponies. It's said yuh got rid of the feller that come lookin' fer yuh at Jube's cabin, an' took what he had, too. Nobody kin prove it. I know yuh an' I know old Bullhead trusts yuh, but watch yerself, Jack. Don't git careless an' set with yer back to the winder. And sleep light at night, hear?"

"Thanks, Bent. I've had to do that so long it's a habit. I'll remember. And you can count on me to return the favor sometime."

As Jack rode up to the hollow, he wondered why it was that he should be singled out as a horse thief, a killer, and robber of his dead friends. Must it always be so easy to blame an Indian?

Bullhead Bailey rode in while Jack was at the Elk Hollow cabin to talk of the cattle, the winter kill, when they could choose the cows and their calves, and finally of what Jack would do in the next few years.

Bailey had reassuring words. "Jack, if you want, you kin work here fer me," he said. "You did a whale of a good job this winter on them wolves and ridin' an' lookin' after the stock. Not many young fellers like yuh! When we settle up, I want yuh to take a yearlin' fer each wolf yuh got rid of. Some fellers'd think that's mighty high wages, but fer me it's a bargain. You saved me a lot more'n that in critters. Take yearlin's instead of calves fer old Jube, too. That way yuh kin trail over a lot easier. I figger you kin git over the Ochocos by mid-May, but we'll wait an' see."

Jack pondered before he spoke. "I was thinking maybe I ought to ride over to the Warm Springs reservation and see what I could find out about Teeah, the girl with us who disappeared. Mr. Hill seemed to think Indians had followed us and saw Stubbs fire at her. They might have killed Stubbs and taken her away."

"If you go there, you're stickin' yer neck out," Bailey warned. "You git to sniffin' around, and even if you're half red, you'll be cross-hauled either way you jump. That place is goin' to be a hot spot purty soon. Fer one thing, nobody knows jist where the reservation's supposed to be. Another thing, there's a big squabble over runnin' cattle there. The Indians don't want it, and the white men do. You're apt to be shot at from both sides, and nobody'll give a good goddamn. But it's up to you, Jack—you kin do as yuh please."

"Mr. Bailey, I never had the time to really figure out what could have happened. I'd like to go back to the gorge, take another look around our camp to see if I could find out anything."

Bailey sighed. "You're set to go, I kin see that. Why don't yuh leave these spotted ponies down at my place, git any sorry-lookin' nag to ride. You're an Injun, and by grab, if you go ridin' around on a good horse without a white man along, you're apt to lose yer life an' yer pony."

"Will you let me have one?"

"Sure thing. Leave all yer good riggin' with me, too. We'll burn yer mark on some yearlin's afore yuh leave. If yuh don't come back, they kin still run with mine." Bailey paced to the door and back. "Jack, it ain't no use to tell yuh you're stickin' yer nose into trouble. When do yuh want to leave?"

"As soon as you have someone to take my place."

"Hell's fire, boy, the cattle're in good shape. I'll have a rider up here in a day or so. Cache yer plunder an' bring yer ponies down tomorrow. We'll pick out a cayuse that don't look like you stole it. You got to be a sorry blanket Injun iffen yuh want to ride through this country without bein' stopped an' held up."

At the Bullhead Ranch next day, Jack stayed overnight

and listened to some of Bailey's early-day experiences. Bailey didn't lay all the present troubles on the Indians, as so many settlers did; he insisted that when he came into the country for the first time he was welcomed by the wandering bands who came through on annual hunting trips.

"Cows come to this country early in the game," he reminisced. "Californy cattle in Oregon to match some that come across country with Whitman's an' the rest. When they seen the grass on the prairies an' hills, the smart ones wanted more. Old Spalding an' Whitman egged the Injuns into tradin' ponies fer cows, an' it warn't long afore there was cattle scattered out purty well over the territory. I done some tradin', got smart, an' went back to bring cattle out along with a wagon train.

"That was about ten years back. I let my little bunch run with a feller that settled down near The Dalles where he could git help from the army, an' went back fer more. I'd heard smart traders talk 'bout what was goin' to take place purty quick with people floodin' into the country an' takin' up land wherever water an' grass come clost together." The rancher smiled. "I wasn't lookin' fer a woman, there was too much goin' on an' no wimmen available fer a young feller with an Injun cayuse and no money anyway. So it was git some more cattle an' then find a place to squat an' keep others off grass I wanted.

"I reckon it was old man Prine put me wise to this place. I met him at the fort an' he'd jist bought cattle to run on the grass here. Anyway, I rode up and staked me a claim, then went back an' got my cows an' a big flatland farmer boy. We built a shanty an' raised cows. I met Injuns an' made peace with 'em. We git along fine. They watch out fer me an' I give 'em a boost oncet in a while." Bailey's tone turned grim and serious. "That's how it is, an' long as I'm here, that's how it's goin' to be!"

15

Jack left next morning riding a Bullhead pony, its old saddle just enough together to hang stirrups on. He looked like a poor blanket Indian going humbly back to the reservation for any available rations. Knowing that in this part of Oregon the prevalent mood among the white cattlemen and stock raisers was that the only good Injun was a dead Injun, he avoided the traveled trails as he made his way across to the proposed boundaries of the Warm Springs Indians' territory, the definite place the government planned for them to live so they could exist in peace, raise their own cattle and ponies, and hunt without being molested.

In Oregon, the idea had sounded like a good one until word spread out that the crazy Indian lovers in the East reckoned to lock up a half-million acres in one chunk for the scattered bands of Indians that made up the Warm Springs tribe and also talked of giving the hell-raising Modocs, Klamaths, and their kin something like a million and a half acres of the best grazing and timber lands near Fort Klamath. Why, it would take a hundred years for those fish-eaters to produce enough cattle and ponies to eat the grass there unless they stole stock from white men! Other reservations were being proposed, always where bunch grass grew heavy and grazing was best. And sheepmen, thanks to the government who encouraged them, were using pasture along the Columbia.

When Jack approached the river gorge, he met three Oregon renegades who thought of themselves as cattlemen. The fact that they rode rough-haired ponies and owned no cows did not keep them from believing they were cowmen. All they needed was to acquire a few hides wearing horns to run on the hills covered with bunch grass, and time would make them rich. They already knew a hot iron on a clean hide denoted ownership. They had ponies and ropes, but so far they had not located the time, place, and stock to start becoming wealthy. When they saw that the lone rider approaching was an Injun, they began to plan.

"Jasper, here comes a pony we kin put our iron on. Better git yer letterin' figgered out."

"I kin do that, all right. You fellers figger what to do with the louse-hauler."

"Toby, git the drop on him. Me'n Jasper'll ask the questions of the poor wanderin' soul."

"I'm with yuh, Huff."

As the three riders drew close, Jack sensed trouble and began to think how to protect himself and his possessions. He could see he was outnumbered and outgunned. One of the riders moved a little away from his fellows. He's the one to watch, Jack thought. He might kill one, possibly two, of them with his loaded .45 before they got him. His father's advice: "Stay alive! Don't take chances!" How could he manage to stay alive against three armed men?

The "poor wanderin' soul" didn't wait for the three to make the first move. At one point, the trail downriver kept close to the rocky bluff. High water from the spring runoff kept it open for travel and formed a little pocket where soft material sloughed from winter rains and slides. Jack urged his pony into it and backed up against the wall.

Jasper saw the move. "He's figgerin' on bein' held up. Don't git edgy, boys. Let's see what he looks like up close."

The three riders came up. Jack saw trouble on their faces. Whiskers, long hair greasy and matted, clothes washed only by recent spring rain squalls. Boots worn and run over, misshapen hats greased to make them shed water. The half-hidden wolfish grins on their partially covered faces and the gleam of triumph in the leader's eyes told Jack his chances of getting away without a fight were small.

"Well, Injun, hit looks like yer pony quit on yuh. Goin' to camp there the rest of the day?"

"If I do, I expect one of you fellers to keep me company."

Jasper stared back in surprise. He hadn't expected a reply like that. Not from an Indian. Jack's language and diction were not those of a lousy, ignorant Siwash. "Now, jist what does that mean, Injun?"

"Just what I said. If any one of you move to pull a gun or knife, he's going to get shot."

100

"Well, now, you talk big! I don't see no gun to back that story up, do you fellers?"

Toby laughed a throaty snort. "Hell no, Jasper."

"Yeah, ten chances to one some old hoss pistol he stole won't go off when he pulls the trigger." Huff glanced at Jasper. "Want me to blast him?"

It was Jack's turn to laugh. "Try it and see what happens. The next shot'll be for that man on the black pony settin' you up to be killed. If any of you get away, you'll be caught and hung. I'll tell you why."

Silence fell, the three men sitting quiet, the only movement that of their tired ponies shifting weight under their saddles.

Jasper spoke up. "Why?"

"Follow this trail and you'll meet a herd moving this way. Fellow that owns 'em has brands on 'em like on this pony. He won't like it if I don't show up."

"That's a lie, Jasper. This son of a bitch is a damned horse thief. Blast him, Tobe!"

"Hold it, Huff, set quiet. An' who might this feller be owns the iron on yer pony?"

"Bullhead Bailey. You're on Prine's range. His riders are movin' Bullhead's stock through on this trail."

"An' what makes you so sure yuh kin git two of us?"

"That's my secret," Jack replied, face impassive. "I got a gun cocked and ready to fire under this jacket. You fellers're so close I can't miss, and before you get into action, there'll be two dead."

Jasper thought it over, and so did the other two, noticing the Indian's pony standing sideways, his rider's hand under a garment on the pommel. The rifle this Indian carried hung in a buckskin beaded scabbard tied to the saddle with thongs. The way he talked, assured, and with no sign of the slurred speech of a blanket Indian, kept Jasper from giving the sign to jump him. A herd of cattle could well be coming. If so, there would be trouble even if they came out alive. The Injun must have one of the new six-shooters he'd heard about.

Let the lousy bastard go, he thought. We kin find other fellers to jump.

Toby and Huff looked at the brand on the hip of the Indian's pony. It showed up through the long hair of winter, and it looked like a bull's head, all right. And the Indian had a gun that would shoot more than once. Someone had given

101

it to him or he had money to buy one. No white man would sell such a precious weapon to an Indian unless he trusted him completely. The thought of meeting a bunch of tough cowboys driving a herd of cattle softened their desire to have the Indian's pony as their own.

They heard Jasper's voice. "Let's go, boys. Injun, if we don't meet up with a herd in the next few miles, we'll call your bluff, jist turn around an' trail yuh down. It'll be our turn when we ketch yuh." Jasper gigged his pony, and the other two moved to join him.

Jack watched them well on their way before he moved his horse back onto the trail. He didn't doubt they might come back and track him down, but how far would they go before deciding there was no trail herd coming? Maybe five miles. If so, they might be ten miles behind him then. Traveling light, with no pack animal, meant they were living off the country or rode just ahead of the law or army. Maybe they wouldn't dare to backtrack.

As Jack rode northwest, the three ambitious scoundrels traveled toward Prine City on this trail suitable only for riders and cattle that wound around rocky cliffs and through narrow passes. Before long, arguments among them began.

"Jasper, that bastard laid out a line of crap yuh could foller by the smell. The old flimflam. We won't never meet up with no trail crew. Who'd be trailin' cattle this time of year? Hell, they're on grass with knock-kneed calves buttin' their maws fer milk."

"Toby, some feller could be movin' 'em downriver to the benches where there's good early grass."

Huff spoke. "I reckon Tobe's right, Jasper. But why go back? He didn't look like money to me. Ragged-assed breed, some hoss thief sneakin' back to that place the blasted gov'ment says they can keep. All we'd end up with would be that bronc and a beat-up saddle."

"He had a rifle in that beaded hide sack."

"Prob'ly an old trade blunderbuss. Maybe somethin' in that bundle back of the saddle, though. Want to take after him and call his bluff, Jasper?"

"The outfit ain't much, but it's somethin'. Main thing is, I don't want no greasy redskin pullin' a bluff on me. So far as the herd comin', we take care of Mr. High-and-Mighty, then see."

102

"This trail climbs to the bench in a few miles," Toby said. "Mebbe we kin ketch him there. If not, jist foller him to where we know we kin cut him off." The way that smart Injun had bluffed a crew who had him outgunned rankled in Toby's mind.

"This time, don't wait. Any one of us gits a good shot at him, let him have it, right through the gizzard." Jasper pulled his gelding around; a jab in the flanks with a spurred boot sent him on the way.

As they passed the place where Jack had backed against the rock wall like a bobcat at bay, Jasper swore, "That's gonna be the first and last time any Injun pulls a stunt like that on me."

Jack had put his pony into a slow lope. Where was a place he could wait and waylay the three cutthroats? He had traveled this trail with Jube and later with the men from the valley; the landscape was clear in his mind. He recalled a narrow place where the river pinched in against the rocky canyon wall and his group had had to go single file, beyond it the benchlands, the trail wider through the bunch grass. He slowed the pony to a walk as he approached the narrow canyon.

Jasper, in the lead, felt confident when he noticed the tracks of the pony ahead of them had slowed. "Boys, he's forgot about us. We leave the river purty quick an' climb to open country. We kin spread out there an' git ahead of the bastard."

Jack's first shot was so close and unexpected that when Jasper's horse went down, the other two men had no time to react before a second hit Huff's mount. His pony reared, stumbled, and in pain jumped sideways over the bank into the river. Toby, between Jasper and Huff, tried to wheel his horse around to get clear, when the third shot hit his mount. The pony screamed in shock as the heavy lead bullet crashed into ribs and lungs. The two men on the ground scrambled desperately, seeking guns and cover.

Jasper got clear of his pony, rifle in his hands, and ran for a protective rock. From the corner of his eye he saw Huff and his pony go over the bank. Toby's wounded mount plunged around on the trail as its rider strove for control. At the rock outcrop, Jasper could not see up the hill where the hidden marksman lay. When Toby finally got off his plunging, screaming horse, rifle in hand, he didn't know whether to hide or scramble down to help Huff, now struggling in the swift, swollen stream.

Jasper called out to Toby, "Git yer rope! Haul Huff in afore he gits too far down the crick!"

Climbing out of Jasper's sight, Jack saw Huff and his pony in the current. He climbed farther up the slope, secure now in the knowledge he was in no immediate danger from the three men below. Toby got a rope from Jasper's saddle, and quickly building a loop, scrambled along the bank, barely able to keep pace with Huff, whose pony made for a drift of trees, logs, and rubbish caught on a rock ledge, but the bullet's effect had weakened him, and before he reached it, he stopped struggling, swept downriver with the current.

Toby's pony stood headdown, dying on his feet. When Jack turned, he saw that Huff had managed to grasp Toby's loop and was approaching the shore, Jasper still out of sight, the dying pony on the trail now slumped to the ground. Jack got back to his mount and continued on his way to the gorge region where the Turpin tragedy had taken place.

16

Jack found no sign of recent travelers at the campgrounds where Mr. Turpin and the boys had been killed by Old Stubbs and his crew, the browse growth not yet enough for stockmen to drift their herds through to the river and any other travelers staying close to the main road. Cautious and wary, Jack picketed his pony among good grasses in a little pocket off the creek valley and made camp where he could watch his back trail. Rifle loaded, he went back once more to the camp.

When he had been with Mr. Hill and the others, no one wanted to take time to scout the country and find a logical trail to the gorge, if, as they surmised, Indians had come from that direction. But Jack knew that if anyone had approached the camp it had to be from the west, where the road and the far gorge of the river ran.

104

At the spot where he had seen Teeah fall, he looked up the hill to rocks and scrubby juniper. Eight months had passed since the shooting. Semidesert landscape changes little with time. Rock and junipers remained the same, fresh bunch grass rippling in the wind and blue, pink, and yellow spring flowers new to the scene. White clouds drifted across the blue sky. Jack climbed up over the rocks, looking for a place where a person might have watched unseen.

He found several such places, but the one he decided he would have chosen, possibly the only one from which the viewer could have seen Teeah fall, was beneath a scrubby juniper firmly embedded in cracks atop the lava ledge. From there Jack saw the campsite clearly and could look across to where Ort and Ace had chased him upward. Anyone seeing Teeah's plight could have quickly scrambled down off the ledge to reach her. Jack recalled that he had heard no shot from the camp after Stubbs fired at Teeah, so Stubbs must have been killed with knife, rock, or rope. He was certain Ort or Ace had not done it. Stubbs loomed too large in their minds.

Jack looked over the country behind him toward the road and river. Had someone scrambled down off these rocks, picked Teeah up, and then climbed back to the bench above? From his vantage point Jack looked for the best way to make such an ascent and saw a possible route. At the place where the imagined trail reached the more gentle slope, he searched carefully for signs of passage.

Grasses would no longer show any disturbance. Rocks could not reveal footprints. Some piece of cloth, hide, hair, or a trinket separated from persons passing that way must be looked for, an impossible task made possible only by concentration and effort. Time no longer drove the half-breed boy. He had no commitments to anyone just now. If it took him all day to examine fifty or one hundred yards of trail, he would do so, looking for some bit of evidence that Teeah had passed by. One clue might lead to more, and . . . perhaps to her.

Like Robinson Crusoe on his distant island, Jack found the first real evidence in a moccasin track near a juniper where grass failed to grow. The pale dry sand held the shape, even indentation, of the toe pressed deeper as the wearer stepped forward. Jack squatted to read all the track could tell him. It had been made by a big man, a man either heavy or carrying a burden. It pointed toward the west and the road. The Indian who passed that way had been careful where he stepped. His moccasin was not old; the sole print indicated stiffness.

The footprint revived Jack's hopes. There would be other footprints. In two days' time he had worked out a probable trail to the gorge, his camp kept close so he could investigate a possible route to the twisting river so far below. Searching for and finding a few footprints and signs of travel, he became certain that Teeah was alive or that there had been an Indian woman with a party on their way to the river gorge, for he was sure more than two people, possibly four, had traveled here, cautious about being seen and about leaving tracks.

Anyone trying to follow this long-ago trail must be patient, take time and trouble. Starting from the south, Jack worked his way north along the rim, often backtracking in his thorough exploration. It was not by accident that on the morning of the third day of searching he found a dim trail that led down into the gorge. He cached his rifle and everything else he would not need for the trip and soon discovered that only an Indian, a goat, or a burro could find the way to the river.

Hidden by brush in a crack in the lava rim, the narrow trail had been used by coyotes, bobcats, and men. Where sand had washed or had been blown by the desert winds and lodged on a bit of rocky shelf, half a moccasin print showed plainly, the toe pointing downward. Jack pressed on through barely visible openings. For animals the path was a way of escape, a place to duck into that led to a safer hiding place.

Crouched under brush grown tightly together, Jack found more signs of human passage, dry twigs broken and removed, scuffings of soil that indicated men had slipped through here like snakes. A hair, black and long! It glistened like a strand of spiderweb in the sun. The seeker's heart throbbed as he reached for it. Was it Teeah's? Jack remembered that Teah usually wore her hair in long braids that hung over her doeskin jacket, bits of blue or red yarn she carefully saved for the purpose woven into the ends.

Hope renewed, he slowly made his way forward, wondering. He came to the end of the tangled brush, to his right a goat track of a ledge following along under the rim's narrow overhang of solid lava left from ancient times when the river cut its way through the valley. In places very steep, it dipped

106

lower and Jack saw crude steps cut or chopped by crude tools to make the way passable. Farther down he saw more indication of manmade improvements. At a narrow place where a cliff edge dropped off more than a hundred feet to rubble below, someone had strung a woven cord of juniper roots along the wall for a handhold. Jack edged down.

The way ended in a great growth of brush and jagged rocks, just past them the roaring, rushing river, its waters green with snow runoff. Before Jack ventured into the open, he looked up and down the river's banks and saw a few deer feeding on twigs on the far side. Beaver cuttings and fresh chips lay under a cottonwood close by. Tracks of bear and coyote crossed the sandbar before him, and high overhead a golden eagle soared effortlessly. There was no sign of humans. Jack moved down toward the river. Above the high-water mark he found a trail that paralleled the stream, used enough to make it seem like a roadway after the tortuous trail down the gorge wall.

He saw no way to cross the river at this point. The Cascades' snow torrent reached almost to trees and battered stumps along its banks. Should he go downstream or up? Placed atop a huge boulder above the waterline he saw a smaller stone, to crown it yet another of lighter color. To Jack that meant: Here is the trail.

As he walked rapidly upriver, he continually watched the opposite shoreline for trails or signs of habitation. More than two miles from where he had reached the river from the cliff trail he found a canoe made of hides stitched together over a framework of split cedar and willow, its seams well covered with pitch, in a tree above it three paddles of cedar showing signs of use. Farther back from the shoreline he came upon a three-log raft and poles for pushing it along, a crudely fashioned sweep for a rudder lying atop it. Jack could only guess at its use—the canoe seemed the better way of crossing. He thought Indians might anchor the raft in the river, spearing salmon from it at the time of the spawning run.

On up the river another mile to a flat on the opposite shore in a bend, Jack came upon a camping place where salmon had been smoked and dried, crude racks there made of poles and posts and stone circles that marked camp lodges now all looking deserted and unused.

This must be the way to enter and leave reservation lands

without being found out by government authorities, the way known only to native Indians. He would retrace his steps now, climb to the rim, and make plans to return soon. His pony would have to be turned loose in case he never got back. He would cache the saddle with things he could not carry with him.

Before he reached the three piled rocks marking the entrance to the cliff trail, he had to pass through a jumble of boulders and great slabs of lava that reached down to the river. As he wove his way between them on the narrow trail, he was halted in mid-stride by a huge Indian who stepped out before him, bow and arrow nocked and ready for release. Jack raised his right hand in the sign of peace. At a slight sound behind him, he slowly turned his head. Another Indian stood there with a cocked rifle. Trapped, Jack knew only luck and his Indian blood could save him.

Silence for long moments. The big Indian ten feet in front of Jack looked as immovable as the blocks of lava on either side. At last the bow and arrow slowly lowered.

"Who you?" It was said in English.

"Jack Tate. Old Bill Tate's boy. Quick Hands. You know Quick Hands?"

"Quick Hands dead, long time. Who bore you?"

"Windflower. Nez Percé. Dead long time too."

"Why you here?"

"I look for Nez Percé girl, Teeah."

"Don't know Teeah. No Nez Percé. We Warm Springs, Umatilla, some Cayuse."

The conversation became a mixture of English, Indian, and sign language. Lowering his rifle, the man behind Jack joined in, the two Indians showing their suspicion of anyone who had entered their territory by the up-to-now-secret route. Once more they asked Jack if he was really the son of Quick Hands the Trader.

Jack spread his empty hands to the two stony-faced bucks before him, suspicious as the two wolves he had shot months before at their den entrance. In the river sand near his feet he saw a red stone, the size of his smallest fingertip, of water-rounded carnelian. Stooping, he picked it up, looked at it closely, waved his hand, and as if by magic plucked it from his ear. The watchers' expressions changed to amazement. With more sleight-of-hand movements, the tension relaxed,

Jack's captors now convinced that this Indian boy really was the son of Quick Hands, who had been well known, at least by legend, to most of the tribes along the Columbia River.

Jack pressed them for information about Teeah but got nowhere. Why was it so important that he find the girl? they demanded. What had happened on the rim to cause her death or capture? Jack outlined the story, but they did not understand. Why had he been traveling with so many men and one woman? Where had they all come from and what had happened to those who had killed the white men and boys?

Jack answered their questions, always keeping in mind that they probably knew the story already. By now he had convinced himself that Teeah, dead or alive, was on their reservation. If they allowed him to leave, he knew he must return again.

The big Indian rose abruptly, motioning the others to follow as he started at a quick trot back down the river and continued past the cliff trail turnoff.

A mile or so beyond, they came to a camp under lava overhang where two women smoked and dried fish, a camping place used for many years, rocks above it black with smoke and soot. Farther on, where the walls raised vertically, smooth and unstained, Jack glimpsed drawings made by the ancient people, crude sticklike men, animals running, or dead and being carried, curious-looking birds, some on stiltlike legs, others flying in wedge formation. At this place, long in use by the natives, one picture showed a mountain with smoke or fire issuing from its top.

"We eat now," the leader said. He squatted. The women dished up bowls of stew and brought pieces of dried fish. As they ate, another man came from downriver, white strands of hair mixed in the black of his braids, only this and his wrinkled, lined face to indicate age, for he walked tall and straight with the springy stride of an athlete. He stood across from Jack, looking directly at him, then squatted and reached for the bowl handed to him. Only the liquid slurping sound of feasting broke the silence. When the wooden bowls crafted of cedar were laid aside, Tall Buck, as Jack had named him, spoke in his tongue to the newcomer, evidently a subchief.

More questions. He knew the men were trying to make sure he did not spy for white men. They couldn't quite believe he looked for a girl. Perhaps they thought he was after

109

the hidden plunder they might have taken from his cache, but no mention was made of it.

The chief motioned for Jack to leave while they parleyed, argued, and considered his fate.

Jack walked to the river. Fish spears lay there. A run of steelhead in the river finned slowly along the edge of a pool. Choosing a spear, Jack walked to the rock and waited while behind him the two women watched.

An egg-swollen female steelhead moved toward the bank, a male drifting behind her. As she settled close behind a boulder to rest from her battle with the strong current, Jack's spear struck and hit his target. He swung the stunned fish to the bank behind him. The woman chuckled and snatched up the salmon for the eggs they wanted. Jack had done it the Indian way.

Jack looked down. The male had drifted away. He stood quietly, waiting for another pair to come within range, but just then the three braves called for his return. They had reached a decision.

17

The man named Jasper crept slowly from his hiding place. He saw Toby helping Huff up the bank to the trail and thought the unseen bushwhacker might be reloading. When no shot came he walked boldly into the open and surveyed the slope above him and the trail where his pony now lay dead, Toby's farther away, Huff's mount drowned in the river, his saddle and supplies gone with it.

Jasper ranted, "That hoss-stealin' red bastard! I should've plugged him when we first seen him. What in hell we goin' to do? Where we goin' to head fer now?"

Huff, none too happy about his plight, let the other two know it. "You fellers're dry an' yuh got yer guns. My guns, my saddle, my pony, an' all my extries gone down the blasted river! Where'd that red son of a bitch shoot from? You see him?"

"Not me, Huff," Toby replied. "How many shots was there, Jasper?"

"How should I know? Hit could've been one or a dozen. Don't stand there suckin' yer thumbs. Let's strip the riggin' off an' find a place to cache it. I got a extry shirt an' vest in my slicker yuh kin have, Huff."

While Huff stripped off wet clothing, the other two cussed redskins, each sure the lone Indian boy had shot their ponies from under them, but loath to confess being outmaneuvered.

"Jasper, how far yuh reckon it is to that bunch of shanties they call Prine City?"

"Dammit, I ain't never been there! If it hadn't been fer that lousy Injun horse thief, we'd be ridin' in by now, I guess. Here's a shirt fer old Huff."

"We got enough money atween us to buy more ponies?" Toby pressed.

"I got mine," Jasper shouted. "Huff, did yer money go swimmin' with yer pony?"

"I got it on me, Jasper, but that's all I got. Next thievin' Indian I see's goin' to git blasted—that is, if I ever git holt of another gun."

Arguing where to cache their extra clothes and the rigging from both dead horses, they finally found a place off the rocky trail, laid the stuff out, and piled rocks on top before they took to the road. Men used to the saddle and not to walking, they soon grew footsore, irritable, and argumentative.

"Jasper, yuh figger we kin find a spot to hole up in till we make us another stake? Money I have won't last long after I git me a new pony and outfit," Huff grumbled.

"I'm in the same boat, with only half a paddle. Naw, we'll jist play our luck, which ain't been too good so far today." Jasper looked back at Toby, stumbling behind them. "Tobe, you got any idees beyond layin' down in the trail an' whimperin' how that Injun done us a dirty trick?"

"Don't blame me fer the fix we're in! It was you wanted to go back an' plug him."

"The hell it was!" Jasper exploded. "We better make up a good story about how we got put afoot when we tried to fight off some red bastards shot our horses. We need to stir up the fellers as lives around here so we kin git that redskin

111

hung if we find him. I want all the natives on our side, an' no questions asked."

Huff couldn't think straight. His wet boots hurt his feet and his borrowed clothes didn't fit. He felt now that if chance let him leave the other two, he would lose no time in doing so.

Toby tried to cheer him up. "Huff, you're the one's the best off. If we git held up agin, you ain't got much to lose. Yuh don't have to pack a rifle an' a buncha useless junk. Even yer boots don't squeak no more."

"The hell with you, Toby. I lost ever'thin' while you two hid in the rocks! You better figger out a good story. I already got mine made up." Huff's tone was truculent.

Jasper stopped. "An' the hell you say! Spill yer spiel—we might meet the crew that bastard said was on the trail."

"Let's set an' smoke, then, if yuh've got the makin's. Mine got wet."

They squatted there along the trail and worked out a story they believed would answer questions as to how they happened to be afoot in this country where horses were always the main means of transportation.

From up on the bunch-grass bench, Lee Wilson made out three footsore travelers on their way up the river trail, a sight so unusual in this vast land that he decided to hold back approaching them. He knew their story would be a hard-luck one; men didn't travel that trail afoot if a way existed to avoid it. He swung his pony's head upriver to get ahead and meet them as if by accident.

Jasper, once again in the lead, looked ahead. "Boys, there's a feller comin' on a pony. Git yer stories ready. Maybe we'll git some good news about ponies an' grub."

Wilson sized them up as they approached, a hot, weary, hard-looking bunch, two with rifles carrying slickers over their shoulders, the last man with a bundle on his back, no gun in sight. Wilson's pony stopped at bit pressure, and he watched until the men were close enough to speak.

"You fellers look like you're down on yer luck," he greeted.

Jasper spoke up. "We was bushwhacked by a buncha yer tame Injuns. Bastards shot our ponies out from under us, but we made it hot for 'em an' got away."

112

Wilson raised an eyebrow. "An' where all did this battle take place?"

"Ten or twelve mile back."

" 'Bout where?"

"Where the canyon pinches in an' the trail crowds the cliffs. The first shot killed my pony, hit him in the head. I pitched off, grabbed my gun an' shot back, but some sharpshooter plugged Tobe's pony an' I never did see jist what happened to old Huff, here."

"And what did happen to yuh, Mr. Huff?" The range rider's voice held a hint of sarcasm.

"I gigged my pony, but then I jumped off and slipped back to where I could git a shot up the hill." Huff's tone turned to a whine. "Then I see this redskin sneakin' fer my pony in the trail. My shot at him hit the cayuse, an' he went inta the river. The redskin crippled outta sight, an' another slug hit my rifle stock. I slipped an' fell in the drink."

"An' then what?" Wilson cocked his right leg over the front of the saddle and rubbed his stubbled chin with his hand.

"They figgered we was too strong fer 'em," Toby put in. "They slipped off through the rocks over the hill."

Jasper Jukes realized the stranger on the blue roan was skeptical, and as he looked at the rider, relaxed in the saddle, eyeing three footsore men below him on the rocky trail, he exploded once more.

"Yuh ain't much consarned with a bunch of Injuns runnin' loose in yer territory, are yuh, mister? By cripes, if you'd a been in our place gittin' hot lead poured at yuh, yuh wouldn't jist set there an' soak up the sun! You'd be ridin' to the army fer help, screamin' bloody murder. I ain't never been no Injun lover. If you fellers live around here don't teach them thieves a lesson, some of us with more guts will!"

"Well, I'm shore glad to hear that," Wilson drawled. "Us gutless wonders kinda managed to live an' git along with 'em up to now. So you fellers're goin' to spread the word there's trouble in the grass country!" Wilson's expression did not change. He straightened his leg and dropped his foot into the stirrup as his bald-faced pony shook its head to the rattle of bit chains. "You'll need some ponies and some grub, won't yuh?"

"Now you're talkin'! Where kin we find 'em?"

113

"Keep on goin' on this trail, yuh'll come to a turnoff leads up a little draw to a dugout shanty 'bout half a mile. Another feller'll be there maybe afore I git back, an' happens we might round up a pony or two. There's sowbelly an' beans on the stove."

"Sounds better'n gunshots an' lead," Jasper grumbled. "How far back to the herd s'posed to be movin' this way?"

Wilson eased in the saddle, alert to something he had already suspected. The only Indian these men could have met on the trail was Jack Tate. If Jack had told them there was a herd coming, he'd done it for a reason.

" 'Cordin' to the boss, there's a herd somewhere back of me," he drawled. "Don't know where they'll turn off. They're movin' to new grass on the benches." His final words came quickly. "Who told you 'bout 'em?"

Huff saw that Jasper might have revealed more than he intended to. "An Injun kid, young feller ridin' a hoss with a funny brand, like a bull's head," he said.

"I've seen him. What about it?"

"We figger he got his pals to bushwhack us fer our plunder. But one thing sure—they can't ride dead ponies," he cackled. "Maybe they're havin' roast ribs now."

"You kin tell the feller at the dugout what you told me." Wilson's tone was mirthless. "And that the Injun kid mentioned Bullhead Bailey was movin' stock downriver."

His heel touched his pony's flank and the roan started away at an easy lope. As he rode, Wilson turned the strangers' story over in his mind. Jack had met them. Jack had said a herd was moving downriver. Why? To let them believe he wasn't alone? But where was Jack now? Wilson rode on to find whatever evidence of the ambush might be left.

Jasper Jukes, pleased with himself, chuckled as he limped along, believing that smart Injun would have a slug in him or a rope around his neck soon. The rider had sent them to where they could eat and get new mounts. They would go on to Prine City and start talk of having a posse round up that horse thief.

Huff Miller wasn't so sure. He wondered if Wilson was going downriver to check their story or just look for cattle. Walking up the river trail in dry leather boots that rubbed his blisters raw, Huff changed his opinion of Tobe and Jasper. Jukes was rough, tough, cruel, and heartless, not afraid of a

114

fight or conflict of ideas, but all he really wanted was to get money or what it represented. He had no qualms about killing or stealing. So far, he hadn't double-crossed Tobe or him, but Huff decided he'd like to cut loose from his partners as soon as he could. Toby was a follower, needing a strong man to look up to, no matter how dissolute, wicked, or dirty. That Indian boy on the trail—now, there was a strong one. Smart, too. Didn't hesitate to call their hand, ready to pull the trigger. And when they rode back to jump him, look what happened! Nope, Jasper had about played his hand out, and unless he had an ace up his sleeve, they'd all be out of the game before long.

Toby Marsh felt only relief. Jasper would git them some ponies and grub. Ponies! His feet hurt, his head ached, his rifle was heavy. All he wanted was to git someplace where he could lie down, rest, and eat. Then they'd git ponies and head for town. What money they had would set them up for the big deals old Jasper had going. Jasper Jukes, Toby told himself, was one to tie to.

18

The Warm Springs Indian chief motioned Jack to sit with the others, then told the half-breed boy he would send someone to check out his story of what had happened on the trail from Prine City and that Jack must declare himself either willing to stay with them or remain as a captive under guard. It was necessary to keep secret the trail leading out of the gorge; until Jack's story was confirmed, they could take no chance he might be lying, a spy of the agency.

Jack considered his words. Actually, the chief's decree was even better than he had hoped. If he stayed here, he might find out what had happened to Teeah. He had no obligation to return to Bailey's place at a certain time, and Jubal and Sarah wouldn't worry if he was late in getting to their place on the John Day. The only thing that concerned him was the pony and rigging on the bench far above the river.

He spoke. "Chief, my pony is up there with saddle and

115

bridle on. He's tied and will die unless you loose him. If you will do that and see he goes to feed with the cattle in Prine's big meadow, then I will stay with you as your guest, not your prisoner."

The old chief nodded in agreement, and signaled to a lanky brave. Jack explained where his pony was tied and where to let him run free, the saddle and rigging to be brought back or cached on the bench nearby. Soon the Indian started at a trot to climb the narrow trail.

Jack went back to the river's edge and found a spear to his liking. The two women watched casually. Jack moved up the bank to where the current cut in around a great boulder, leaving a clear space in its shelter. The women below him saw his arm poise for a throw. Then the flashing spear entered the water like a gleam of sudden light. The thong attached to the wooden haft straightened and the spear thrower began to retrieve the taut line, slowly pulling it in to reveal another large fish for the drying racks.

As he stood waiting for more steelhead or an early salmon to enter his field of vision, Jack wondered just what the chief would do next to satisfy the element of suspicion that Indians living along the river felt. Long moments later, one of the women came up to Jack and smiled. She picked up the four fish he had speared.

"You go see chief now," she told him.

The chief squatted, legs crossed, smoking a long-stemmed pipe of red pipestone, its smoke curling up from the bowl with a mixed fragrance of willow, kinnikinnick, and a slight scent of tobacco. Jack knew the odor—when tobacco supplies were low, the pouch was filled with ground-up bark and leaves to make it last until more of the white man's real thing could be had. He squatted opposite the chief and waited.

The chief filled his lungs with a final slow draw, savored the taste and feel, and expelled a thin blue curl of smoke, then laid down the pipe, half-closed his eyes, and began to speak in a monotone.

"Many winters and summers so long ago that snow stayed always on the hills, my people came to this river to live and hide, for there were many enemies, men who killed and ate other men's flesh rather than starve. My people survived by keeping secret." He pointed skyward. "They had to go above to hunt deer. Now only we, who have lived in the rocks,

116

know the trails, the caves, and all the secret places. If the white men find them, we are no more. Even now the secret is half gone, vanished like smoke in the wind, for you are half white. We must seal your lips, blind your eyes so that you cannot find the way again. Think on this."

As if to further darken Jack's thoughts, a cloud from the southwest cast its shadow into the canyon, and from down the river a chill breeze touched his back. He knew the chief's problem. He must somehow stop any possible investigation. Troubles between whites and native Indians escalated, and no one knew what the end might be. If this particular Warm Springs band thought secrecy absolutely necessary for their survival, then his chances of getting out of the gorge diminished by the minute.

The chief spoke softly. "You carry the white man's new gun, the one that shoots more than once. Show me how it shoots; then we will talk some more."

Jack had considered killing the chief, the two women, and whoever else might come to their rescue, dismissing such a plan when he realized he might never have a better chance to locate Teeah. If he killed anyone here, he would never again be able to enter any part of this Indian stronghold without being open game. Reaching slowly, he withdrew the revolver from its holster, but before he handed it over, he withdrew and pocketed the bullets. Then he handed it, butt-first, to the man squatting in front of him.

The chief did not know how to open and roll the cylinder. He held up the gun as if shooting but not sighting. Then he handed it back. "Tell me," he said.

Jack took time to show each detail, his observer watching intently. When satisfied he knew how to open and load the weapon, the chief spoke his command.

"You shoot."

Jack reloaded the gun, then pointed it at a large rock fifty yards away. Each time he fired, rock dust flew from the boulder. The chief looked on in amazement. Five carefully aimed shots; the revolver was empty once more.

"Good . . . good," the chief muttered.

He watched Jack reload. At the half-breed's movement to replace the gun in the leather-laced holster, the chief reached for it. "Me shoot rock," he said.

The weight of the weapon surprised him. As he lowered it

to get the feel, then raised it, Jack saw that his eyes were closed. At that moment the gun went off, the recoil of the charge lifting gun and the hand that held it high in the air. Jack dared not be amused at the look of shocked amazement on the chief's face. For a moment he thought the weapon would not be surrendered to him, but at last the chief reluctantly handed it back. Jack showed him how to hold it, telling him with gestures to look at both gun barrel and the object at which he pointed it when he fired.

The chief took the gun; this time he looked as he fired, sand and silt flew from the ground below the boulder, and he uttered a sound of triumph. Again the gun boomed.

Jack stood up and motioned. Together they walked closer to the target rock. "Now shoot," Jack said.

Splinters and rock dust flew. The gun boomed in the canyon. Echoes rolled along the river, and black powder smoke lay heavy in the air until the breeze carried it away. The chief did not fire again. He handed the weapon back to Jack.

At the camp, the women still worked at fishing and tending the fires that dried and smoked the steelhead slabs. The chief once more squatted in spring sunshine out of the small cold breeze and leaned back, dark eyes almost closed.

"Jack, you look for Indian girl. You give me gun and powder, I send for girl. I keep gun. You take girl. You don't come back. You do, you dead. If other men come, we find you, and kill you." He sighed. "No safe place for me. You want girl, I want gun." His eyes questioned.

Jack nodded. He could find another gun somehow, but there was only one Teeah. If he could find her, maybe she could tell him where the gold and guns were hidden. His mind raced ahead. He would take Teeah to the cabin on Bullhead Bailey's range. She could help on the drive to the John Day, where Jubal and Sarah had a range of their own. Jack's heart pounded at the thought of seeing her once more.

He handed the gunbelt, holster, and gun, along with the small bag of powder, caps, and lead, to the chief, now fully alert.

"I send for girl when man comes from pony," the Indian said.

The older woman tending the fires went to a red blanket hung drying on a frame of poles. As if at some secret hidden signal, she replaced it with a blue-and-white one, and with the

118

red one folded in her arms went to the overhanging rock to lay it away. Within minutes an Indian brave appeared in camp, and soon others drifted in from the lower trail and up-river. Jack had no idea there were so many guards near the camp.

He went back to fish while the chief explained to a council what had transpired. His occasional sideways glance and the occasional outburst of words told Jack there were differences of opinion, but in ten or fifteen minutes Jack was summoned. Evidently all had agreed to a decision.

"I will send for the girl," the chief said. "She is yours. When she is here, you will leave by the secret trail. Neither of you must ever return. If you do, death waits for both. It is done. The gun is mine, the girl is yours. I have said it. We are agreed."

It was now late in the day. Jack thought they could not go up the gorge trail that night. Bad enough in daylight, the trip would be impossible in darkness. A misstep on the narrow, twisting ledges could mean a long, battering fall to death on the rocks below.

Jack saw a courier coming with the girl. Shadows crept up the eastern wall of the gorge. Waiting with the chief and others of the band near the entrance to the trail, he could see that she was small and slender, dressed in short skirt of doeskin and soft boots of buckskin. Her jacket seemed familiar . . . but something was wrong! This girl did not walk like Teeah! Had she been hurt? Her face was obscured by a pack she carried over her shoulder, but when she was close to the waiting group she shifted the bundle. Jack closed his eyes in despair. It was not Teeah!

Sick with disappointment, his trip, his hopes, all for nothing, Jack opened his eyes and looked at the chief, his eyes black and expressionless. In the silence, Jack spoke softly.

"This is not Teeah, the girl that came from above the rocks."

"You take this girl and say no more, white boy. Take her or we kill her and throw her to the river."

There was no choice, no alternative. Jack saw the girl tremble in fear. A sudden chill swept down the river out of the shadows. He stepped forward and reached for her burden, then stopped in sudden shock. In the covered bundle was a baby! With willpower he hardly believed he had, he again

119

reached out, but the girl stepped back, crying, "No, no! I carry!"

"Then follow me. We go up."

Together they slowly struggled up the narrow, crooked, almost impassable trail until on a slightly wider ledge where they must negotiate a step more than three feet high Jack stopped to catch his breath, his emotions now under control, anger cleared by an effort, determination to survive renewed.

Fearfully the girl-woman looked at him, eyes and nostrils expanded, breathing heavily from her exertion and her bewildered fear. For the first time, Jack felt pity, realizing that she too had been trapped in some circumstance beyond her control. How had she come to the Warm Springs Indians? Who was she that the chief could so easily trade her off for a gun he desired? Both of them had been double-crossed and cheated. Now it was up to them to work and stay together in order to survive.

His words came down to her. "I am Jack. You come with me. We keep on—the bad part is near the top. Dark soon."

"My name Ahseeah. I come, stay with you."

Jack reached down "Give me the boy." She handed him her burden and took the other hand offered her. She had accepted his help, and in return she would help him.

19

Lee Wilson smiled to himself as he left the three footsore travelers, not ready to believe their story until he found where the action had taken place. If those buggers had lost their ponies by gunfire, the evidence would still be there. He doubted that Indians had attacked them, certain that the only Indian they could have met was the boy Jack from the Bullhead range upriver, and if Jack shot their ponies, Wilson felt damned sure they had tried to kill him first.

The first pony lay on the trail, headed upriver, its blood track leading back to where it had been hit. Just beyond it he saw Jasper's dead mount, headed in the opposite direction. Wilson dismounted and looked at the bullet hole in its head, then up the rocky slope. It didn't take brains to calculate where a sharpshooter could hide there. Studying the tracks, he saw that another pony had jumped on the trail, then struggled over the edge into the river.

"Well, that accounts fer the one with wet pants. If Jack was doin' the shooting. . . ." He shook his head. "I reckon the breed was too dern smart fer them thieves. Nothin' I kin do now but head back to the cabin an' lissen to their lies."

Wilson had no need to write down the details of what was written there before him on the trail and in the rocks. His memory, storing and recalling the brands, colors, marks, and actions of cattle, horses, and other denizens of the country, worked as well as that of a clerk perched on his high office stool recalling details of his accounts ledger. He mounted his pony and wheeled, sure in his own mind of what had taken place here.

Walking on blistered feet, Jasper grew more irritated as time went by. Hungry, and angry at his two lagging companions, he believed they both blamed him for their being afoot. Forced to stop occasionally and wait for them to catch up, he needed all his willpower to hold his temper and keep on the trail.

The laggard Huff tried to endure his own pain, weariness, and hunger, while Toby Marsh, like a dog that wants attention and affection, thought he might be in better favor with Jasper than he had been before the shooting, having noted the look on Jasper's face when he observed Huff trailing far behind. All three men looked forward to reaching that cabin.

At the dugout, Ross saw the travelers slogging flat-footed up the trail and realized that the men must already have met Lee to know their way here. He sized them up—not members of a missionary society unless there was something going on in the world he had missed. Their rough looks made Ross decide not to turn his back too long while alone with them.

Not much food in the shelter, he thought. More would have to be added if those three stayed long. Even the coffee beans were low in the sack. He looked at the moldy sowbelly, the last slab of it half gone. Flour—they could have sourdough biscuits. Not much meat. Deer were still winter-thin; the last one they killed had been tough and stringy. A couple of sagehens hanging outside. They had a strong taste of sage

121

leaves, but he could throw them into a stew and make some dough gods to go with it.

"Hi in the shanty! Yuh got company!" he heard Jasper call.

Ross went to the low doorway. "Well, iffen it ain't Santy Claus an' two helpers! Santy, you're late—I see yer ponies got tired. Git off an' rest—dinner ain't quite ready. The cook overslept."

"What's the name of this eating house, anyway?" Toby tried to match Ross's humor.

"This here's the Gateway Hotel, the entrance to boomin' Prine City. You fellers travelin' or just goin' somewheres?"

"Jist lookin' at yer beeyootiful country," Jasper replied. "Throw down yer luggage, boys. The man says we're welcome."

"Strangers're few an' far between in this gulch," Ross responded. "Wilson say he'd be in soon?"

"Said he had to make a swing downriver," Toby answered. "Said to let yuh know."

"Well, set easy. Ain't no room inside 'cept fer dishes an' the cook. I'll have coffee soon."

The three visitors sat, and, as if pushed by the same hand, lay flat back and closed their eyes. Huff said not a word. Jasper lay still, feet throbbing, and contemplated his next move. He would tell this cowboy his story about the Indian ambush and ask for ponies to take them into Prine City. He had a little gold. Huff had some, Toby a little more. Huff would need a gun, and that would cost as much as an Indian cayuse.

"Come an' git yer brew!" came Ross's call.

They arose, wincing, and hobbled to the doorway on blistered feet. Ross held out a battered tin cup, another of white chipped china, and a small bowl. Each man took a drinking vessel. Ross brought the coffeepot and poured out the steaming black liquid. They sipped and slurped just to prolong the joy of having something so good to drink, and their spirits rose as the hot coffee dispelled some of their gloom.

"Boys, from now on, the only way is up," Toby enthused. "If that feller kin make grub good as this coffee tastes, we'll sure help him eat it. Huffy, old scout, you look better."

Huff didn't give a whoop how he looked; it was how he

122

felt. He wished his empty bowl could be refilled. Finally Ross appeared at the door of the dugout again.

"You fellers kin come in one to a time so's not to crowd the stove. We only got two plates. Let the feller with the bowl come first."

Huff began to think his luck had turned, getting first dip at whatever was in the pot. He straightened and walked to the door. Jasper Jukes noticed the new attitude and swore softly to himself, "That smart son of a bitch's gittin' too big fer his britches!"

Serving himself, Huff made sure he had some meat in his bowl. In the doorway, Ross called out, "The feller with the tin cup kin come fer a refill an' a plate."

Jasper, slavering like a dog at a coon tree, felt ready to explode, the leader now at the end of the line, like a mule whose only view was the hind end of the one in front of him. By godfreys, if he ever got loose from this lousy outfit in a gopher hole in a mudbank he'd kick a coupla butts, put Huff and Toby back where they belonged!

Toby, his plate full, a cup of steaming coffee in hand, grinned at Jasper, adding insult to injury. "You'll have to take whatever's left, Jasper," he jeered. "Me'n old Huff got the good stuff. 'Course, you don't need it like we do."

Jasper could have killed him if he'd had a gun handy and wasn't so anxious to fill his own plate and cup. There was still plenty of food in the pot. He dipped out meat, spuds, onions, and chunks of dough gods, filled his cup, and staggered outside to savor the food. Ross grinned as he went to see how much they'd left for Lee and himself.

Wilson rode in just as they finished eating. He put his sweaty pony in the corral and hung blanket and rigging on the pole fence. Bowlegging it to the dugout, he grinned to see the three travelers take turns swishing their dishes clean in the little stream that came off the hill, ready now to settle down and rest up.

"Well, fellers, looks like Ross filled you partway to the top. Leave anything fer me?"

"Clean plates an' an empty pot." Toby laughed. "Take yer choice."

"Well, in that case I better shoot the old nag I was 'bout to loan yuh. If we're outta grub, we gotta eat Old Yeller, poor old pony."

Huff spoke up. "Look in the pot afore you draw yer gun, cowboy. Something in there still smells gosh-awful good. The cook's prob'ly savin' the best fer yuh."

Wilson walked to the dugout. "Yuh jist saved that yeller claybank cayuse's life. Now he kin help you fellers down the road tomorrow. Lucky fer both of yuh. You told Ross 'bout the attempted massacree took place down the river?"

"Nope, we was jist too derned tired to bring it up," Jasper replied. "You run into any of 'em?"

"Naw. Guess you fellers run 'em clear back to where they come from. Ross'n me'll eat."

The two took their time getting their plates filled inside the dugout, enough for Lee to brief Ross on his suspicions. Outside, squatting, Prine's two riders appeased their appetites as they listened to Jasper's story, almost believable to anyone who had not read the tracks and surveyed the evidence Lee Wilson had seen.

"When I ketch up with that redskin, I'll take his hide off like a dirty shirt an' have it tanned fer a saddlebag," Jasper concluded. "He sized us up, figgered we had money, an' cut fer his relatives to waylay us. We lost our ponies, but by God we saved our skins!"

Lee gave Jukes a level glance. "Well, all I kin say is, you're three lucky fellers. You kin take Old Yeller. I'll ketch up Roanie fer yuh, too. He kin pack two of yuh and Yeller'll take the other an' yer plunder. Don't gig the claybank. He'll turn into a pinwheel an' corkscrew all to once, but Roanie's like some folks I know—he jist don't give a damn."

They rolled out at daylight. Jasper elected to ride Yeller, and they tied the extra clothing behind his saddle. Roanie, sleepy-eyed and docile, stood quietly while Toby climbed on bareback and Huff jumped behind.

"Good riddance to bad rubbish, as Maw used to say when she cleaned out the henhouse." Ross grinned as they rode down the trail. "Three rats lookin' fer green cheese. I do reckon little Huff's got some good stuff in him somewhere."

"Let's us saddle up an' scatter fer cows," Lee remarked. "Iffen you git a shot at a big old groundhog, git him. Maybe his grease'll taste better'n that stringy buck meat."

"Tired of sagehens?"

"That an' moldy sowbelly, too. Reckon we could spear a steelhead t'day?"

124

"Try it, then fry it! I'm on my way. See you tonight."

But Ross did not see Wilson that night. Lee rode downriver with the idea of working the south slopes to check on the calving, but before he turned his pony's head to the hills, he decided to go farther, see if he could find any trace of Jack. He followed Jack's trail tracks until they turned off at the top of the open bench to circle back and intercept the three men in case they had decided to follow him, his pony in a lope, its tracks plain across the bunch-grass bat. At the edge of the river bluffs, Wilson saw where Jack had tied his pony and gone on foot. Now I'll follow the trail back, Wilson thought. He pushed his pony into a lope.

Jack carried Ahseeah's baby until they reached the twisted rope of roots that clung to the wall as a handhold. He stopped to wait for the girl, shifted the child to his right arm, and said, "Be careful. Let me cross first."

Step by step, he inched forward. Once the child squirmed and whimpered. Across, Jack looked back to see the girl coming slowly and cautiously. What would happen to these two once he left them? But how could he leave them to shift for themselves? The chief had given him the girl, actually sold her for the gun. Had he forced Ahseeah on Jack as a joke? A tragic joke for him, Jack thought.

They reached the rim just before dark. Jack found the place where the saddle and his rifle had been hidden. Somewhere, trailing the leather rope, the pony was loose. Jack told the girl to make a fire while he looked for his mount.

He started out at a dogtrot, headed for a little flat where the pony might be, and heard him nicker. Whistling a small soothing sound, he approached and grasped the trailing lead, mounted, and went back to the spot where firelight flickered on rocks and junipers.

Ahseeah had found the jerky. She handed a piece to Jack and smiled up at him, but he could think of nothing but Teeah held somewhere in the Indians' hideout. Alert to their danger, knowing that if the chief had cheated him once, he would again, Jack slid off the pony.

"We must leave at once," he said. "We go where the chief will not send his men. Get the child."

When Jack was in the saddle, she held up the baby. Jack reached for her hand and pulled her up behind him, then urged the pony in the direction of the Prine City trail. The old Indian-bred cayuse knew his way across this land of rock and junipers; soon they crossed the main north-south road. On the trail that led to the river, the baby commenced to whimper and cry. Ahseeah spoke softly in Jack's ear. "He hungry. We stop."

In a sheltered hollow off the trail a hundred yards they slid off the pony. It was light enough to see in the soft gleam of the half-moon. The chill desert breeze caused Jack to shiver, but Ahseeah took the baby. In the protection of a lava outcrop she arranged her doeskin shirt so the child could nurse. The pony tethered to one side, Jack slipped back up the trail, carrying his rifle.

The half-breed squatted among junipers, his ears pricked for desert night sounds. He was not sleepy. New problems kept him alert, and he continually turned solutions over in his mind, the burden of Ahseeah and the baby something he had never imagined. He must plan a way to get to Elk Hollow and somehow rid himself of the girl and her child.

A sliver of sound behind him. Slowly he moved his head to glimpse Ahseeah coming among the junipers like a shadow. At his side, she whispered, "Jack, you sleep. I watch." When she spoke his name, the slurred syllable sounded like *Szack*.

"We watch here," he whispered back. "They come soon— or not at all."

In the half-light he saw the sling that held the baby in front of her. She had groomed her hair while the child nursed; now braids hung and framed her face. Unconsciously, Jack looked to see if colored yarn adorned it, but only strips of deerskin tied the ends. In the darkness, close to him as she whispered, he smelled the Indian odor of hides, fish, smoke, and the faint scent of milk from her breasts.

Jack's thoughts went back to the hide-and-canvas tepee where he had lived with his mother as a child. Did the girl croon to her baby as his mother used to sing to him? Oh, if it were only Teeah!

Ahseeah moved away in the shadow of the scrubby trees to where she too could listen and watch back up the trail for intruders.

20

Over open bunch grass where short sagebrush gave cover to jackrabbits and nesting birds, Wilson saw a pony carrying two people slowly coming his way. He rode toward them until he recognized Jack, the half-breed Indian boy, then pulled his mount to one side and waited. He saw that the other rider was an Indian girl. Could it be the one lost in that bloody canyon massacre? Wilson wanted to hear Jack's story.

"Well, Jack . . . I see you're still alive. Say, you've picked up a family! You must have come through that little affair along the river all right."

"You meet up with 'em?" It was Jack's usual impassive tone.

"They come by with flat feet an' blisters. Reckon they got tired of sittin' on their ponies!" Lee guffawed. "You folks're travelin' purty light so far from home. Et anything lately?"

"Jerky and dried fish." Jack turned his head. "I got Ahseeah and her baby as a gift from a Warm Springs chief after he stole my gun."

"Lucky it warn't yer hair an' hide! Let's go to the gopher hole. Maybe we kin dig up somethin' besides dough gods an' sowbelly to eat. Kin yer woman cook?"

"If she can't, I can. You out of beef?"

"Old Prine ain't much fer killin' his own cattle. We could sure use one."

"Lead the way. I'll see we eat better tonight." Jack knew a real cattleman like Prine wouldn't blink at a yearling killed to feed hungry men and that he could repay the old man if there was any complaint. Whatever happened, he would take the blame.

Grinning, Wilson looked over Jack's outfit. "S'pose she'd squall if I held the kid to spell you off?"

"Ride close, we'll find out. You want to practice bein' a daddy?" Jack saw Wilson's humor.

"Not quite yet, Buster. What is it, bull or heifer?"

"It likes music, I know that. If it starts squealing, you can sing to it," Jack told him.

"The hell with you, horse thief! Stolen pony, stolen woman, an' now a stolen kid! Wait'll Ross sees this outfit a-comin'! We jist got rid of three hangers-on—now we git more. I sure as hell hope there turns out to be a cook in this bunch."

When Jack handed her child over to a stranger, Ahseeah did not protest, evidently trusting his judgment. She had made out enough of the conversation to know the cowboy would lead them to a place up ahead. She noticed that he held her baby carefully. During life with the Indians, she alone had cared for the child; no other person had ever taken him from her arms. Though Wilson's action was new and strange, somehow she was glad to see a man reach for the baby, and she felt he was safe with Wilson.

Lee Wilson chuckled. He knew nothing of what had occupied Jack Tate the last day or so except that he had put a bunch of thieves afoot and then disappeared. Now, here he was back, a woman and her baby in tow. The child squirmed, and unconsciously Wilson rocked it a little. He tried to remember when he had last held a baby in his arms. Long time ago . . . the little boy dead, burned when the lamp overturned in the covered wagon. Lee held him while his father dug the hurried grave. They had smoothed it over . . . walked the cattle across it . . . Indians might have dug it open. Wilson cradled the Indian baby a little closer.

Surprised when Lee asked to spell him off, Jack could now move freely in the saddle. As he shifted, he felt Ahseeah's warm softness against his back. One of her arms reached around his waist as the pony broke into a trot to keep up with Wilson, and he looked down at her small brown hand, nails short to the fingertips. The movement of her body against his back with the pony's gait was strangely disturbing. Thoughts of Teeah came to him. Was she alive somewhere back there? He must seek a time and place to ask Ahseeah what she knew.

At the dugout, the Indian girl slid off, walked to Lee's pony, and reached up for her baby, smiling as she pulled back the blanket. The baby blinked its eyes in the light, cooing in response to Ahseeah's voice. Wilson softened at the sight, remembering that he was two thousand miles from where he was born, two hundred miles from any relative. It had been two months since he'd even seen a woman, or heard a woman's voice.

While the two men put the ponies away, Ahseeah changed and washed her baby, then sat down to nurse it. Jack told Lee of his confrontation with Jukes and his partners on the river trail, and their attempt to follow and trap him.

"I shot the ponies," he said. "Thought they'd be kinda discouraged without something to ride."

Lee grinned. "I seen the dead ponies on the trail."

"I slipped out over the hill," Jack went on. "Never thought they'd end up here."

"How's yer bullet wound healin'?"

"Bullet wound?" Jack smiled.

"That little feller Huff said he took a shot at yuh as yuh went up the hill."

Jack's hand came down in a short chop. "I healed up quick!" he said. "Want to kill some meat tonight?"

"Wait till Ross comes in. Let's go see what we kin dig up fer grub to hold us over."

The Indian girl watched each move the men made. A strange place in a country she'd never seen. When the chief sent for her, she had no idea what was in store. Captured far away by a band of young men on a daring raid for ponies, she had been spirited across rivers, mountains, and grassy rolling benchland to the strange and wonderful river hideaway of the Warm Springs tribe, where she had been abused and used as a captive girl belonging to no one. She had heard stories told by women in her mother's tepee about what happened after the raids, some bitter at their women's fate while others laughed and cackled at their various experiences. All had agreed that the best thing was to somehow survive and find a strong man who would take them into his lodge.

Ahseeah did not know which young man was her child's father. Now she had been sold to the white Indian, who seemed shocked at receiving her, though when he reached for the baby at the steep, treacherous place on the trail, she had seen no sign of anger or hate on his face.

From then on, she trusted him. When he handed the baby over to the tall laughing rider with the beard, she felt the two wanted to help her. Now they talked, perhaps about which one would choose her to share his bed.

129

She watched Jack take a tarp and soogan Lee handed him and look for a place to hang it. Ahseeah thought he had a place in mind, but she pointed to another. She laid the baby down close to a tree. "Sun here in morning," she said, and picked up pine limbs and cones to clear a spot.

Jack went for an ax to cut poles and uprights, and as fast as he cut one, Ahseeah carried it to the shelter spot. Once a wagon sheet was hung and anchored, she gathered pine needles to cover the floor. Jack left her to go to the dugout. This was woman's work.

When Ross rode up the trail, he smelled smoke drifting down the little valley. Wilson must be in; but who had ridden the other horse whose tracks he saw in the trail? He pulled his horse up short at the sight of a shelter under the pines, a fire in front, and an Indian woman doing something with a kettle. As he rode on up to the corral, Lee appeared at the dugout doorway.

"Put up yer pony an' wash yer handsome face," he called. "We got company an' a cook."

"Who brought her?"

"Bullhead's Indian wolfer come in with this woman an' her kid. He heard you was tired of my cookin'."

"How'd he escape the massacre?"

"Jack'll tell yuh all about it."

At the fire, Ahseeah saw the rider and heard Wilson welcome him. Would she be used by all three of these men tonight? If she ran, they would hunt her down and abuse her. She tried to act calmly, but her heart pounded.

Ross could only laugh at Jack's dilemma—one man's trouble, another man's humor. Jack's rescue attempt, the trade of his gun and ammunition for the wrong woman and a baby, seemed a big joke to both cowboys, and even Jack saw the humor in the situation as Wilson and Ross tossed ideas his way. Jack with a family! Now he could begin his own tribe, start a new reservation, hire the squaw out to Bullhead Bailey as a cook. Or he could be a summer rider, and in the winter trap and hunt while his woman tanned hides and cleaned skins. But underneath their fun, Jack sensed genuine interest.

"What's next, Jack?" Ross asked, grinning. He held the one battered tin cup in his hand.

"I'll probably go back up to Mr. Bailey's place until I find someplace Ahseeah can live."

"Boy, you got more brains than good sense. Take her and the kid up to old Bullhead—swap her like yer friend the chief did. Think the old hide-skinner'd go fer it, Lee? A good-lookin' young woman to cook, hoe the garden, and keep his soogans warm?"

"Yeah, and one with a young 'un comin' on to ride the range! Ross, I think it'll work. Jack, it's time to figger out what Bailey's got yuh kin use."

Jack wondered. Bailey wouldn't go for a trade, but he did need a woman on the place. Sarah had teased him about getting him one, and Bailey had joked about it with her. Yes, he could take Ahseeah and her baby to Bailey and say that he had done what Sarah had told him to do.

"I might do that," he said. "Could we hang around here a few days till she gets kinda used to white men? I'll kill a beef to help out on the grub. Besides, the chief might send scouts after us, and there's those three bushwhackers."

Lee spoke with a twinkle in his eyes. "Jist a little honeymoon to git acquainted afore yuh trade her off to Bullhead? Yeah, stick around, Jack. You an' Ross kin kill that yearlin' down on the flats. Bring him back up here. We'll skin him out an' hang him high to cool tonight."

Ahseeah had her own meal by the fire at the lean-to, then held the baby. Lee strolled over. Jack and Ross had gone for meat, she knew. Why was Wilson coming to her camp? He squatted down not far from her and rolled a smoke of leaf tobacco.

"A boy?" he inquired.

Ahseeah shook her head and shrugged her shoulders as if she did not understand the question. Lee scratched his head, pointed to the baby, then to himself, and then to Ahseeah. She shook her head violently, thinking he wanted to help her make a baby. Lee laughed.

"Me boy," he said slowly. He pointed to her. "Girl . . . you girl." He pointed to the baby, inquiring again, "Boy?"

Ahseeah smiled and nodded.

Still pointing, he said, "Girl?"

She laughed aloud, and said softly, "He boy."

Intrigued by trying out English words she knew, he tried "knife," "fire," "gun," "friend," and "horse." Pointing to him-

131

self, he said, "Lee—my name is Lee." He pointed to her, a question in his eyes.

The word came softly. "Ah-see-ah . . . Ah-see-ah."

Then and there, Lee Wilson became sorry for the Indian girl. He watched her gentle, loving look as she picked up the baby. He wondered about her past life and how long she could last in the world of white men she had entered. She pulled back the covering from the baby's face and held him toward Lee. The baby cooed and smiled.

"Cute little rascal," Wilson mused. "What yuh gonna call him?"

The girl looked bewildered.

"My name's Lee, you Ahseeah." He pointed at the baby. Ahseeah smiled. "Szack . . . he Szack."

"Why not call him Lee?"

"Lee. Szack." She smiled up at him. "Szack Lee . . . Szack Lee. You like?"

"Sure do, sister. First kid I ever had named after me, even if I am in second place."

Ross and Jack came in with the yearling tied on Lee's pony as packhorse. Lee had a limb picked out, a rope slung over it. Sharp knives peeled off the hide, and Ahseeah stood by with her knife and a bucket to get trimmings. The kettle went on the fire, and she added a few roots and bulbs she had dug up nearby. Ross gave her the beef heart. She cut it up at once and put it in the simmering pot. They would slice and fry the liver for breakfast.

It was not quite dark. Ahseeah took the fresh hide to a dry log with no bark on it, spread it flesh-side-up, and began to scrape bits of fat and ribbons of flesh from it. She meant to save it for tanning.

The men squatted by the fire and talked quietly, slapping at buzzing mosquitoes. A cool breeze holding scents of sun-warmed pines, sage, and juniper drifted down the valley. The coals glowed red, the pot simmered, and odors of stewing meat and bulbs filled the air.

"Ross, me'n Jack've got one up on you right now. You're jist a driftin' saddle bum, but we got a family, got people named after us," Lee began.

"The hell you say! That makes you and Jack special?"

"Well, the young lady liked our looks and high-class ways so much she named her only boy after us."

132

"You mean Alice or whatever her name is has named her squinch-eyed kid after you two thieves?"

"Call him a squinch-eyed kid again an' you'll do the cookin' for a week," Lee told him lazily. "Yup, she named him Jack Lee. If you was better-lookin', maybe she'd tack somethin' on fer you, but that'd spoil it. This kid's ourn."

"I don't believe it. I'm gonna ask Alice myself."

"There yuh go, stutterin' like a half-wit. Her name ain't Alice, it's Ah-see-ah. Real high-class name! Jack, we've got to see the kid has somethin' to take with him when he leaves. You find a place fer him an' his mother, and you'n me kin kinda look after him. Poor little feller, lucky fer him he has folks now."

"Oh, shut up, Wilson, you make me sick!" Ross jeered while Jack smiled. He stomped over to where Ahseeah worked on the hide, standing there undecided until she looked up at him. Her little smile did the trick. Ross grinned. "Jack Lee," he said.

Ahseeah nodded, arose in a graceful movement, picked the baby up, and showed him to the cowboy. Ross was strangely moved at the sight of the sleeping brown baby, its black hair straight as wire strands. The range rider watched a little smile come and go on the boy's round, full face. Early memories of home stole over him. He pointed one finger toward his own chest and said, "Me Ross. He Jack Lee Ross—okay?"

"Szack . . . Lee . . . Ross," she repeated. "Baby Szack Lee Ross." She rolled out the syllables, smiled, and patted her child's cheek.

21

The coals grew faint in the rising darkness. Lee Wilson stretched his arms and yawned. "Fellers, I'm gonna turn in. Stay and fight the gnats and skeeters if yuh want. See yuh at daylight."

"You goin' to sleep in the tent or under the stars, Jack?" Ross teased.

"I'll lay close by her outfit—keep you fellers away." Jack's smile was wry.

The cowboy turned serious. "Don't worry about that, boy. I was brought up with some things in my head I ain't about to change now. Sleep where yuh want. I guess yer own girl's still on yer mind."

"Yeah," Jack replied. "I won't sleep too good anywhere till I find what happened to Teeah. Nobody down in that hellhole seemed to know anything about her, but I'm sure they took her."

"If yuh ever need some help that way, Lee an' me'll be glad to oblige," Ross assured him, and sought his bedroll.

Jack walked toward the lean-to. He paused to listen; all quiet in there. Coyotes yipped and yodeled their quavering song from hills above the river. Air moving down the draw brought the scent of pines still warm from spring sunshine that caused their sap to run and the olive-colored pollen to drift away. Jack's heart beat faster. Under the canvas lay a young woman who could be at his mercy—the Indian way with captives. He rejected the thought. His religious training at Lapwai and at Lee's Mission on the Willamette denounced such an attitude. He and Teeah had been Christians. He would keep to himself.

Inside the shelter, Ahseeah lay still. She knew Jack stood outside. A piece of wood caught flame, the light flickering on the canvas roof and walls. Somehow the Indian girl felt safe. These men had helped name her baby and smiled at him. Jack, perhaps younger than she, was strong and brave and sure—she saw that when he talked with the chief at the river. She wondered about the girl he called Teeah. Who was she? In the Indian camp she had heard no rumor of a girl by that name.

Jack entered the low tent on hands and knees. Ahseeah lay still, hardly breathing. He pulled off his knee-length boots with their soft buckskin soles and laid them aside, then stretched out on the soft pine needles.

"Szack?" came her soft whisper in the darkness.

"Yeah?"

"You sleep here?"

"Yes. You sleep too, Ahseeah."

Conscious of each other, so close, yet separated by race and taboos, they lay still. Jack's heritage told him to take her in the Indian way, but his white blood and training said that would be a sin.

Sleep came to tired bodies and settled the problem.

Before the morning star faded and the coyotes' morning song began, Ahseeah was at the fire, feeding coals under the ashes with pine-pitch slivers. The nearby kettle was still warm. She went into the pines and brought back with her a few dry, crisp cones to feed the flames.

Jack came out, alert as always, and before he stepped into the clear, looked carefully around. When Ahseeah came to the fire, she smiled at him in the dim light of morning and spoke softly. "Szack?"

The Indian youth looked down at her. "Ahseeah, it is good to see you doing the cooking."

She smiled and nodded, not quite understanding, but sure that what he said had something to do with food. She turned back to the fire, and Jack went to wash at the spring that fed into the creek. Lee appeared at the dugout door; smoke soon issued from its rusty stovepipe. Ross went to the corral to grain the ponies and saddle up while Lee cooked a cattleman's breakfast.

Jack had borrowed coffee from the dugout supply, the beans ground in the hand-cranked grinder that also ground corn for cornbread. Now he measured it the range traveler's way, a handful to the pot of water he had brought from the spring.

Ross came by the fire to say howdy. He looked in the shelter where the baby lay sucking its thumb. "Jack Lee Ross—that's my boy!" He grinned at the girl by the fire.

"Szack Lee Ross," she echoed.

Ross and Jack went down to the dugout, and Lee put fried liver and sourdough bread on two plates. "Fill up on Ahseeah's stew," he advised. "Then we better figger out what we'll do today besides chase all over the country fer old man Prine."

In full light, the glow of the sun on western slopes turning them rosy pink, Jack and Ross squatted by the fire. Ahseeah took two cups and filled them from the pot. Jack watched her move around the fire, doeskin skirt and black braids swinging, reminding him again of Teeah, but Ross broke into his thoughts.

135

"Jack, iffen you an' the girl stick around here for a few days, we'll send Lee in town fer grub an' to find out what them three rannies put out about the massacree."

"We'll stay. I ride with you or we can split. She can keep camp and cook. She won't use the stove, don't know how, but she will feed us the Indian way."

Wilson came out with the skillet as plate and dipped more food from the stew pot. Ahseeah filled his bowl with coffee and looked to see the others had plenty. Lee grinned at Ross.

"Well, what'd yuh think of Jack Lee?" he asked.

"Purty fine-lookin' boy. Too bad he had to have you fellers' names on the front end."

"Front end? What yuh talkin' about?"

"Well, Jack Lee ain't so much. So I give him a good name. That little feller's now Jack Lee Ross!"

Jack stopped his hand halfway to his mouth, speechless. Wilson gulped a hasty swallow of coffee.

"What's that name again?"

"Jack Lee Ross. How you fellers like it?"

"Well, I'm amazed! Suits me'n Jack fine. Glad yuh did the right thing by the girl."

"Say, I figgered you birds would squall like blue jays when I put my name on him," Ross countered.

"It jist so happens that Oregon's a state now, and legal things like marriage an' havin' kids an' raisin' hell all gits a look from the law," Wilson pointed out. "It's up to you to see this boy of yourn grows up to be somethin' other than a saddle tramp. Right, Jack?"

"That is right, Lee. It ought to be a Christian marriage. You could look up a preacher in town and hire him to come out and give Ross's boy legal protection. I won't have to see Mr. Bailey after all."

"The hell with you sonsabitches!" Ross exploded. "Jist 'cause I give the kid a decent name don't mean he's mine."

"Don't try to squirm out of it," Lee told him. "Jack an' me're witnesses to the fact yuh give yer last name to the boy as his'n."

"You fellers're crazy as a locoed steer! He's all red Injun, anybody kin see that!"

"Right in court is where you'll be, cowboy, iffen you try to back out of yer deal with this pore little child. Git ready to pay off the preacher."

Ross began to eat in gulps, not too sure that Lee and Jack were joking. Folks *would* take it the boy's last name was Ross, and so far as he knew, he was the only Ross in the country. His joke had backfired.

Silence. Ahseeah looked from one man to the other. She knew something had disturbed Ross and that Jack and Lee seemed to have the advantage.

Ross got up, slung a few drops from his cup, and looked down at the two squatted by the fire. "By grannies, that boy's worth a good name, but I ain't about to marry the woman. One more crack 'bout me an' her an' the kid, an' I'll git ready to fight. I ain't never been no Injun lover, but this here's a fine girl, an' the kid's somethin', too. Now, let's Jack'n me git down the meat an' wrap it up. Lee, reckon you want to drift into town. Don't look fer no preacher yet unless yuh figger on a killin' out here."

Lee laughed a huge easy laugh. "There'll be no killin' around here unless them buggers show up lookin' fer Jack. I'll be back tonight an' have the other ponies along, 'cause we're gonna need 'em."

"Keep yer trap shut about Jack and Ahseeah," Ross warned.

"Yeah, an' you tell her to keep her eyes open, an' take to the hills iffen anybody shows up here." Lee looked at Jack, then turned to the dugout.

Ahseeah took a dish of stew into the shelter. The baby was now awake, murmuring and cooing in his blanket. Ross, finished sketching out the day's ride for Jack, stood up to leave. He saw the baby's waving arms, and went to hold one finger for the little hand to grasp. The cowboy shook his finger lightly to feel the little one's clutch tighten, then pulled away and left without looking at the baby's mother.

With Indian talk, gestures, and a little English, Jack told the girl to help Lee with the meat. He would show her the food in the dugout. They would be gone all day, and if anyone came, she must take to the hills and hide. Bad white men, Indians too, might rob the camp and take her with them. She nodded in sober agreement. Jack saddled up and rode off with Ross.

They lowered the beef, quartered it, and cut a chunk for steaks. Ahseeah helped Lee wrap the meat and hang it in the shade. At first she was reluctant to enter the dugout, dark

137

and gloomy after the morning sun, but when Lee showed her flour, beans, rice, dried prunes, and various other articles kept in covered tin cans, she showed interest, pointing to the prunes, nodding that she knew what to do with them as well as the rice and beans, at the same time deciding that when Lee left for town she would look in the hills for food she knew. On the ridges she could find bulbs; along the stream, salad materials.

In Prine City, Wilson went first to the livery barn to see if Yeller and the roan were there. The barn boss laughed.

"Yuh sure sent us three fine citizens yestiddy," he said. "Where'd yuh pick them rascals up?"

"They come flat-footin' up our trail with a story 'bout a shoot-up with some Injuns. I let 'em stay the night, fed 'em, and after I heard their side of the desperate battle, I loaned 'em two ponies to git to this mudhole yuh call a town."

"They shore started somethin' here! They got half the town laughing' at 'em an' the other half loadin' guns an' buyin' powder an' lead! Damnedest thing since the Injuns killed the Whitmans!"

"Me an' Ross figgered that might happen. I come in to git some grub an' collect my stock. Don't fret 'bout no Injuns on the warpath. They're all along the rivers catchin' fish while the squaws dig bulbs an' feed the kids."

"Well, what did happen? Somethin' must've put 'em on the ground 'sides hard luck or horse cholera."

"I read their tracks. Them ornery galoots met up with Half-breed Jack, the one wolfed fer Bullhead up in Elk Hollow last winter. They figgered him some ignorant breed with a gun and a pony, and decided to collect, but Jack was a little smarter. He got up the hill an' shot their ponies. They had to stomp ten or twelve mile afore they got to our camp."

"Jack's the one come out of that killin' up in the canyon, ain't he?"

"Yeah. Don't mix it with him if yuh don't want trouble. That Injun's either plain lucky or smart enough to keep on livin'."

"Well, yer ponies're here. Have a drink, git yer grub, an' lissen how them fellers're tryin' to stir up a posse."

Wilson found the story of the Indian attack to be no laughing matter in the town. Most of the residents had at some

138

time or other come in contact with Indians, the Whitman massacre still fresh in their minds. To the east in the Boise Basin and along the Snake the Bannocks were on edge, while the desert people, the Paiutes, raised hell with little skirmishes and raids on cattle and horses. Scattered homesteads and small places where people had settled suffered, and each incident became enlarged in the telling.

At The Mercantile & General Supply where Wilson did his buying, he was questioned. Mr. Prine, out on a cattle-buying trip, was not there to be consulted. Prine could stop any false reprisal attempt by his word alone, but Wilson was judged just an ignorant rider with not enough brains under his hat to boil beans before dinner. If the army didn't run the bastards back to the brush, a few citizens would, Wilson was told, and anything he said had to be to a few old-timers with sense enough to size up the panicked storytellers and issue judgment as to who was lying.

Jasper Jukes had used up what gold he and his fellow travelers had to buy sleeping quarters, ponies, and some grub. As they made the rounds, they spread the story of the attempted killing and robbery, each time embellishing it to make a more convincing tale. They got to believing most of it themselves, and Huff Miller went along with the lurid account. Jasper began to again look like a man to follow, as Huff saw men's eyes widen, listening to Jukes's tale of the fight at the river.

The three had left town by the time Wilson arrived, but before they left, a saloon swamper had taken Jukes aside to tell him about an Injun hater who would sure help to run the red bastards back across the Deschutes River where they ought to be. He described a cowman west of town who had come from real Indian country and lost his family, stock, and equipment in a raid. He kept a rough bunch of riders with him and made open threats to kill and skin any red man or woman that ever showed up on his range.

"Dingus is his handle—Big Red Dingus," the swamper told Jukes. "He's from the South, he hates niggers an' what he calls red niggers—Injuns, yuh know. He'll be in it with yuh, but don't never cross him, 'cause he's p'ison."

"Yuh think he'd take a few days' ride with us?"

"Try him out. He's the only one I know mean enough to go out of his way to kill Injuns."

"How kin we find his place?"

139

"Head west. His outfit takes off on a little road out four, five miles. Set of elk horns nailed to a post on yer right."

"Thanks fer yer advice, mister. If we git him to go with us, there'll be somethin' in it fer yuh when we git back."

22

At the Dingus ranch, the only person around was a woman who came to the shanty door and told Jukes and his partners the boss was out after cattle and wouldn't be back for a while. When Jukes inquired when, the answer was, "I dunno, mister, an' I doubt that he does."

"I guess you wouldn't mind if we decided to stick around?"

"I reckon not. I'll fry up some grub if you're hungry, but Dingus says anybody who eats here has to work fer it. If yuh want to git busy an' cut a little wood, there's an ax." She pointed, then went back into the shanty.

It was something the three hadn't encountered before. "To hell with the old biddy!" Jasper said. "Probably can't cook worth a damn, anyway."

"Well, I'm fer cuttin' some wood, an' let's see what she kin cook up. Hell, man, we could be here fer hours, an' I'm hungry right now."

"All right, Huff, grab the bucksaw an' start in," Toby suggested. "I'll use that grubhoe she calls an ax an' split what yuh cut. Jasper kin set an' watch."

"Oh, fer hell's sake, you fellers beat anything I ever heerd tell of," Jasper grumbled. "Go ahead, then, I'll pack it to the porch, but by grab, if she wants me to fill the stove, I swear I'll throw it through the winder!"

In due time they were served a hot meal with fresh bread and pie. The woman never admitted to being Mrs. Dingus, and they didn't press her for her name. When they gave her curt thanks for the meal, she said, "Nobody has time to split wood on this farm. They ride out at daylight an' don't come in till dark." Her voice turned querulous. "Ride, ride, ride, eat an' sleep, an' do it agin the next day! When I try to cut the wood I need, saw won't cut, ax ain't sharp, an' the juniper's hard as iron! I swear I was better off back in Missouri!"

Huff spoke up, feeling sorry for her. "Ma'am, yuh give us a fine meal. While we're waitin', I'll put an edge to that ax. I seen a grindstone out there. Tobe'll turn the wheel fer me."

Just before dark, Dingus and three wild-looking men rode in. Huff, sitting on the corral's top rail, saw them coming. He whistled to Jasper and pointed. A big man riding a long-tailed white horse was in the lead, the brim of his wide hat turned up against the crown. Two of the other riders wore caps, the last man's headgear a short-brimmed, flat-crowned affair.

Their leader sat straight in the saddle. Strength showed in his movements, and his horse was large and powerful, different in size, color, and gait from plains and western Indian ponies seen in this country, outweighing the other riders' ponies by three or four hundred pounds, Jasper guessed, an eastern-bred horse probably. All the men carried guns on their saddles, and as they drew closer, Jasper saw knives in their belts, men loaded for trouble and looking as if they could handle it. Jasper felt shaken.

Dingus rode up to the corral and without dismounting asked bluntly, "Jist what brought you fellers here?"

"Indians," Jasper replied, walking toward him.

"How many an' where?" Dingus' hard blue eyes bored into Jasper's.

"Don't know how many. They was on the crooked river trail maybe fifteen miles down from Prine town. They killed our ponies."

"You kill any of 'em?" The big red-faced, red-haired man blared the question.

"Not fer sure," Jasper replied. "Huff here figgered to got lead into the one killed his pony."

"When'd this big fight take place?"

"Yesterday, jist 'fore noontime. We had to walk into a cow camp. They give us some ponies an' we rode into town, picked up the ones we got now along with some grub. Heerd you liked to fight the red devils. Air yuh interested in wipin' out this bunch?"

Dingus sat still, staring hard at Jasper on the ground below him. Finally he turned to his riders and said, "Turn yer ponies loose in the corral—we ain't goin' anywhere for a spell."

141

He looked at Jasper and Toby. "What's yer names?" he grated.

"Jasper Jukes. This here's Huff Miller an' Toby Marsh. We come to Oregon to find us a place we could run cows. Yer red friends give us quite a welcome."

"Don't never call anything with a red or black hide my friend, Jukes," Dingus said in a venomous tone. "An' I don't buy this tale of yers. I think yuh dreamed it up. Even if yuh didn't, yuh wouldn't stand no chance of catchin' up with them Injuns now. What cow camp lent yuh the ponies?"

Dingus' insulting words made Jukes furious, but he dared not show it. His hand had been called, and he could do nothing about it as things stood. "Fellers by the names of Wilson an' Ross was there," he answered evenly. "They ride fer Prine, I guess."

Dingus swung out of the saddle to the ground.

Jesus, he's a big man! Huff thought. Two-fifty or more, an' better'n six-and-a-half high. He could fight grizzly bears an' rassle wild bulls. Jasper better pull in his claws.

Dingus ripped off the saddle and slung it on the pole fence, all his motions angrily vigorous. He snatched the blanket off his horse and shook it out before putting it alongside the saddle, then held the reins with one big hand and rubbed the neck and back of his mount with the other. Looking at Jasper once more, he said, "I know Wilson, and I've heard of his buddy. If they didn't work up a sweat at your story, I sure as hell ain't goin' to. Iffen there was a bunch of Injuns there yesterday or even this mornin', they ain't there now—them red rascals jist melt away. They got some way to cross that blasted canyon an' river, an' nobody ever ketches 'em. You might as well drift back to town an' fergit 'em. I am."

The last remark increased Jasper's irritation. "I'm goin' huntin' fer redskins!" he snapped. "We lost our ponies, an' I ain't goin' to let 'em git by with it."

Dingus spoke quietly. "Stranger, I don't know where yuh come from, an' I don't give a damn, but you got a lot to learn 'bout *this* country. You lost three ponies an' one outfit. Hell, I lost a family, wagons, an' a herd of stock. You stir up them river redskins, an' if yuh live through the first skirmish, they'll tack yer hide on the ground the second time. The army don't like sech goings-on. They're havin' trouble over on the Snake an' the Clearwater, more comin' on the Grande

142

Ronde, an' they don't want nothin' stirred up over here till they git that kettle cooled down."

Jasper swung around and walked to his pony, tied down at the corral fence, Huff about to follow until he heard Dingus ask, "Who sent you fellers out here to see me, anyway?"

"A swamper in the Rider's Rest told us you was hell on Injuns and might want to join in with us, said you was a nigger-hater too."

"He wants to be picked up by the scruff of his neck an' throwed out in the street fer talkin' that way. I'll do it myself next time I'm in there fer a drink. Now, let me tell you somethin'. The redskins is a lot different than them with black hides. These people got bows that can shoot arrers that kin kill. Some have guns, powder, an' lead. All their ornery lives they been used to killin' an' fightin', an' they know ever' hidey-hole an' ambush in the country. You smart Injun killers wouldn't last through the first day. More'n one that's tried it never come back, an' their riggin' wasn't never found, either. If you want trouble, you know where to find it—I'll lissen fer what happens!"

Impressed by this towering man, Huff thought his theories made sense. He himself had thought Jasper crazy to try to get even, knowing he'd get no help from Wilson and Ross. Jasper Jukes would get him in deep trouble yet, possibly killed. Alone with Dingus, he spoke.

"Mr. Dingus, I reckon you're right. Let me ask yuh a question."

"Shoot yer wad."

"I want to split with Jukes an' Marsh, go on my own. You have any idea where I could git a job?"

"There's lots of work around fer fellers that kin ride, cut wood, split rails, make shingles and shakes, and build shanties an' corrals." He smiled grimly. "If I git ahold of that swamper's scrawny neck, there'll be a job open in his saloon. Naw, I ain't got no room." He looked down at Huff. "Yuh seem like yuh mean it," he continued. "Go into the livery stable, not the one this end of town, but on the far end. Tell the barn boss I sent yuh an' see what he kin come up with."

Dingus put up his horse, and Huff turned away. The three drifters mounted. As they trotted toward town, Jasper rode alongside Huff. "What'd that big boar hog have to say to yuh?"

"Said to leave the Injuns alone and not stir 'em up less'n a war started, then organize an' clean out the nest with the army's help. Said to lay low an' wait."

"You believe that crap?" Jasper scoffed. "I sure don't. I'm goin' to git my belly full at that boardinghouse, then make the rounds of the saloons an' find somebody'll join us lookin' fer that red bastard put us afoot!"

Toby spoke up. "I'm with yuh, Jasper. I wanta git even with that Injun." He shook his head. "I'd like to see old Red Dingus git gut-shot, too."

Huff objected. "That old boy'd lay out a few corpses afore he died, I betcha. If it was me doin' the shootin', I'd try fer his head an' let him flop like a chicken when the slug hit him."

Jasper was nettled. "Huff, you rattle like a loose wheel on a buggy. Don't let the old boar bluff yuh. Him an' his crew was a leetle too much fer me to mix with, but the day'll come when we meet equal, an' then I'll whittle him down to size or die tryin'."

But Red Dingus with his size and fierce openness had impressed Huff far more than anything Jasper had ever done or said. He changed the subject. "You fellers taken in the saloons. I'll look in at the livery stables, maybe pick up some idea of where that Injun feller might land if he comes back. I heard he worked fer Bullhead Bailey last winter."

"Well, find out what yuh kin about him, an' while you're at it, try to git some idea where we kin settle down—not close to town, but kinda out in the hills. Git some barn swipe to talkin', buy him a drink or a bottle."

In Prine City, Huff sauntered down the street after he ate supper, and stopped at the far end to see the barn boss at the Ochoco Livery Stables and Corral, where a hostler was brushing down a light team near the door. Whistling a soft, slow tune that seemed to quiet and soothe restless horses, he looked up when Huff walked in. As he brushed the sweaty back of a bay gelding, he nodded at the stranger.

"Yuh lookin' fer the boss or fer a hoss to ride?"

"The boss, maybe. You work here long?"

"Come a year back. They call me Frank."

"Big feller by the name of Dingus told me to see the boss of this outfit."

"Big Red comes in now an' then," the hostler replied. "He

an' Ike Cafferty git along purty good. You was here with those ponies of Wilson's, wasn't yuh?"

"Yeah. They still here?"

"Naw, Lee rode in an' got 'em. Packed a load of grub put on the roan. Must be feedin' a crew. You know Wilson an' his pardner Ross?"

"We stayed at their cowcamp. Wilson let us have the ponies so we could rest our feet on the way to Prine City. We'd walked twelve or fifteen miles the day before.

"Yeah, the story's goin' round that yer ponies got shot by an Injun or two."

"Yeah, that's right. I got a chunk of lead in one of 'em, I hope. The boss around?"

Cafferty, a man fully muscled and quietly alert, moved gracefully as a well-conditioned and trained boxer, the slight crookedness and hump of his nose a sure indication it had been broken at some time. His sharp, bright blue eyes studied Huff.

"So Red told yuh to see me 'bout a job," he said in answer to Huff's statement. "Yeah, I could put you on here. You was with them other two fellers in the Injun war downriver?"

"Yeah."

"When'd you see Red?"

"Few hours back."

"How come he sent yuh here?"

"I let him know I liked the way he talked an' told him I was thinkin' of quittin' Jukes an' Marsh. I want no part of tryin' to run down those Indians. It'd come to no good. When I asked him about a job, he said see you. I got a little money, but I want somethin' to do."

"Bunk here in the barn an' help with the horses fer a few days till I sort yuh out," Cafferty said. "Yer pards won't git their tails in the air over it, will they?"

"I'll give 'em a story to quiet 'em down if they do. I got some plunder at the boardinghouse—the pony's tied in the yard there, too."

"Go git 'em, then. My rules is no smokin' in the barn, no drinkin' on the job, no repeatin' what's told to yuh in confidence."

Huff stopped in the saloon where Jasper played cards and Toby watched from behind his chair. When Toby came outside at his motion, Huff told him about his move.

145

"I'll work in the horse barn fer a few days, git acquainted with the town an' what goes on."

"Huffy, yuh come up with a good idee. Me'n Jasper'll play the town an' see what we kin find out. We'll see each other now an' then. You gonna eat at the boardinghouse?"

"Unless a better place shows up. I git a buck a day an' a place to sleep at the livery stable."

Ike Cafferty had not been generous because it was his nature; he suspected Red Dingus saw something worth watching in this man. The three drifters' tale of what might be a phony fight with Indians could lead to an undesirable confrontation. Wilson had laughed at it. Around the barn, Huff could be watched and that loudmouth fellow Jukes headed away from trouble.

So the three settled down for a spell in and around the little town struggling to become more than just a stopping place on the way to the John Day and across the mountains to the Snake River and Idaho. Mines were springing into life all over the region, boom times loomed ahead for both miners and cattle raisers if only some calamity like an Indian war or a financial panic didn't strike them. It was an ideal period in Oregon territory for adventurers, con men, and rascals after quickly gained wealth.

23

Jack learned the river country. Most cattle fed on bunch grass now, spring well on its way. Sudden cold, windy spells with skiffs of sleet and rain were followed by bright blue skies, white schooners of clouds billowing, crowding together, and splitting apart as the wind pushed them eastward. The Cascades were white with snow, the Three Sisters showing no dark shadows at all. Meadowlarks and bluebirds sang and fluttered up here and there. It was a time when riders carried rifles ready for a shot at an old gray wolf or his cousin the coyote. A country of waving grasses, sheltered draws, and gulches for cattle cover, its higher slopes and mountain meadows would provide feed during summer's heat.

146

The Indian boy and Ahseeah and her baby found Ross and Lee easy to live with. Jack did not know how old the girl was, and nothing she said helped him guess. At times, she seemed mature, then suddenly only a girl growing into womanhood, unsure of herself. Jack thought she might be a little older than Teeah. He saw the same hesitation, yet a certain assurance in Ahseeah's actions and looks bothered him.

The second night, after Lee had brought a variety of food from town, they ate well and later sat by the fire talking. He asked her if she had known a Nez Percé girl named Teeah in the camp along the river. She nursed the baby as she talked, and the sight of her smooth round breast, the nipple oozing drops of white milk, stirred Jack. The way she exposed the other breast while she put the child to the oozing milk fascinated him, and he missed some of her answer. But when he heard her say "Teeah," he came alert.

"What did you say about Teeah?"

Ahseeah realized Jack's mind had been on her body and her appearance as she nursed the baby. "This girl Teeah—did you marry her?" she asked.

"No. We rode together. She was going to the Indian school, the mission school in the big valley, to learn the white men's ways."

"White men's way better?"

"Maybe so. I will have to live it. Indians must learn to live with white men. War will come. Indians get killed. Many bad times. Teeah was to live with whites, then with me. We live together somewhere, have cows and ponies someday. She is gone, but I still look for her."

The baby squirmed in Ahseeah's arms. She moved him to the other breast, and Jack saw its shape and gleam in the firelight. He wanted to reach out and feel its smooth roundness, rub his face against Ahseeah's as he had rubbed faces with Teeah long ago.

"You Jesus man, Szack?"

The question startled him. Was he a Jesus man? He had been taught in several missions that Christ was the only one who could lead him to the white man's God and that if he wanted to go to the white man's heaven he must live by Christian rules. Mr. Craig, Big Thunder, and Mr. Hill had all wanted him to go the white man's way.

147

He nodded his head. "Yes, I was baptized at Lapwai Mission."

Ahseeah looked puzzled and tried to say the word.

Jack explained to her with signs and Indian words. She had heard Indian women tell how the Black Robes and the preachers put water on the babies' heads or submerged them in the water of river or stream to clean them of all sin. It was the white man's way. Most Indian women laughed. They knew Indians were clean—they had their own sweatbaths, swam in the rivers, and washed in the summer rains. What did the words "clean" and "sin" have to do with going to the white man's heaven?

Jack couldn't answer that. Ahseeah pulled her jacket together, put the baby over her shoulder, and patted him on the back, smiling. She arose in one graceful movement and took the child into the shelter. Jack watched her as she arranged him in a nest of pine needles, two black braids framing her face. On hands and knees she turned toward him. "Szack, you come, sleep?"

Jack shook his head, got up, and walked into the darkness to look at the starry sky, wanting desperately to enter the shelter and lie with this girl. But if he did that, he could not keep looking for Teeah. To find Teeah was his goal. Ahseeah had given him no reply, no clue that would help him in his search.

Resolved to subdue his desires, he crawled reluctantly into the shelter, turned his back to Ahseeah, and thinking of Teeah, soon slept.

Next morning he rode with Lee Wilson to a new territory across the river where they checked cattle on the slopes exposed to the warm sun. When they reached the upper benchlands, high enough now to see the far mountains white with snow, the great cones of Mount Hood and Mount Jefferson looking like guideposts to travelers, they got off their ponies. After cigarettes were rolled and the first puffs of fragrant smoke emerged, Jack spoke, his tone quiet.

"Lee, you know I was raised around the missions at Lapwai and in the valley, so I got baptized and was brought up as a Christian. My old man never said much about it—he wanted the best for me. He had his winter women, but he never told me about the girls or women in camp because I was too young at the time. Mr. Hill was a Christian, and he

148

talked Bible talk to me once in a while; he never said not to sleep with girls, but I never knew him to go with a woman on our travels, so I guess that way of living rubbed off on me.

"When I asked if Teeah could go with us to Oregon to live with the Turpins, Mr. Hill didn't object. He did say to watch the boys and the older men we traveled with—they would be after Teeah. Old Stubbs wanted Teeah. Of course he wanted the money, the ponies, and all the rest too, but he wanted Teeah. I think he would have used her, then killed her. She knew it, too. Mr. Turpin couldn't believe that Stubbs and the others would kill us, and he was careless. He'd lived in the valley too long, where people who acted that way were few, and if caught, they were hung. Teeah kept a knife with her, and I had a little gun, but I was at the ponies when they started shooting. I saw Stubbs shoot Teeah. But when Ort and Ace took the ponies and dead people away, Teeah was not there."

Jack took a deep breath and paused as the scene flashed through his mind. His cigarette had died out. He relit it and went on, trying to be brief as he told his story. Lee Wilson listened, and as the moments passed, took in fully at last the meaning of Jack's trek and his faithful dedication to the search for Teeah.

"My problem is this," he heard Jack saying. "I have to leave Ahseeah with someone. If I stay with her, you know what will happen. I might marry her, but I'd always wonder about Teeah. Maybe we better leave in the morning for Mr. Bailey's ranch headquarters."

"I know what you mean, Jack," the cowboy mused. "It would solve yer problem if Bailey'd take her in. But if he don't?"

"Then we head for Jubal and Sarah's place over on the John Day, cattle and all, soon as the pass is open."

Lee nodded. "What kinda place they got over there?"

"I don't know. Jubal nor Sarah never said, but Jubal wants to quit trading and start a cattle herd. He traded ponies to Mr. Bailey for cows and calves, and I have some cattle coming for the wolves I killed last winter."

"I reckon it'd be a smart move on yer part, Jack. The talk around town is that Jasper Jukes and his two idiot sidekicks're after yer scalp. They're out tryin' to round up help in wipin' out the crew shot their ponies. I don't think they'll git many to go along, but you'd better watch out for 'em."

Jack pulled on his smoke, waiting.

"Might be better fer the woman an' her kid, too. If Bailey takes her in, she'll have a few years of peace, but, hell, that's all any of us kin figger on. I can't see ahead more'n one or two myself, kin you?"

Jack had never thought of it quite that way. All he was really interested in from now on was how and where to find Teeah.

Bullhead Bailey had never thought he'd get a proposition like the one before him now. A young squaw and her still-drooling kid live with him and learn to cook and keep house? He couldn't believe his ears. Should he run this jackass of a half-breed down the river with the girl and her papoose? He looked once more at the silent, impassive Indian boy waiting for acceptance of his outrageous scheme. Ahseeah faced the rancher directly, no fear or apology in her face, either. The child in the sling around her neck awoke and waved one arm in the air as if saluting Bailey.

"Jack, kin she understand white talk, or do I have to flap my hands like a crow in a cornfield?"

"She understands some words. She's learning fast. She's a lot like Sarah. If you let her stay here, she and her boy will be safe and she will repay you in many ways."

"Jack, one of us is plumb crazy. I don't want no woman around, especially with a sucklin' kid. Jesus, Jack, what got into yuh to bring her here?"

"There was no other place. You got good cattle, good ponies, a good range and house. Like Sarah said, 'All you need is a good woman.'"

"You an' Sarah!" Bailey jeered. "Well, come on in—we'll eat an' talk. If she stays, what'll I do with old Brew?"

Jack ignored the question. He spoke to Ahseeah, led the way into the cook shack, and Bailey followed, scratching his head.

They stood by the long table. "Mr. Bailey, you need a woman to cook and help you here. No white woman would come to this place. Ahseeah will stay. Her boy will grow up to be a help to you. If you ever find a white woman, Ahseeah will leave—that is the Indian way. Sarah and Jube live and work together—it's easier for both of them. Ahseeah was a slave in the Indian camp. The chief took my gun for her and told me if I didn't want her to cut her throat and throw her and the baby in the river. I couldn't do that, but I can't keep her with me, because I want to find Teeah."

Bailey was silent a moment. Jack saw him look at Ahseeah, whose eyes roved over the stove, the pots and kettles, the food in cans and sacks on shelves.

The rancher sighed hugely. "Oh, hell, Jack, she kin stay! But by godfreys, if I find out yuh lied about her an' played her off on me fer a joke, I'll have yer hide!"

Sarah had told Jack that Bullhead Bailey was a bluff fellow who tried to cover up his inner kindliness by being hard on the surface. She often said Bailey needed a woman on the place, somebody he could care for and who could care for him. Now he had her and the baby too.

"Mr. Bailey, you will not be sorry," Jack said.

"And now that you've got me saddled up with a woman an' her kid, what're yer own plans for the next little while?" Bailey snorted.

"I'll drift up to Elk Hollow and look things over before leaving for the John Day place."

"Maybe you better help me build some sorta place fer the woman to hole up in. She'll look awful good to some of these fellers. Even old Brew gits snorty at times."

Jack knew this problem was not so easy to solve, and that if Ahseeah seemed apt to be a source of trouble, the rancher would want no part of it. He had enough to worry about with cattle, wolves, feed, rustlers, and prices for steers.

"I guess you could use another little cabin or shack," he replied. "I can take two ponies up to where I split shakes last winter and bring back enough to side up the walls and roof. We could use corral poles for the frame."

"Now, that's an idee! But suppose when it's done we kick old Brew out, let him live there. Then she an' the kid kin take over the cook shack, where she'll be close enough fer me to keep an eye on her. Let Brew grumble. I been wantin' to git him outta here. We'll make his cabin big enough fer a couple bunks an' a leetle stove, an' when some rider comes in that wants to hang around, we'll move him in with Brew. By grannies, after a night or two listenin' to Brew grindin' his

151

teeth an' snortin' an' snorin', the feller'll be willin' to take the trail in a howlin' blizzard."

They laid out the place where the shanty would be, and Jack took to the hills with the two packhorses while Brew and Bailey carried poles for the framework. Ahseeah was reluctant to proceed with the cooking until Brew decided to show her the ropes. He bustled about, explaining how to feed the fire, where food was kept, how to wash dishes and pans. He made faces at the fat baby, even tried some baby talk, a line of communcation which fascinated everyone.

In a few days, a rider came up from Prine City, saying the pass was open over the Ochocos. That night, Bailey talked with Jack and suggested he take his cattle and Jubal's over at once. It was all Jack needed to start him again planning a search for Teeah, still convinced as he was that she was alive and in some camp in the Warm Springs country. He must find her, he told himself.

"Jack," Bailey was saying, "I better send a feller along with you. An Injun with a good horse an' good cattle wouldn't stand much of a chance if some fellers wantin' a start in the cow business decided to begin with his bunch. Bent knows the lay of the country purty good."

"If you can spare him, I'd like to have him go with me. Bent and me git along real well."

"We'll round up the stock tomorrow—you an' Bent kin git rigged and packed. The four of us'll push the bunch up to Elk Hollow, then me'n Rusty'll drop back."

Ahseeah realized Jack was leaving, but if she worried, she didn't show it. She had become accustomed to her cookhouse and the men that drifted in and out; the story of old Bullhead Bailey and a young squaw and her kid had spread, and if a rider had a chance to make a trip in that direction, he was sure to stop in to look over the situation. The baby intrigued them all, especially his name. Bailey had learned it first. When he asked Ahseeah what she called the child, she proudly answered, "His name Jack Lee Ross."

Bailey looked across at Jack. "How come she named him that?"

Jack explained.

"Jesus, we can't have two fellers named Jack on the same range. How we gonna keep yuh sorted out? Why not call him Ross? But would Ross ride in and steal him?"

152

"Knowing Ross, it won't be until the boy is old enough to cook and help with work," Jack retorted.

The riders talked it over. "If the kid ain't earmarked an' branded with Ross's iron, he'll git burnt with Bailey's," one of them said. "That old thief ain't goin' to let anything on his range without his mark. The papoose'll be called Bailey's kid afore long. How's that fer a handle—Jack Lee Ross Bailey! Why, hell, it rolls off the tongue like good whiskey!"

24

A rider came through as Bent and Jack packed up to leave. Questioned, they told him they were taking a bunch of stock across to the John Day country for old Jubal Street. The rider mentioned it in Prine City, saying the snow must be out of the hills because Bailey's Injun and a rider were taking a bunch of cattle over the pass. Jukes heard it first and told Toby, who went to see Huff.

"Jasper says we kin git ahead of 'em when they hit the main trail, an' latch onto enough stock to start our herd. Jasper's dern near broke, an' I ain't fur behind. I tell yuh, Huffy, this may be the start of somethin' good."

"Sounds okay to me," Huff went along. "Yuh say there's only two fellers with the herd?"

"Yeah, Jack the Injun an' a rider called Bent with a bunch of cows an' heifers an' four ponies. I'll bet a plug of rough-cut tobaccy that Injun's got that gold an' plunder they tell about with him. We could be in tall clover with a sharp scythe there." Toby slavered at the thought of such wealth.

"I'll git word to you or Jasper if I hear more about it," Huff said.

"You figger on gittin' a pony or two fer us and some grub," Toby urged. "Hell, Huff, you got more of the spondu-licks than we have. Me'n old Jasper've really had to rustle, but maybe the winds're changin'. Money to spend, new boots, new clothes, an' new wimmen—if there's any to find!"

When they made up the bunch of cattle, Bailey ran in an

153

old roan cow with an early bull calf. Bent looked at her curiously. "Cullin' yer herd of baggers, Bullhead?"

"Could be, cowboy."

"Well, I guess we'll jist have to toll her along. That old biddy might make wolf bait or tradin' stock to some bunch of renegade redskins."

It wasn't until the second day on the trail that both Jack and Bent saw good reason for having the old roan in the bunch. Rousted off the bedgrounds, she and her calf started to follow Booshway and Jack, and soon others swung in behind her. One day they fought snow, hail, and wind; the cattle tried to break for shelter, but eventually all came back into the trail behind the roan cow and her bawling calf. That night they made camp in a shelter of jack pines where grass lay exposed by the spring sun and wind. The cattle fed and bedded there under the limby trees while Jack and Bent warmed up, drying out beside a fire of dry lodgepole timber.

Taking turns sleeping and feeding the fire, they were glad to see streaks of the coming dawn in the eastern sky. The snow stopped, and while Jack brought up the ponies, Bent got a pot boiling. The smell of coffee drifted across the flat. Coming back with the ponies, Jack saw Bent crouched near the fire and suddenly thought of Teeah and their camps along the trail. How little time they had had together! Was she lost to him forever?

"I'll shore be glad to see the sun!" Bent declared. "I bet old Bullhead knew we'd hit snow up here. He was right about one thing."

"Yeah?" Jack reached for a cup of steaming brew.

"That old roan bagger. Bailey knew she and that limber-legged calf would lead the bunch."

"Mr. Bailey's smart. In some ways he reminds me of Mr. Hill. You think they're old and cranky, but they're not. They just keep thinking ahead all the time."

Bent had his mouth full of meat and bread as he stood with his back to the fire getting some of the night's chill out of his bones. Cattle were bawling a little, looking for grass clumps. Bent took a few swallows of coffee and turned to look at Jack.

"Jack, when we meet up with Jube an' Sarah, yuh oughta brace 'em fer some way to git inta that bunch of Injuns over the river an' find out what happened to yer friend. I got an idiot's hunch they'd have an idee as to how it could be done."

Jack was alert. "You think so?"

"It's worth a try. Old Jube's got a lot more under his hat than hair. His woman thinks like redskins do. Put the two together an' yuh might come up with schemes us whites don't savvy."

Jack wanted to do it on his own, go and puzzle out the trail, find Teeah and get her back so they could make plans for the rest of their lives. But perhaps Bent was right. Jube and Sarah . . . Yes, they might know what to do.

With hope and optimism in his mind, Jack brought the ponies up to the packs. Today the sun would shine and they would drop down into grassy slopes and canyons along the river.

The cattle trailed well once they learned to follow the roan cow. Jack stayed alert to possible dangers ahead, his instincts warning that this broken country was ideal for ambush and holdups. He didn't like going down the close-walled draws and water-cut canyons at the mercy of anyone above, and he expressed this concern to Bent.

"Yer seein' things an' havin' bad dreams, Jack. Who in this busted-up country's gonna hold us up fer a few critters an' rack-of-bones ponies?"

"That's what Mr. Turpin thought," Jack countered. "If you can handle this bunch, I'd like to scout ahead."

"Take to it, Injun. I kinda forgot you'd been through a few scrapes. You feel like a gunshot wolf?"

"Well, I don't feel good about riding down a trail boxed in. A little bunch of cattle is easy to steal and get away with." He looked at the rocks above and around them. "I wish I had the gun the thief got away from me. These long guns're no good for close work. If they get the drop on us, we can't fight back."

"Keep talkin'."

"If we get jumped, forget the cows, take off. They won't stray too far. We can split up and pick 'em up later."

"That makes sense. I allus figgered my hide was worth more'n a cow's, but fellers like old Bullhead and a few others I could name look at it different. Jack, it's yer herd!"

Having never been over this trail before, Jack learned by riding out into the country. Bent drifted the cattle along while they fed on good grass. The Indian boy killed a year-

155

ling mule deer that had wintered well. They trailed through warm days and cool nights, the country new and fresh with no sign of recent travelers. Although he thought Jack too cautious about scouting ahead, Bent let him do it with no objection, surprised though when Jack came in early one afternoon.

"How you makin' out, Bent?" he greeted.

"Driftin' easy. Old Roanie an' her snotnose keep leadin' the way."

"We got company comin' in a day or so," Jack told him. "Why don't you go on ahead with the ponies? I'll foller the critters and we can talk about it around the fire. There's a good camp spot about a mile ahead where a little creek comes in."

"I'll jist do that little thing, an' git to cookin' while you tell me this big story. Old Roanie'll find the camp."

Around the fire, drinking coffee and eating the juicy roast venison, Jack told Bent what had happened that afternoon.

"I was up pretty high where I could see down the valley we're driftin' into. I saw this rider coming, way down. I knew I'd seen him before. I kept out of sight. Just the way he turned in the saddle to keep a look behind him, I knew it was Jubal Street. I thought I'd surprise him, slip in behind him, but no chance—he had me spotted before I got within gunshot. He was on his way to meet us."

Bent knew Jack was pleased. He reached for more coffee. Jack tossed his rib bone aside and sliced another off the backbone. In the evening cool, the breeze drifting down-canyon brought the scent of warm grass mingled with a faint smell of bedding cattle.

"Where'll we meet up?"

"He's with two horse thieves out to steal the cattle and plug us both," Jack said.

Having received this bombshell, Bent slurped his coffee. "Nice sort of feller, ain't he? Horse thieves do manage to meet honest people now an' then. Who's goin' to plug us?"

"Two of those bastards I set afoot down on the crooked river this spring. Jube said one named Jasper has another named Toby Marsh with him. Maybe somebody shot or hung the other one. Jube looks like a horse thief, and when these two met up with him, he went right along with their game.

156

Said he was looking for a few cows to stock his own place and wasn't particular about their brands."

"Seems like they've took on somebody they don't know nothin' about."

"They're greedy. Old Jube knows the country, and when he heard them say they were waiting for a bunch of cattle coming through, he knew it must be us, so he agreed to scout ahead and pick a place for the showdown. Jasper had already told Jube about me and that I was his meat, that he'd be the one to knock me off, even up an old score."

Bent rose and kicked the fire together, straightening up with his hands on his hips to twist his spine and stretch. "An' jist what'll we do about it?"

"We'll be the innocent cowboys trapped by fellers who got the drop on us. I'll be in the lead, you bring up the tail. My gun'll be in the sack so I'll look unarmed. You stay back, but within shooting range, and be a witness to the holdup. When you hear shots, be ready to plug somebody, though."

"When and where will the party take place?" Bent inquired laconically.

"Probably tomorrow or maybe midmorning the next day. Old Jube wants it well up from the river, where there're a few little places settlers got fenced in. Nobody in that country'll know those two, and nobody in Prine'll miss 'em. It'll be good riddance to feed coyotes."

"You don't figger on diggin' graves?"

"Piling rocks on 'em'll suit me, unless we find a sandbank. Seems we come without a shovel."

In Jasper Jukes's camp, Jubal Street told his plan to the eager outlaws.

"Boys, we'll be splittin' up a herd by this time tomorrow. Talk about easy pickin's! These two fellers're driftin' a leetle bunch of critters with nobody out to scout. The redskin's in the lead, ridin' a speckled pony. In the tail, a feller rides a bay and leads two pack ponies. I figger there's about twenty head of cows and heifers an' one calf we kin butcher fer camp meat. I know of a place we kin hole up where nobody'll bother us till we git the brands changed. If you fellers wanta build a little spread right there, it'd fit the picture. I'll take my split an' mosey on downriver to my own hideout."

"Sounds like you got the deal pretty well laid out. How do yuh figger to git to these fellers?"

"You said the redskin knows yuh. He shore don't know me. You'll be off the trail, one on each side. I'll ride up to meet him, git the drop on him, an' tell him to keep his pardner back less'n he wants a hole in his gizzard. Jukes, you say you want his hide—it'll be there fer yuh to take, jist like ridin' to church on Sunday mornin'. Both these sorry riders'll never git their guns out a-tall. But I want the spotted pony the Injun rides—you kin have the other three."

"Hell, you make it sound easy!" Toby worried.

"It'll be easy. Keep yer guns down, act like we don't want shootin', jist the herd."

Late in the day, Bent saw a rider come from out a side draw ahead and stop Jack. After a moment, Jack signaled him by waving his hat to allow the cattle to graze. Bent saw two men ride in, one from each side.

Jube held up his hand in the sign of peace, his rifle across his knees, and pointed at Jack. He kept his voice low. "Got yer leetle gun ready, boy?"

"All set, Jube."

"I'll take Jukes. When I fire, you git Tobe—he'll be watchin' an' keepin' ready fer your pardner. Have yer knife handy."

Jukes rode up to where Jack sat on Booshway, and Toby stopped alongside of him. Grinning at Jack through his bushy black whiskers, Jukes spat a stream of tobacco juice at Jack's pony. "Well, yuh red bastard, I reckon we've caught up with yuh!" he said.

Jack's face remained impassive. "I don't see the thief that took a bath in the river."

"Still the cocky rooster, eh? It ain't none of yer business, but he's still alive an' kickin'!"

"That so? I figgered you shot him in the back for his outfit."

Jukes, sure of his quarry, laughed as Toby pulled his pony to where he could see back of the cattle. They had Jack dead to rights.

"You smart son of a bitch, you made blisters on my feet an' I hain't forgot it. Make one little move an' yer dead, an' that goes fer yer pardner, too. We got yuh surrounded. Huff's on yer back trail. This time yuh ain't gonna pull no tricks!"

158

Jack stared at Jasper Jukes and Toby Marsh. "It ain't me that's surrounded—it's you! Take a look up that hill. That's not a rock, it's a feller with a gun. Mr. Bailey made sure his cattle would reach the river once he heard you'd left town."

"He's lyin', Jasper. Shoot him!"

Jube spoke up. "Hit can't be so. I scouted this country too dern well fer that. You fellers take a look—I'll keep this rooster settin' quiet."

As the two turned, Jubal swung his gun. Centered on Jukes, he pulled the trigger. Jack put both the derringer's bullets into Marsh. Startled ponies jerked and reared, and Jukes fell sideways as his mount wheeled away. Smoke and flash from the "leetle" gun had erupted almost in its face. Toby's pony buck-jumped, then took off running.

"Git the guns!" roared Jubal. He spurred his steed to catch Marsh's pony, where Marsh rode bent over, desperately clinging. Alongside, Jubal raised his rifle, his right hand grasping the stock, and swung the heavy barrel down across the neck of the wounded thief, who fell forward off to one side.

Jubal stopped his mount with a jerk, and on the ground, knife out, made sure Marsh was dead before he looked back to where Jack and Bent stood looking at Jukes's body.

Marsh's pony slowed down, and with nothing more to frighten him, started grazing along the trail. As Jubal rode back, he caught Jukes's mount.

Bent looked up at the old trapper, beard untrimmed and bushy, glittering black eyes squinting under his wolfskin cap, ragged, greasy, and smoke-stained as he was, and thought: He shore looks the part of a thief—I'd hate to have him against me!

"Well, boys, next thing to do is find a place handy to bury 'em."

Bent had a grin on his face. "Wal, there's a good place back up the trail a ways. The spring runoff's cut under a bank 'nuff so a little stompin' an' shovin'll make 'em a nice blanket. Say, how come these fellers took to you like they did?"

"They're a couple of greedy guts, that's why. And how'd you git a name like Bent?"

"Allus bent, never broke, as the sayin' goes." The cowboy liked his joke. "As it happened, I was born in Bent's Fort, so

159

my pappy named me that. These gents got anythin' we kin use?"

"Not much 'sides a little money in gold an' silver, along with their knives, guns, an' ponies," Jubal said.

Jubal and Jack, the two dead men tied on their ponies, went to bury them under the cutbank while Bent moved the cattle on down toward the night camp. Around their little fire that evening, Jack told Jubal Street how he had continued to look for Teeah and of his meeting with the Indians in the gorge.

When he described the chief who traded Ahseeah for Jack's gun on false pretenses, Jubal said, "I've heard of him. Sarah knows some of those people. We might make a trip over to where they have the big powwow and whoop-te-do this summer. They like a big git-together where they tell lies, play games, an' race their ponies. Sarah could mix with the women kinda easy-like. She jist might find the girl or learn what happened to her."

Jack's face relaxed. "Bent told me you and Sarah might have some idea about what to do," he said. "But the chief told me that if Ahseeah or me ever showed up there again, he'd have us killed."

"Don't fret about that, Jack. If ever' feller red or white that said he'd kill me had done it, I'd've been gone long since. Kin your ponies run like they used to?"

"Neither one's slowed down much. All they need is another pony to run against and a kick in the ribs."

Jubal filled his black smelly pipe with real tobacco, tamped it gently with his finger, then with his blackened, callused thumb. Gesturing with the pipe to accentuate his words, he said, "They go crazy bettin' on horses!"

In the quiet as Jubal reached for a burning coal to drop on his pipeful of tobacco, Jack and Bent squatted with cups of coffee, awaiting Street's next words.

"Now, that being the case, if we git there to drum up some races, they won't suspect you an' me know each other. If Bailey'll let Bent come, we kin skin us a few hides along with tryin' to git the girl back. You kin lose a run or two until the big one. Me an' Sarah'll be there to trade with 'em, jolly 'em along. If the girl's there, I'll bet on the big one with my ponies an' riggin', an' the chief kin throw in the girl. But this time you gotta make sure it is *yer* girl, not some squaw stole from another tribe!"

"By God, it might work, Jack! I'm all fer it," Bent declared.

Once more Jack's hopes soared like a hawk in flight. Would it be possible he might see Teeah again? Even to hear what happened would console him and put an end to his constant wondering about what really took place at the camp and where the gold and plunder he had buried lay now. The trip *would* be worth a try, he thought soberly.

"Will Bailey let you go, Bent?"

"If he don't say yes nice an' easy, I'll leave nice an' easy."

"When does the powwow take place, Jubal?"

" 'Bout as soon as we git these critters home an' kin ride back to the Warm Springs main camp. You fellers push the cattle along a bit faster an' I'll take off ahead with the extry ponies an' make sure everything's ready. I kin have a feller watch the stock an' the cabin whilst we're away."

The whole idea was too interesting to let alone. Jack and Bent asked questions about the race course, the distances run, and whether whiskey and rum would be allowed. What about the Indian agent?

"Fellers, no agent or the army's goin' to keep them Injuns from their big powwow," was Jubal's judgment. "They air goin' to drink if there's whiskey there, they air goin' to bet on anything that kin run, jump, or crawl, an' they air willin' to lose their shirts an' outfits clear to the last set of moccasins an' breechclouts. Oncet I git that old chief warmed up, he'll dig up the girl, your gun, or his best bow and arrer if he thinks he kin win."

"What should we do to make sure we don't lose?"

"Yuh can't never be sure about that. Jist try to see the odds are on yer side. The Injuns ain't stupid. The first thing is to stay separated so we don't seem connected at this free-for-all comin' up. In this country, yuh can't tell thieves from honest folks. I'll go on ahead, you deliver the cows, an' head back without me. We'll make our plans before you leave, and I won't see you after that until you ride into camp at the Warm Springs reservation."

161

25

Jubal's John Day hangout lay just off the road, a cluster of buildings made up of a log house and a few pole sheds roofed with shakes and covered with sod from which grass grew and blended in with the steep rough hills that rose behind them. A corral of poles made from jack-pine timber enclosed an open-sided shed, and stake-and-rider fences had been put around a patch of ground where ponies grazed, raising their heads as the herd of cattle approached. The gate poles were down; as Jack rode close, Jubal appeared to greet him.

"We'll put the critters in the corral fer now, Jack. I'll salt 'em down, let 'em git used to the place afore I turn 'em to the hills."

Sarah came from the log house. She greeted Jack and Booshway and looked at the cattle following behind him with Bent and the pack pony.

"Jack, you get girl and baby for Bailey. He happy?" She smiled up at the half-breed boy so long her companion at Elk Hollow.

"Hard to tell yet. I think the baby made the difference. Even Brew changed after he saw the boy." He swung down. "I brought along a young feller for you, Sarah. I'll trade him for some of your cooking."

"Jack, you know Jube goes to Warm Springs to look for your young girl. Mebbe so I keep you here with me." Her lips curved and her shoulders shook in silent laughter.

"Naw . . . old Jube might shoot me. We all go to Warm Springs, have a big time. You can look for Teeah. We'll run the ponies and bet."

"Jack, hear me. You practice hand magic. Win at that if pony lose. All Indians like magic." She smiled. "You Quick Hands' boy."

A look of surprise crossed Jack's face. He *could* fall back on the hidden-pebble trick. He would talk to old Jube about it first, though.

As they saddled up to leave the next morning, Jube told Jack and Bent, "Next full moon'll mark the beginnin' of big doin's at Warm Springs. Let 'em git goin' three days afore you come in. Bring some ponies fer tradin' an' bait, an' git a couple jugs of sorghum 'lasses and cut in some whiskey to flavor it. If you kin worry the sawbones in town to give out some oil of peppermint, add that, tastin' as you work up the mix. Most of the stuff Injuns git fer whiskey'd gag a hound followin' a gut wagon. If yuh mix the stuff right, they'll keep a-comin' back fer more. That'll lead to tradin' an' bettin'."

"We'll do it, Jube," Bent agreed. "I'll help with the bettin'."

Jack kept his goal in mind. "You and Sarah find out what you can about Teeah," he reminded them. "I'll run the ponies."

"One more thing afore yuh take off—put a pack on yer best pony and make him look like he's not much, jist fit fer totin' yer plunder."

Bullhead Bailey, intrigued with the story of Bent and Jack Tate's adventures, went along with the idea of their going to the Warm Springs powwow to race and gamble, and said he'd round up a few ponies to swap or put up for the betting.

Ahseeah hovered in the background as the men talked. Jack picked up Jack Lee Ross and laughed to see him smile and gurgle. But Ahseeah's every move brought a picture of Teeah to his mind, and he turned impatient to be on the way. Each night he watched the moon change in size. Days grew longer and the warmth of the sun lay on the land, grasses waving tall on the hills. Cattle scattered; some of the older, range-wise stock drifted higher.

Bent left to go to the cabin near the north edge of the range until time to leave for the powwow, but Jack asked Bailey if he could stay close to headquarters and run his ponies on the flat to keep them in shape.

"Well, boy, there's enough to do here, and plenty more. Which two hosses you figger on runnin'?"

"Booshway on the short race against Jube's pony, Speck. On the big race out and back, I'll run Pardner against all Jube has and what the chief puts up. Pardner needs practice on the turn. I got to get him used to sliding and bending around a tree or stake."

"Yuh know this range ain't no playpen fer ponies, boy. Yuh do it on yer own time, which is when there ain't anything else needs doin'. Yuh done me a favor or two, Jack, but don't never lean on me. That clear?"

"Sure is, Mr. Bailey."

"Well, git yer ponies used to the run, an' mebbe I'll find some to run agin yuh, just fer practice."

Jack raced his ponies, sometimes in the early morning, sometimes in the heat of the day. Evenings were best, when it was cool and Bailey or one of the boys coming through would try out a mount against either one of Jack's. Pardner soon learned to turn around a stake or tree, leaning into it as he slid his feet to slow, then taking rapid jumps into his stride for the finish line. Jack taught him both the left and right turn, signaling with two hisses through his teeth for the right turn, one for the left. Pardner was soon ready to turn without the jerk on the reins so common with the Indians' handling of their ponies.

The moon gained in size. One day, Jack had both ponies near the shed where Bailey kept a forge, anvil, extra horseshoes, some bar iron, and odds and ends of equipment. As he looked through the keg of horseshoes, Brew came to see what was going on.

"Yuh jist lookin', Jack, or about to feel fer somethin'?"

"I want to put shoes on the ponies so they'll be used to 'em before we race."

"Them Injuns don't have shoes on their cayuses, do they?"

"Probably not, but if the ground is slick, I don't want mine to go sliding off in mud or dust. Stick around. Once I find what I want, you can turn the blower. How're you and Jack Lee Ross gettin' along? You savvy his talk?"

"All blab an' blubber to me. But he's a cute little button. Never figgered I'd take to a kid ner to a squaw neither, but them two help keep this place alive. Old Bullhead seems easier to live with. Never thought I'd see the day!"

"I'll be going into town for grub and a few things I need tomorrow. You want anything?"

"Yeah, a bottle. An' say, look fer some red-an'-white stick candy for the kid to suck on. He's about to chew off his right thumb. Guess he's cuttin' teeth. He slobbers a lot." Brew paused, then added, "Mebbe yuh kin find out somethin', too."

Jack came alert. "What's that?"

164

"Last time I was there, I heard the two rapscallions that squalled fer war on the Injuns left fer a trip over to the John Day and never come back. Their pardner, Huff, works at the horse barn. He asked if you was back yet. Guess he's curious as to why Jukes an' his pard didn't show up."

"I won't miss 'em if they never come back," Jack said. "They let the word out they were looking for cattle or ponies to start up a spread of their own. I guess somebody took it serious and set out to change their minds."

"I git the drift. Fellers git a few cows an' a leetle gold, they hate to have drifters horn in."

That night Bailey put together an order for supplies. He showed his list to Jack. "I'm leavin' ahead of yuh—first light. I'll leave this order at the General Mercantile fer yuh to pick up. Put anythin' else you want on when you're there."

"Would you write down two jugs of whiskey and four of sorghum and get a small bottle of peppermint oil from the doc if you have time? They might not sell that stuff to me."

"Why not? Yuh work fer me. But why the joy juice an' molasses? Oil of peppermint! What you an' that half-witted Bent figgerin' on? You could get throwed in the calaboose fer sellin' whiskey to the Injuns."

"It goes to old Jube. He'll mix drinks for his friends to get the bets up. The peppermint's for toothache."

"Well, I'll git the stuff, but if the army picks yuh up fer sellin' whiskey to Injuns, I don't know nothin' about it, see?"

At the General Mercantile & Supply, while the Bullhead Ranch order was being put together, Jack found the red-and-white peppermint sticks for the baby and bought enough extra to take with him to the powwow. He looked over the bolts of cloth and bought pieces of red and bright yellow cotton for Ahseeah. Intrigued with the spools of ribbon, he bought several to take along. The curious clerk looked at the stuff Jack had piled up on the wooden counter. He knew Jack worked for Bullhead and that there was a young squaw on the place, but no one had talked much about who laid claim to her.

"This stuff going on the ranch account?"

"No, I'll pay for it."

"Taking it to the ranch fer the cook an' her kid, I s'pose."

"Yeah, some of it. The rest I'll take over to the big dance at Warm Springs next week for trade goods."

"You an' Bent gonna run yer ponies over there?"

"Yeah. Mr. Bailey's sendin' one too."

"There's a story around that you put three fellers afoot sometime back."

"Could be."

"Only one of 'em left in town, an' he ain't talkin' much," the clerk pressed. "His name's Huff—works at the livery stable. Say, here he comes now."

There was no way to avoid meeting Huff at the long wooden counter where Jack's goods were being wrapped. He looked directly at Jack and grinned. "Seems like I remember you," he said.

"Yeah. You ever git dried out?"

"Got blisters on my feet doin' it! Say, were you bluffin' there that day?"

"You took to the river," Jack evaded. "I guess your pardners talked you into believing I had help."

"Seen either of 'em lately?"

"Yeah, we met over east of the mountains, Jukes dirty as usual and his pardner tailing along like a coyote pup." He eased to face Huff. "I figgered Jasper had shot you in the back."

"I left 'em. I'm workin' fer Ike Cafferty now at the horse barn. Hear old Bailey has a squaw fer a cook."

"Don't let Mr. Bailey hear you call her that. He thinks she's a fine lady."

"No offense, Jack. Shake hands an' let's fergit what happened on the river."

Jack stuck out his hand, and Huff grasped it. The clerk had wrapped the package, and Jack took it, went to the end of the counter, and paid his bill in gold, getting back some change. Huff followed him out of the store; some instinct told Jack he wanted to find out what had happened to Jukes and Toby. On the dusty walk, with no one close, he spoke.

"Jack what really happened to them two drifters I used to hang out with?"

"I have a hunch they went to some hideout or maybe they had business down the line. Ain't seen or heard from 'em since that day we met over the pass."

"Jack, I owe you thanks fer not killin' me when yuh had a chance, and I owe Red Dingus a favor fer puttin' in a good word fer me with Ike. I figger on stayin' around here. If

166

Jukes an' Tobe never show up, they'll be doin' me a favor too."

Jack grinned. "Good. Huff, I feel better now. Whenever I come in town, I'll look you up."

On the way back to Bullhead's place, Jack thought how things had changed. Three enemies gone. If he could only find Teeah and get her back, he would be happy and free of worries for a while, at least.

26

Jubal Street and Sarah entered Warm Springs country from the road crossing to the Willamette from Prine City. They swung north to the Metolius River, where they found the big dance and powwow were already taking shape, old Jube and his pack ponies welcome, for those who knew him well wanted to trade and bargain. Sarah inspected gloves, mittens, moccasins, and other Indian work for quality and workmanship, while the old trader bargained. Some pony racing had already taken place, and trade goods and trinkets found owners. Jubal began to size up the ponies Jack's might race against.

Jack and Bent rode in with their pack animals, and found a spot away from the main crowd for their camp, but almost immediately Indians appeared to see what might be in those packs. Jack, wise to Indian curiosity, didn't show them much, and kept the jugs out of sight, wishing he had someone to stand guard.

Bent was to circulate and find Jubal and Sarah. He saw Jube at the race course, watching half a dozen young bucks line up for a race, and stayed back, knowing Jubal had seen him from the corner of his eye. The ponies took off in a flurry of excitement, their yelling riders whipping and kicking their cayuses. They swung around the far turn, two or three falling over each other in a cloud of dust while the ones that had missed the fracas came on in a rush. One or two of the crowd packed close to the track were almost bowled over. Laughter and applause greeted the winner, and bets were paid off. Old Jube must have lost on this race; he scratched deep in his wallet and brought out a small gold piece. An Indian held out his hand, then shook his head.

"Me want whuskey."

"No whuskey yet, chief. See me tonight. I give whuskey fer gold."

"No lie, Jube?"

"No lie, chief. Bring gold, I give you big drink good whuskey."

Milling Indians, laughing and joking, surrounded Jubal, who elbowed through them to reach Bent at the edge of the crowd.

"Howdy, stranger, yuh here to drink, bet, or swap ponies? They call me old Jube. I'm from over the Ochoco Mountains."

"I aim to run a pony. I'll stay an' trade too," Bent replied. "I ride fer anybody's got stock runnin' loose. That's why they call me Bent-about-to-go-broke."

"I got some trade stuff. You runnin' yer pony today?"

"Nope. I want to see how these boys do it first."

"Well, yuh won't learn much till yuh git into one of these free-fer-ever'body races. When some of the young fellers git juiced up, yuh'll see the real thing."

The men talked as though strangers, Jubal suspicious of listeners nearby. When time came for him to bet against Bent and Jack Tate, he wanted the tribe on his side.

With hundreds of men, women, children, dogs, and ponies of all colors there, Bent looked for some sign of the army, supposed to be on hand as a symbol of power and control, but so far all he could see was a pleasant, happy crowd enjoying themselves, and evidently doing their own policing.

A group of half-naked kids surrounded Jack. He talked in a mixture of Indian sign language, English, and the native tongue. Jack's little pieces of candy had drawn the children. He put a piece in his mouth, sucked on it, and licked it, not even noticing the kids who came silently, watchful and waiting to see what the strange white boy had in his pack. He dressed like a white man and had a white man's outfit.

Not cussed and driven away, treatment they might have expected from white men, the boys' curiosity overcame their fear. At first there were three. Soon more came and edged closer, until a dozen youngsters stood whispering and giggling. Jack offered the candy to a little fellow, who backed away in fright, but was stopped by the pressure of those behind him. An older boy reached out his hand. Jack put the candy in it, took another piece from his pocket, and licked it. The boy touched his candy with his tongue, then began to lick it. At once his companions reached for a taste, chattering back and forth. Finally Jack gave each boy a piece and waved his hands.

"Come back tomorrow. I trade and run my pony now."

Reluctantly they left, sucking candy and grinning. Jack knew the word would spread, too good to keep to themselves. In a few minutes, women appeared to size up this man who had given their children something sweet and unusual to suck and swallow. Why had he given something away to children? They had nothing he could use. If this half-breed had something to offer free, they wanted in on it too.

One of them as she was, Jubal Street's woman, Sarah, heard about Jack's largess. She pulled the flap of her tepee closed. The men and older boys were at the racetrack, busy with betting and getting matched up. Sarah saw Booshway and the speckled pack pony, Pardner, two other horses picketed nearby. Jack squatted with a smoke in his hand near a lean-to shelter made from a tarp.

The women drew up in a line, standing nervously silent, like a bunch of hens in a farmyard looking at a strange dog or cat, heads turning here and there to take in everything in sight. An older squaw walked close.

"You trader?"

"Yes. You like this?" Jack pulled out ribbon he had cut into small pieces. The one she reached for was bright red, about a foot in length and four inches wide. The woman smiled, then laughed outright as she held the ribbon up against her jacket. She pointed to herself, to Jack, and then to the tent. The meaning of the gesture she made could not be mistaken.

Jack laughed and shook his head. "No . . . you keep."

"You like better?" She pulled a younger woman from the crowd and motioned again. Jack handed a piece of yellow ribbon to the girl, who took it and laid it against her cheek. The group pressed closer. Jack gave out more small pieces. Presents to Indian women were unheard of without something demanded in return. It wasn't a woman in his tent this youth wanted.

When the ribbons were gone, Jack told them to come back the next day, and finally only Sarah waited before him.

"You and Bent bring jugs?"

Jack held up four fingers. "You want one now?"

She nodded and asked, "What did Bailey say?"

"He said the trip turned out good. You find anything about Teeah?"

"Not Teeah no more," Sarah said in a curiously matter-of-fact tone. "She Woman Not Die now. Not here. Maybe tomorrow she come."

Teeah alive! A thrill like Thunder's lightning symbol ran over Jack's being. "You see her?" he demanded.

"I hear talk about girl who came from deep river where white men kill other white men and boys."

"Where is she?" Jack was standing. "You know?"

"She gone. Man with her. White soldiers come. Ask about men killed. Some people afraid, so they leave." She looked at him, her glance shrewd. "She come back. Her man race his ponies tomorrow."

The words "her man" shocked Jack's spirit. Time had passed. Teeah had had to adjust to a new life to survive. That meant a man, and unless she were a slave, she would have to marry. But she was alive! He looked at Sarah, the little piece of ribbon in her hand, then went into the lean-to and brought out a jug wrapped in a blanket.

"Sarah, I have present for you." He went back to the tent and came out with a package wrapped in brown paper. "Take it with you. Open it before Jube comes back. He can have the jug. This for you."

The package felt soft and flexible. Sarah took it like a curious child, then picked up the jug and went to her camp.

Bent appeared, a grin on his face.

"Jack, I've got good races lined up, some tonight, more tomorrow. Old Jube's comin'. He's been sizin' up fellers with good hosses, them as ain't so much, and some of the real bettin' bucks in camp. He won a few this afternoon, an' figgers to lose some tomorrow to git the boys hot. How'd yuh make out?"

"The kids came first. They told their mamas, and then I had company. I could've found you a woman, Bent! The ribbons brought 'em like honey draws flies." While Bent laughed, he added, "Sarah was here."

"The hell yuh say! What's the news?"

"She said Teeah is in this camp. She hid when army fellers come looking and asking questions about something happened across the deep river. I gave Sarah a present and sent a jug back for Jube. I'll bribe some boys with candy to watch our things while we take in the fun tonight."

"They're gittin' ready fer it. When the sun goes down, the ground's gonna shake an' the coyotes'll take to the hills!"

"You find anything to drink?"

"Nary a drop, but if there's any in camp, you kin bet it'll show up tonight. Jube kin put us wise what to expect. I saw a couple fellers looked like squawmen."

"Any good-lookin' girls?"

"Not many at the races."

"Couple in the bunch of women came here. Take some ribbon to the dance with you and first thing you know one'll throw her blanket over your head and Bent'll be broke to lead."

"You talk like you know how it's done."

"No, I was just a boy at the powwows on the Clearwater. But at a big doings with a full moon and a warm night to put ideas into the girls' heads . . . There's always a big crop of Indian babies in the spring. It's all part of what happens."

"Kind of like the mating dances of the sagehens," Bent mused. "The old boys strut, throw out their chests an' go boom, boom-boom, an' all the hens come a-lookin' fer a feller to take 'em off in the high grass."

"Same idea. The women'll dress up for it. Wait till they shine in the firelight with their buckskins all beaded and the quills dyed and set in patterns. Their braids'll have colored yarn wound in, sometimes little bells. It's pretty easy to get worked up. When the couples drift away, everybody sees 'em gets happy about it."

Trader Street came riding up on his bay pony and looked down at the two squatted on the ground. "Which of you two fellers mixed up that mess in the jug my woman Sarah brung in?" he growled.

"What's wrong with it?" Bent demanded.

"Guess I'll hafta wisen up a couple bent an' broke cow

171

chasers," Jube scoffed. "Kin you smell my breath from where you squat?"

"You ketch a peppermint-flavored skunk, Jube?"

"Boys, you guessed it! I got to my wigwam, an' there Sarah was, all decked out in red, green, and yeller cloth an' smellin' like a field of weeds in the spring, the brown jug settin' close. She opened her eyes an' asked me to give her some more. I knew what it was afore I tried it. Better'n I figgered, boys. Sarah won't be goin' to the dance, she went plumb out on me. How much of the stuff yuh got?"

"Three gallon jugs an' a couple bottles."

"Mixed like I said?"

"Jist about."

Jube snorted. "What the hell yuh mean?"

Bent grinned. "Well, hell, Jube, you know how it is. We mixed some an' tried it, then mixed more an' tried it. Ever' time we tasted, we figgered it lacked somethin' to give it fire, maybe cut the sweet taste. Jack dug out some whiskey he'd got fer Brew an' dumped a little of that in and stirred it around. Well, we kept mixin' an' drinkin', but it was goin' too slow, so Jack went to the cookhouse an' come back with a big kettle. We dumped ever'thing in it—sorghum, whiskey, rum, peppermint, vaniller. Purty soon Jack staggered out fer air an' never come back. Brew an' Rusty showed up to see what all the singin' an' laffin' was about, and they had some ideas as to what the stuff needed. None of us rightly know what all went into that batch of joy juice. Old Bailey's been squallin' about not findin' the horse liniment or his last bottle of Dr. Potter's Gentlemen's Rejuvenator."

Jubal dismounted. "Don't tell me nothin' more. I jist wondered if there was wolf poison in it. One minute Sarah was singin' an' yodelin', an' the next I knew, she was snorin'!"

Laughing at the thought, Jack said, "Set awhile an' let your pony pick grass. You think the stuff'll do the trick?"

"Like a mess of coons swingin' through the grapevines! Iffen them bucks drink enough, there'll be sights an' sounds around these parts ain't never been heard or seen afore. What took place the next mornin'?"

Jack looked over at Bent. "Tell him what you saw when you came to in the rainstorm."

"You git rain over there?" Jubal asked.

"Naw, I dreamed it. Rusty was pourin' the stuff in the jugs

172

fer us, an' old Brew was tryin' each batch an' gittin' louder an' wilder. Lucky fer us old Bailey was gone—he'd a canned the whole bunch. Brew got to croakin' out his songs, as he calls 'em, an' comes up with the bright idea we need company. He staggers fer the door. Rusty sees him an' asks where he's headin'. Brew says he's takin' a drink to Alice an' Jack Lee Ross. Rusty tried to talk him out of it, but it was like tryin' to slide uphill with a sled. Rusty picked up a chunk of wood an' clouted the old feller where his hat sets, then drags him on out the door an' lets him lay with his head hangin' down so he won't swaller his own puke.

"Rusty bottled up what we'd mixed, and altogether he had four jugs an' a bottle. He didn't tell us where he put 'em till we sobered up an' got ready to leave."

"But how did you fellers feel next mornin'?" Jubal wondered what Sarah's disposition would be when she awoke. Once long ago he had narrowly escaped being scalped by a drunken woman.

"That's when I thought I was in a rainstorm," Bent chortled. "Old Rusty gets up first, comes out, an' sees Brew layin' like a throwed-away rug outside the door, me down the trail, an' off to one side sprawled out flatter'n a stepped-on toad was Jack. Rusty got a bucket of water from the crick an' dribbled it in my face an' mouth. I comes alive gaggin' an' spoutin' like a whale. He sloshed what was left in the bucket on me an' told me to wake Jack up. Well, I was all shivers from the wettin', but I sloshed old Jack. You shoulda seen him jump in the air like a belly-shot coyote. He comes down wild-lookin', an' I thought I'd have to hit him afore he saw who I was."

Jack was grinning. Jubal squatted to smoke his pipe, and Bent rolled a new smoke. Horses picked grass, and the sounds of the big encampment came and went like distant waves of water on a rocky shore, the soft warm air of summer carrying noises muffled by distance, the whole atmosphere one of peace and contentment. Somewhere someone tried soft drumbeats that pulsed like an erratic heart.

"I was dreaming that old thief of a chief was after me." Jack took up the story. "Just as he was about to grab me, I fell off the cliff backward into the river canyon, fell forever until I hit the water and started to swim. When I got out, I thought the chief was there, a club in his hand to clobber me, and it took me a minute before I saw this bastard of a cow-boy with a bucket in his hand. He told me to wake up Brew up at the shanty.

"I walked over to the cabin, and the old feller still laid there with his head hanging over the porch edge. I thought he was dead till he gave a jerk and a kind of gurgle. I looked in-side, and everything was gone—kettle, jugs, bottle. I was sure happy about that. It was clear daylight by then, with the sun just coming up. I saw smoke from the cook shack, so I knew Ahseeah was probably getting breakfast. I rolled Brew over and pushed him off onto the ground. He come up wild-eyed like a bobcat backed in a hole, put both hands to his head, and started groaning and cussing. Rusty told him he got the big bump on his skull from trying to butt his way out of the cabin through the log wall. Hot coffee settled our guts a little." Jack smiled. "I never had any real hangover, did you, Bent?"

"Naw—I come out of it purty dern good, 'cept fer 'nother dream or two that night."

27

Bent went into the lean-to and came out with three bottles, all with illustrations on their wrappers. Jubal held one so the soft light from the western sky lit up the picture of a stallion, head in the air, tail stiffened, all his equine pride and power represented. The label said in big letters: "DR. JACKOB'S FA-MOUS LINIMENT, GOOD FOR MAN OR BEAST."

Jubal began to read the rest aloud: " 'Use sparingly for sprains, splints, swollen joints, foul foot, ringbone, glanders, saddle and collar sores, sore backs, tail itch, and any infec-tion. Tried and proven in the U.S. and all foreign countries. Patented as a miracle cure by veterinarians and stockmen.' " He guffawed.

"Fellers, that'll fetch any Indian!"

"Yeah, that's why we poured it in the mix. Lookin' at that old pony with its tail in the air jist makes yuh want to try some, don't it?"

The next label showed a man dressed in the long suit of a boxer, hands clenched and muscles swollen to show his great strength: "DR. POTTER'S GREAT MEDICAL REJUVENATOR! THE WONDER DISCOVERY OF THE AGE!"

Again Jubal slowly read the label, running his blackened fingernail along beneath the words as a guide: "'This marvelous discovery was produced through years of research going back to the Golden Age of the Greeks, who used it to develop the greatest athletes of all time! It can be used for the developing male from puberty through the rest of his active life. Guaranteed to bring results! Will cure bed-wetting, sleeplessness, and general apathy in young boys, produce strength and develop body hair in young men! Stops balding, generates vigor and power in older men, and satisfies the elderly gentleman! Guaranteed by U.S. government patent.'"

He swore softly. "Jesus, boys, where'd you git this bottle?"

"Dug it outta Brew's boar's nest. No wonder he chomps his teeth at night. But it'll make the old chief think big. Give a gander at the other side."

Jubal turned the bottle over. There an Indian chief in war bonnet stood sternly, arm pointed, feathers trailing down his back to the ground. The words proclaimed: "CHIEF EAGLE EYE OF THE POTAWATOMI TRIBE and all his people give thanks to Dr. Maxim Powers for this medical discovery which saved his tribe from death! Its rejuvenating powers doubled the population in just TWO YEARS! Think what it can do for you! RESULTS GUARANTEED BY LAW."

Jubal was ready to explode. "Holy smoke, boys, the army won't stand a chance in a few years! Brew mighta populated this country if he'd ever found wimmen to put up with him!"

Bent enjoyed the old trader's amazement, then handed him the last bottle. "Take a look at this'n, Jube. It'll make yer feathers stand on end!"

Square in shape, short-necked, glass and cork stopper, the label yellow, crinkled paper, words printed in blue. But the picture was of a lady dressed in the style of English royalty, a voluptuous pose, wasp-waisted, bosom projecting like a pouter pigeon's, hair piled high, arm half extended with a small glass in the right hand, the little finger daintily held away from the rest. Jubal stared. He could almost smell the perfume.

His nostrils widened, he threw his head back, pawed the

ground with his left foot, and gave the snort and whinny of a bugling stud horse.

"Do wimmen dress like that where she comes from?"

"Durned if I know, but she looks like she's broke to harness, don't she?"

"I shore would like the chance to gentle her! This fer me?"

"Read what it says on the bottle."

Jubal read: " 'LADY LYDIA GOSSAMER OF LONDON, ENGLAND. At great expense, Lady Lydia Gossamer had the royal chemist develop this wonderful remedy for female troubles. From a sickly, underdeveloped girl she grew into this striking woman, allowing this remedy to be placed on the market to help other women with female complaints a physician could not alleviate. One bottle of this remarkable discovery will put any growing girl or mature female on the way to abundant health and a beautiful body. A dozen bottles will cure any real or imagined complaint. All our products are unconditionally guaranteed to please. This elixir has been registered in England and the United States. Dr. Alexis De Asimov, Chemist to the Queen.' " Jubal swung on the two.

"You fellers believe it'll do all it says?"

Bent's face went deadpan. "The stuff's guaranteed, ain't it, Jack?"

"Sure is, Jube. All we ask is you bring back the bottle."

"Aw, the hell! I plumb fergot you jokers mixed the stuff! Let's us figger how we're goin' to peddle it."

"Jubal, she's all yers. Call it cough medicine, stomach soother, or plain old joy juice, anything but whiskey. Me'n old Jack'll lay back an' let yuh deal with the tribe an' play us fer suckers."

"That'll be easy to do. You fellers won't have to change one leetle bit," Jubal joshed. "I'm a-goin' to set up to win yer best pony, old Booshway, an' talk yuh into layin' ever'thing yuh got on the line fer the last race. Now, Jack, you want the woman. She ain't here, but she will be. I'll lay bets I kin have the chief bring her out jist afore that so you'll know it's the right girl. You still want that six-gun yuh give him?"

"I do, Jubal, you know that! The old thief tricked me out of it."

"Well, easy come, faster gone, like the old woman said when she shot her old man. We'll git it back, but you let yer

176

pardner keep it till you're out of camp or he might take it away from yuh agin."

Bent spoke up. "Sing that tune over, Jube. I'll take the gun an' look after the girl, too. Feller lets a girl an' his gun git away an' only gits a spavined pony outta the deal needs a man to look after him."

"When the last race's over, you fellers better be on the jump, 'cause some of these fellers is goin' to be madder'n bald-faced hornets when their nest is wrecked," Jubal warned. "I'll have a jug or two laid back to kinda git 'em slowed down while they sharpen their knives an' prime their guns, an' by the time they git their wits together you should be where the army kin come if you holler real loud."

"You work it out and we'll go along with you," Jack told him. Could this old trader really produce Teeah and gain her release? he wondered to himself.

"I'll take a jug. You keep the bottles here with the other two jugs," Jubal went on. "I'll bet the Injuns with ponies'll gang up on yuh! But remember we can't be friendly after yuh win the first race. By that time the camp'll be ready an' willin' to bet you'll sure enough lose the last one. We'll take lots of time argyin' an' dickerin', have a lot of yellin' goin' on. Bent kin be drunk an' put the pressure on you to copper the bets. I'll have the chief oiled up so he'll git the girl if he has to drag her in by the hair, an' this'll make the crowd go wild."

Jubal rode off. Chuckling, Bent suggested a drink, but Jack warned him to stay sober awhile. At the dance grounds, the drums throbbed and the two men stepped to the beat as they walked that way.

To their surprise, the crowd opened up for them so they could see the dancers. They glimpsed squaws wearing pieces of ribbon, and a boy came up to grin at Jack, then stick his finger in his mouth as if to suck.

"See you tomorrow at the races," the half-breed promised.

The boy disappeared in the crowd. Jack saw a woman with a red ribbon around her hair look his way. A tall buck came over and stuck out his hand.

"You got whiskey?"

"No whiskey now, chief. Maybe tomorrow."

"Want whiskey now. Dance and sing."

"We get some tomorrow. You run pony tomorrow?"

177

"Run pony! Beat you!"

"The hell you will! I'll bet on your pony."

"You crazy, white man. You dance?"

"Naw, I watch you. Tomorrow I bet on your pony." Bent watched the man go off through the crowd.

Some of the Indians already had whiskey. Two drunken bucks staggered into the line and tried to keep pace with the drumbeats. Soon both were grasped and hauled out. Another eruption took place on the other side of the crowd, and people near the dancers swirled to look. Suddenly two shots rang out somewhere near the main center of the lodges. Yelling and wild whooping commenced just as Jack saw someone he recognized. It was the tall scowling brave who stood near the chief when he traded Ahseeah for Jack's revolver.

When the chief himself turned and caught Jack's attentive gaze, he scowled back in anger. Someone grasped the chief from behind and jerked him over, and a flurry of action began. The big brave grabbed another buck and wrestled him to the ground. It led to a general mix-up.

"Let's git the hell outta here!" Bent said to Jack. "I see trouble comin'!"

They walked back. The crowd surged forward to see what was going on, but the drummers kept up their monotonous beat.

"Jesus, what was goin' on back there?" Bent breathed.

"That old boy got pulled down is the chief of the renegades who got Teeah and my gun, the one old Jube's gonna get worked up to bet her and the gun against whatever I have. Something sure happened back there—maybe Jube can tell us about it tomorrow."

More shots and yelling. Through it all the drums beat continuously. Jack and Bent moved the ponies close to their lean-to, fearful of what Indians getting drunk and wilder by the hour might do.

"Jack, let's take a swig from the jug, see what haulin' it this fur done."

"Just a little one. I ain't forgot what we put in it!"

"Well, here's to luck, Jack, and a good day fer runnin' ponies tomorrow."

They took their drinks and told each other it was smoother and slicker than before. Jack had pulled off his boots and was rubbing an itching foot when more shots were heard and

178

screaming broke out. Bent got up to look, and saw a glare of flames. More yelling and whooping.

"See anything?" Jack asked.

"Looks like a lodge caught fire. There she goes! Some pore feller gits to sleep with the skeeters tonight."

Jack chuckled.

War cries, a shrill yelping of many voices.

"Jack, them war whoops're whiskey crazy! They got another fire started! They'll burn the whole dern town yet!"

"Don't get excited, heads'll be cracked. The sober chiefs'll round 'em up. I'll bet they're not all drunk."

"Well, let 'em play all they want—it's not my stuff they're burnin' up," Bent said as he returned to his soogan.

Jack pulled his shirt over his head and was soon asleep.

When morning light brightened the tall yellow pines with the rising sun's gold, Jack looked at the ponies, then strolled toward the main camp. A few dogs skulked between the lodges, and no one seemed in a hurry to start another day. Only ashes remained of the two lodges that had burned. One lean dog, tail tightly curled, sniffed there where a sliver of smoke lingered. The hungry animal wanted to reach something in the hot ashes. Hunger overcame his caution and he picked it up in his mouth, then leaped, whirled, and dropped it, yelping. Two more dogs came on the run, and there was a snarling mix-up as they fought over a piece of dried salmon smudged with ashes. The day had begun.

Jube came out of his tepee to stretch and yawn in the morning sunlight. He scratched his beard, then made his way toward the half-breed, his mind on the races.

"What pony you want to lose to me on the first run, Jube?" Jack greeted.

"I'll run Sarah's agin this'n of Bailey's."

"Guess Bent'll do the riding and betting. I'll stay back, let you fellers argue and deal."

"The next bet'll be for a jug agin some goods an' hides. I win the jug and start to oil up fellers fer the next race. When it's gone, Bent'll make another run an' git the second jug. From then on, the crowd'll want ever'thing you boys brought along with yuh. Late in the day, when ever'body's happy an' well oiled, you an' Bent got to act like you're soused, an' I'll git the chief to bet the girl, the gun, an' even his own hide."

179

"What happened to him last night? I saw somebody grab him, then some fights started."

"Them fellers was whiskeyed up and figured the chief was holdin' out on 'em. They was goin' to drag him out an' search his outfit, an' this ain't usual—nobody touches the chief!"

"What started the fires?"

"Two drunks so soused they lost all good sense—if they had any in the first place. In the wickiup they laid in they got the top off a can of somethin' stole from some settler or the army. It scalded 'em and one kicked the can into the fire. It turned out to be coal oil or turpentine, and fire busted out so sudden it follered across to the drunks 'cause they'd spilled it on theirselves. They hollered an' left fer open air. Another drunk tryin' to help picked up something with fire in it an' carried it off to put it away inside the next tepee, and it went up."

Jack snorted held-back laughter. This was like old times with the distant tribe on the Little Salmon.

"And what was the shooting all about?"

"Jist fellers feelin' good, tryin' out their old fusees to see how the fire flashed in the dark."

"One time we heard shots, then yelling and screaming."

"Oh, that! I got there jist as it happened. Drunks agin, tryin' to see who could shoot clostest to the other feller's foot. You kin guess from the noise what happened. First feller lost a toe, so when he had his shot, the other drunk got a bullet through his foot. The wimmen mixed in, an' then's when the screamin' come on. I'd had a few drinks myself, an' I reckoned all that was real funny, but a couple of chiefs had their camp soldiers dunk the drunks in the river, then haul 'em out to drain. They had a harder job with the wimmen than they did with the bucks!"

"How'd you find Sarah when you got to your tent?"

"All togged out an' no place to go. Slept clear through, still snorin' when I left. You ain't et, have yuh?"

"Nope. Bent's up. Maybe he has some ideas about that."

"We kin go over to where they was roastin' meat last night. Some's good, and some don't ask about. I seen a lot of diffrunt things brung in an' I got choosy 'bout what I sliced off. The big chunks'll be red an' juicy when yuh cut in deep enough. Git old Bent to boil coffee. We'll mosey on over an' cut us a few slices, then squat an' eat at yer diggin's."

Bent already had a fire going. Tousled hair poking out from under his pushed-back hat, he greeted Jube with a grin.

"Bet them shots I heerd last night was yer old woman givin' you a dose of yer own lead fer leavin' the dance with that young tender-lookin' squaw. When I saw that blanket bobbin' down through the trees, I figgered you'd be late gettin' in."

"Sarah's still out an' dead to the world," Jubal told him. "Stick around whilst me an' Jack go rustle up some hot meat from the stuff they been roastin'. Name yer critter."

"What all they got over there?"

"I seen deer, elk, sheep, mule, horse, bear, cat, dog, coyote, and woodchuck. I don't know what's in the stew kittles. How about some salmon jist been smoked? Jack, fetch some of that candy along fer the old wimmen—it'll git us all the grub we need."

Jack gave each of the two old women watching the fire a striped stick of candy and a ribbon. Cackling with pleased laughter, they showed the two men what they had in the blackened pots and kettles, and let them sample the contents with two spoons traded or stolen. Jubal cut into a big haunch. Red juices dribbled out to hiss in the coals.

"This'll make a man of yuh," he said, handing a chunk to Jack. He cut a piece for himself, poised it on his knife point, opened his mouth, and shoved part of it in while juice leaked onto his black whiskers. "Good, ain't it?"

Jack nodded. A woman handed a battered tin pan to Jube. "Take now. You bring back?"

The pan filled with meat, they went back to find Bent squatted, drinking coffee. He whistled.

"Godamighty, you leave any fer the pore folks?"

"When this is gone, we'll go fer some high-class stew," Jubal assured him. "Fill yer craw whilst we fill our cups with coffee, an' don't complain about what it tastes like."

While they ate, the kids came back for candy. Jubal sized them up, then talked to them in their own language.

"Boys, we need you fellers to guard this camp while we race the ponies. Jack here has some candy fer yuh, an' I'll hang ribbons on yer arms so's people'll know yer important policemen. Yuh want to watch the camp fer us?"

There was no need to urge.

Jubal tied a piece of red-white-and-blue ribbon around the

oldest boy's right arm. "Yer the chief, savvy? See the others keep on the job an' don't run off ner go to sleep." The next boys got yellow, green, and blue ribbons, and Jack gave each a stick of candy. Jubal drew a line around the camp with a crooked cedar stick he picked up.

"Now, fellers, don't let nobody or any dogs git inside that line. Yell fer help if yuh need it, an' we'll come."

Jack watched the boys swell with pride in the ribbons denoting their authority. The ribbons were trade materials and would surely be confiscated by their mothers, or perhaps by their fathers to tie in a pony's forelock. But for the time being, the boys could cherish them as a symbol of power.

28

Already, younger Indian riders were out racing their ponies and betting against others. Older people who had retired sober moved about, some standing or squatting around the piles of meat, talking and gesticulating, making plans for the coming competition.

Jubal, too, got into action.

"Bent, you want to run that pony Bailey sent over? Ride him down to the track an' I'll brace yuh fer a race, jist the two of us, bettin' a leetle somethin', but not the ponies—that'll be on the next race, when we begin to drink."

Jack and Bent had raced the bay gelding several times while training Booshway and Pardner. He was fast over a short distance. If Jube's pony beat him, it wouldn't be by much.

As Bent rode to the race course, he passed part of the camp where a group of women sat cross-legged, gambling, so intent on what they were doing that he stopped his pony to watch. They used flat pieces of cedar painted with figures, the counters small pink-and-white shells. From the pile in front of one squaw, Bent thought she was well ahead of the game. He shrugged. At least they could amuse themselves while their men danced, ran races, and gambled.

A race had just finished. While the riders laughed and argued, Bent put the spurs to his pony and loped down the track for a few hundred yards, swung him in a quick turn, and came racing back, a clear indication to the crowd that he was ready to race anyone who wanted to match ponies with him. His pony blew, snorted, and caught his wind, loosened up now and anxious to run. Several riders hesitated, not knowing how to approach the stranger. Jube rode up on his running horse.

"Yuh want to make a run an' git beat, cowboy?"

"I ain't racin' jist fer fun, old-timer. Got somethin' yuh want to lose?"

"I need a new hat. Bet my cat-fur cap agin that old sunshade of yourn."

"That old flea cage all yuh got to put up fer a race?"

"The day's young—like you air. Maybe I'll have more to offer later on."

"Name the course—I'll go along. Down an' back suits me."

"See that pine down the stretch? We run down, turn there, an' come back here. We'll git two fellers to stand apart—the first one goes atween 'em gits the hat."

"Yuh mean cap, doncha?"

"Cap, hell! It's yer hat I'll be wearin' when this's over!"

Two big bucks stood at the starting line.

"Git yer pony in line!" Jube shouted. "The feller waves his hand down, we take off."

The ponies rolled their eyes and belled their nostrils, off in jumps at the signal, neck and neck until the turn, where Jube's pony took the lead and went around the tree in a wide circle, Bent's bay cutting in close to gain. Then it was neck and neck to the finish line, with Bent winning by a nose.

Jube whirled his pony to where Bent sat grinning. "Lucky fer you I didn't bet ponies with yuh," he said. "You'd had to walk to yer camp."

Jube sailed the fur cap at Bent. "That wasn't a fair race, mister. Want to run agin? What've yuh got to bet 'sides yer pony?"

"I might have a jug to put up."

"An' what's in the jug?"

"I'll give yuh a little snort. You go bring me a rifle an' I'll go fetch the jug. If yer old fusee looks good enough, we'll have us another run."

The listeners got warm. The two white men were going to

183

bet whiskey against guns! This meant they'd be drinking. When white men got drunk, any sober Indian could beat them in a horse race! While they waited, the Indians ran a race of their own, and the crowd got bigger as the sun climbed closer to its zenith.

When Bent arrived with the jug, Jube took a big drink.

"You old thief, you drank 'bout a quart of it!" Bent accused.

"Hit'll be my jug after this race. I kin drink my own whiskey, can't I?"

"Not afore yuh win it. I don't even know if that old piece of iron'll fire, let alone shoot straight. Lemme try it out."

"The hell with that idea. Sail yer hat in the air, I'll ventilate it."

"Then git off that bag of bones an' git yer piece cocked an' primed."

"She's primed. I'll pull back her ear. When I holler, sling yer bonnet out toward that bunch of trees."

The crowd backed away. These two white men were going start shooting already!

"Let her fly!" Jube sat his pony, rifle half-raised.

Bent sailed Jube's fur cap over the meadow. Smoke blasted out in a cloud of burned powder as the soft lead bullet left the trader's rifle barrel, the cap jumped, and fur flew. Furious, Jubal jumped off his pony, which took off at a run as he shook his rifle at Bent.

"You dirty skunk, you made me shoot my own cap!"

"I won that cap fair an' square. You said sling yer bonnet, an' I done jist that." Bent laughed. "You cheat at races an' then whine about it!"

"I won't lose that ole gun, you kin bet yer shirt. I'll git my pony an' show you somethin', young sprout."

"Then take yer shirt off, old man, 'cause yer goin' to have to bet it."

Young Indian riders were bringing back Jube's pony, the crowd now enlarged as word spread that the traders were betting whiskey and guns. Bent pulled his shirt off and laid it down with the jug. Jube took off his greasy jacket and wrapped it around his rifle. The onlookers chattered. Bent's white skin had a thin spread of brown hair over the chest, but old Jubal Street looked as hairy as a hibernating bear. They saw that the cowboy was slender, Jube barrel-chested

184

with broad shoulders and powerful arms. If the two fought, the big man could crush the other like breaking a dry willow stick!

They lined up for the race, Indians of all sizes and ages on both sides of the course. If the white men got drunk enough and had more whiskey, maybe they'd pass the jug around.

This time Jube made the turn close to the tree. Bent's pony swung wide and lost by a length. It was Jube's turn to laugh. As he climbed down and picked up the jug, Bent called, "Hey, old man, give me a swig."

Jube thought about it, swished the jug, took out the cork, and tried to peer in. "I will if yuh bet yer pony agin mine in the next run."

"Damn betcha! Give me the jug."

Bent drank, handed the jug back to Jube, who hoisted it to his lips. The Indians licked their lips and eyed each other in growing excitement. They wanted some of that too!

"Well, smart feller, still think yer pony kin beat mine?"

"Ain't had enough, have yuh? Let's see yuh bet that sorry plug on it."

"Pony, saddle, bridle, an' yer cap agin yer hull outfit, includin' the jug an' what's left."

"Fair enough. Pull off yer boots."

"You're crazy. I need them boots to ride!"

"Wal, yuh said you'd bet 'em!"

Bent pulled off his boots. Jube slipped off his dirty moccasins and put them beside the jug. They climbed back on their sweating ponies. The buck's hand swept down, and they were off. This time, Jube swung his mount into Bent's on the turn, almost upsetting him, and came to the finish line well ahead. He slid his pony to a stop, got off, and went at the jug. While Bent sat protesting, he offered it to their starter and the other judge, then grinned up at Bent.

"Figger what else yuh kin dig up to lose? Here, take a drink, it'll make yuh feel better."

"The hell with you, old thief. I'll git another pony an' win it all back."

"Run on home. We aim to drink this up whilst yer gone."

The Indians chuckled and laughed to see the cowboy walk barefoot back to his camp. As they passed the jug around, Jube told the crowd he'd show those Ochoco cowboys, win everything they owned, and let them walk back. Jack heard the cheers and shouting, and when Bent hobbled into camp, he knew Jube had piled up the winnings.

"Looks like you lost pony, shirt, and boots. What's next?"

"I'll take my pony and a bottle, the one with the stud horse on it. I'll trade it to old Jube fer my saddle so I kin ride against some Injuns. Jube kin get 'em excited, give the chief a swig from the bottle, an' work him up fer the big swindle."

"I'll ride Booshway over. Did you see the chief there?"

"Yeah, he's been watchin' all along, an' he's tryin' to figger what yer doin' here."

"I'll get Jube to have him toss his scalping knife on the pile when the big bet comes up. It's a good thing you brought extra boots."

They rode to the track, Bent bareback, a rope looped over his pony's nose. The crowd parted and they rode up to Jube, now surrounded by admirers who had tasted some of the drink and were hoping for more. Jack's chief had edged in, and Jube gave him a couple of swigs. Now he bragged to his tribesmen how he'd get everything these cowboys had with them.

"Old-timer, I need my saddle," Bent said. "I got somethin' with me I think yuh'll like."

Jube spat at the ground. "Fetch it here."

The trader looked in awe at the bottle with the picture of the stallion standing statuelike in all his glory, then commenced to read the words on the label aloud, the chief at his side with half a dozen others.

Bent interrupted the reading. "Hell's fire, old man, yuh want it or doncha?"

"Take the saddle—I'll win it back anyway, cowboy. Say, chief, when I win this race, we'll have a snort of this stuff."

Jubal pulled the cork and smelled of it, put the neck of the bottle to his lips, then closed his eyes, thrust his head well back, and gave a wolf howl that made his pony back away in fright. "Wahhoooeee!" came the full-throated squalling echo from the cliffs back of the timber. If anything impressed the chief, this was the climax. The liquid in the horse bottle must be powerful to have that effect on the bearded trader!

"Old-timer, what'd yuh say yer name was?" Bent egged old Jube on.

"My handle's old Jube, an' Jubal Street's my full name. I

heerd yuh called Bent, but yuh'll be broke afore this day is done!"

"Let's run a straight flat half-mile."

"I kin beat yuh runnin' around a tree, over jumps, trottin' in circles, or swimmin' the river. Makes no difference," Jube boasted. "What yuh gonna bet?"

"This pony an' my rifle agin yer pony an' the riggin' on him. My riggin' ain't in it, 'cause I borried it."

"Well, I do declare! Talkin' big, but 'fraid to bet."

On the flat, with no one to hear them, Jube told of making progress with the chief as they rode out. "He's sniffin' like a cat at a rat hole. The drink's gittin' to him. I'll win this race an' you'll be busted flat, so you jump Jack fer Booshway an' Jack won't let yuh have him 'cause yer luck's gone sour. So Jack rides Booshway and bets me the other jug along with the pony agin both yers an' the riggin'. I win the whole she-bang, an' all hell breaks loose atween you an' him, with me buttin' in."

They reached the place set for the run back to the crowd. Jube looked over at Bent. "Make it look close, boy," he said.

When Jube yelled, the ponies jumped and dug in, running flat out like startled rabbits pursued by hungry coyotes, neck and neck until Bent checked his pony just enough for Jube to cross the line ahead of him.

War whoops, yells, and shouting drowned out the cussing Jack gave his partner for losing not only the race but their pack ponies and most of Jack's outfit. Jube opened the jug and brought it to give each a drink, then passed it to the chief and on to a few of the braves.

Jack had kept in the background while Bent handled the racing and betting, but now he took over the dealing, and every time Bent proposed racing Booshway against Jube's ponies, Jack shouted him down, while the Indians drew closer to watch the half-breed dominate his white partner. Jube came over, the bottle in his pocket and the jug in his arms.

"What's the matter, boys? Can't figger who's boss? This old pony looks like he could run."

"Don't wanna run him," Jack said, slurring. "My pony's old but he's best damn runnin' pony in camp."

"Wanna bet?"

"Don't wanna run him. Best damn pony in whole damn world."

187

"Yuh ain't got Injun blood in yuh, yuh cheapskate. Yuh come braggin' 'bout yer ponies, cry 'bout losing the jug, an' now yuh won't run yer pony. Two leetle boys that play like big men!"

Bent made as if he couldn't stand it and wanted to fight. "You old skunk-skinner, if you'd run yer race fair an' let an Injun ride agin Jack, he could beat yer old plug!"

"You git that feller brags on his speckled cayuse to run him an' I'll git any Injun that kin set a pony to run agin him!"

More wrangling and shouting, some of the Indians having their say. The chief sided with Jube, and they traded drinks from the bottle and jug; then Jube strode over to make his proposition. "Young feller, I'll bet you all three of my ponies an' their riggin' that I kin beat yer speckled pony with you ridin' him an' an Injun ridin' mine. Now, iffen yuh got guts besides all that wind yuh been spoutin', you'll take that bet."

"Take him, Jack, you kin do it," Bent said. "Old Boosh-way'll beat any pony in the park!"

Jack went to Booshway and tightened the cinch. This betting had become so real that for a moment he feared old Jube really meant to clean him out. He recalled the chief's smirking face—the main point of all this was to recover Teeah! He led Booshway to where Jubal talked with the chief, carrying on about what he intended to do with his winnings from these two Prine City cowboys.

"I'll race your pony," Jack told him. "Get your red brother on him, pronto!"

"The run's down an' around that tree an' back to here," Jube said. "Hit'll be yer last ride on that speckled dog of a pony. Once I git him, my woman'll use him to pack her blankets on."

It was an Indian insult. Jack coughed up a gob of spit that almost hit Jube's feet.

"You smart young jackass! You ate army mule an' Injun dog fer breakfast an' yuh'll eat crow fer dinner tonight if they let yuh hang around camp. Runs-A-Pony'll beat you. Git ready to run yer stock, boy!"

Jack weaved a little in the saddle as the race began, and at the turn he leaned the wrong way and almost fell off. To the bettors' delight, his pony made such a wide circle that he lost all chance to win.

Triumphant, Jube whooped, hollered, and bragged, while Bent, disconsolate, cussed their run of bad luck.

29

Jack and Bent walked back to their lean-to, where the small, earnest guards were still on duty. Jack seemed drunk as he paid them off with more candy; he let them keep the ribbons, and when they left, entered the shelter to hear Bent chuckling. "Old Jube'll be over soon pretendin' to rub it in an' crow over what he done to us. Jack, yuh figger any of them fellers suspicion we're about to roll a fast one?"

"You never can tell. Jube'll know about that, I reckon."

Jubal brought a surprise: Sarah, dressed in all her ribbons, riding Booshway, preening herself like a peacock in the spring.

"Fellers, I know how you feel, down on yer luck," Jubal said in mock sympathy. "Yuh got one chance to git even. The chief wants a bottle of that stud-horse whiskey. If yuh got one more pony that kin run. I'll match yuh fer a race— all I got from yuh agin the pony yuh got left, another jug I hope yuh got hid out somewheres, and a bottle of stud-horse."

"You old thief!" Bent shouted. "You stole the races, all our plunder, an' our best ponies already."

"Jubal," Jack pleaded, "get the old chief to show up with Teeah and my gun. If we make some sort of deal there, I might run my pony against yours. I've got to see the girl you and Sarah have told me about first to know if it's Teeah."

"What if the chief won't?" Jubal knew the risks.

"Tell him we got a couple bottles better'n the stud-horse," Bent said. "If he brings out the girl, we talk up a bet. If not, we pack up and leave."

Jubal rode off, with Sarah on Booshway trailing behind.

"Bent, let's take a sip of the jug," Jack proposed. "Then it'll be easy to convince the chief we're drunk."

189

Half an hour later, two young braves, colorfully painted and riding ponies decorated with feathers in manes and tails, galloped up and slid to a stop in front of the tent. One shouted, "You come now! Big race! Chief says come!"

Jack sat up, rubbed his eyes, and held his head, then waved his hand at them. "We come to bet on our pony. Tell chief!"

The two riders whirled off to carry the news. Jack turned to look at Bent, who lay on the soogans grinning. "Go on over with the bottles and the jug while I fetch Pardner. Get the chief excited about the race. Old Jube'll go along, so all we have to do is make sure the chief really wants to win."

Pardner nickered at Jack as he untied the picket rope, and nudged the boy in welcome. "Run this race, old pony, and we'll have Booshway and Teeah with us again! We'll leave this country for a place where we won't have to run and be cheated!"

He knelt and looked over each foot to make sure Pardner's shoes were set and tight. Satisfied, he selected a hair from the pony's tail and again knelt. When he arose, Pardner lifted his foot, then set it back down as if in pain, and when Jack walked him around, he saw that the pony was limping as if from a sore foot or a sprained tendon. Nevertheless, he led his horse to the tent and saddled and bridled him.

At the course, Bent was drunk and showed it, but Jube seemed drunker. The chief, curious about the bottles Bent had, tried to make out what the two white men argued over. Bent turned to him and held out the bottle displaying the powerful man. "We had to send clear across the big seawater fer this, chief. Now, this feller here, Jack, wants to see the girl he says you got here in camp, and he's ready to bet ever'thing he's got to git her back. We know we got a pony kin win. If Jack wants to bet all he's got, we'll take it, won't we?"

The chief, pretty well swacked, agreed, nodding and gesturing. Bent looked up to see Jack coming and almost forgot he was supposed to be drunk. Pardner was lame!

"Jack, yuh can't run that pony! What happened?"

"You're drunk and don't know it. If Jube and the chief're ready to bet, I'll beat 'em if they put up enough. We'll get back your pony and saddle, too!"

"How kin yuh win a race with a lame pony?"

"I'll beat him with a club or hit him with a rock to make him run circles around 'em." Jack's bravado seemed real. "He'll run!"

Jube joined in. "Bent's plumb right. Yuh can't run a lame pony, Jack. Better call it off."

Jack raved at them. "I'll run this old pony on three legs and beat you. Put up your betting money—I'll get all my stuff back. I got ribbons and lace and candy and a jug about full. Got a pretty lady on a bottle, too."

Trying to pull the bottle out of his shirt, he almost fell off the pony, but Bent grabbed him and said, "Shut yer trap. Yuh can't bet that bottle! We got to save it fer Bailey to pay fer the pony we lost."

"I'll win him back. Old man, put up what you bet."

"Well, kid, we already agreed—all I won from you, except the whiskey, agin this lame pony."

"Not enough. Want your ponies, your blankets, your woman. We bet trade stuff, whiskey, bottles, and guns."

"Pile ever'thing in a heap, an' whoever wins the race gits it?"

"Yeah. The chief's gotta put up Teeah. I want to see her right here. No cheating again."

"Okay, bring the jug an' the other bottle, an' git the trade ribbons and lick-sweet."

Jack turned and rode off on his mission, Pardner still limping, but Bent stayed to argue a bit more.

Teeah had come back to the camp, and now she stood at the edge of the crowd with a tall, heavyset brave. She had watched the drunken battle. She had seen Jack, and for the first time since the killings near the river she was sure he had survived. Rumors that a white boy, part Indian, had penetrated the canyon looking for her but had left with another girl and her baby had reached her. She had seen the new gun the chief wore around his waist. It had come from the stranger, they said. Jack hadn't had such a gun while they traveled together. Now, listening to the great bet being placed, she could only hope that somehow its outcome would bring her release. The tribe would not let her go easily, but they might sell or trade her. If Jack lost, he and his friend would have no chance to take her away from the chief.

* * *

191

At the lean-to, Bent now had the pack pony saddled and ready for the load of goods. At the main camp, the Indians raced and whooped it up.

"Jack, yuh must have a trick up yer sleeve I don't know about. If Pardner's as lame as he looks, you won't have no chance against any of the chief's ponies he's so hot to run."

"Three drunks'll make a dandy race," Jack replied. "But the chief might be putting it on about being soused. Keep your eye on him. He has Teeah well guarded."

Bent shook his head, despairing. "That big feller standin' next to her with the mean look in his eye is prob'ly the feller's got her in his tepee. I wouldn't want to tussle with that old boy."

They loaded the pony with all their plunder. On top of the pack lay Jack's rifle in its beaded and quilled scabbard. Bent led the way back to the race grounds. Sarah was holding the ponies, and Booshway nickered as Pardner came up. Jack saw that Teeah was still there, the big Indian close by. The chief paid her no attention, but looked to see what loot on the pack animal might be his if he won this race.

Wrangling and arguing began again. Jube would not agree to throw Sarah in on the deal. The chief wanted in. Jack and Jube pretended to argue him out of it, but finally Jack said, "Old man, let him match us. He must put up his pony, the girl, and the gun he got from me. Make him show you the gun first, and point at the girl."

Jube and the chief talked. Finally the chief brought up his pony and displayed the six-gun. An argument began between the brave with Teeah and the chief, settled by the chief's offering part of the winnings if the brave allowed him to put up the girl as part of his bet.

Now Jack insisted that Jube throw in Sarah with his bet, and he produced the bottle with the figure of the lady. Jube showed it to the chief and began to read him the label. As the Indian listened, amazed, Jack asked the trader for the bottle with the big horse on it.

"What yuh want it fer?"

"To see if I can cure this pony's lame leg. Just a few drops. Pour some on my hand."

Jack rubbed a little of the fiery liquid on Pardner's knee joint, felt around the leg, then straightened up. "If it works, he'll be fixed up before long."

"But it's his foot. Yuh rubbed it on his knee!"

"Putting it on the joint above where it hurts does the trick. It sends the stuff to wherever the pain is."

"Okay, you throw in the bottle with the woman an' I'll throw in my woman. Hell's fire, I'll sell you the girl fer twenty in gold when I git her."

"It's a deal. The gun is worth ten ponies. You ready to line up?"

"Let's make it a longer run, the chief says."

The chief insisted on the long race, while Jack argued for the turn around the tree, finally settling the matter by an agreement they would go to the far end of the flat, then run to the tree, circle it, and wind up at the finish line, where the goods, ponies, guns, and two women would be waiting for the winner. Teeah had been brought over to where the chief's pony and the six-gun were. Jack and Jubal examined the gun to see that it was loaded. While the chief looked at the coveted bottle, Jack made sure the caps were in place and that it was ready to fire. Then they climbed on their ponies and jogged to the distant starting line, Pardner limping as he trotted along.

Just before they reached the point where the race was to begin, Pardner started to act up. Jack jumped off and rubbed the sore leg from knee to fetlock. Pardner stood there snorting, but when Jack finished, he put down his foot, lifted it again, and when Jack led him a few steps, there was no limp!

"Chief, looka that! That stuff in the bottle really works!" Jubal was dumbfounded at what he saw, and the chief sat amazed at what had taken place. As the ponies walked to the starting line, both men watched closely, but the limp did not come back.

The racers placed themselves ten feet apart, Jack in the middle. Jubal and the chief eyed him. Jack lifted his hand to signal ready, and as the hand dropped, spurs and quirts went into action. The ponies leaped. Pardner's iron shoes dug into the soft earth.

Jack beat the others to the tree; he hissed twice and swung right while the others swung wide to make the circle. Jack made the full, close turn, and was ready for the straightaway when he heard a shout. His glance caught the mix-up—both ponies and their riders now sprawling, rolling in the dirt. Jack let Pardner have his head and raced across the finish line.

193

The half-breed leaned down to Bent, both of them cold sober. "Git yer gun and all the others. There's going to be trouble when those two come in."

Bent picked up his own rifle and Jack's, found the six-gun and its pouch. He carried the weapons over where Jack sat on Pardner waiting. The two racers were walking their ponies to the finish line, Jube shaking his head and saying, "That weren't no fair race!"

"We run again," the chief insisted.

"No," Jack said in his old impassive tone. "You fellers mixed up. I'm taking the pot I won, all except the jug and the bottles. Get off your ponies and I'll hand 'em to you."

"We never had no chance. You tricked us both!" Jube waved his arms and shouted.

Jack had a reply. "You drunken fools ran into each other, old man. You figgered to box me in, make me lose the race so you could split the loot. Tell your woman to load those ponies."

Jube kept up the pretense. "You talk mighty big, but afore yuh leave here yuh'll have to deal with me'n the chief!"

Something had made Jack determined not to delay. "Bent, see the women tie the string of ponies together and pack up the stuff," he said. "Jube, git that jug hid. Look who's coming down the trail next to the hill."

When the Indians saw the detail of soldiers, they panicked until older and wiser ones started riders racing again. With the jug and bottles, Jubal rode to his camp while Sarah and Teeah packed up Jack's winnings. The soldiers came on at a trot once they reached the meadow.

Jack put his saddle on Booshway, and Teeah rode Pardner. Sarah took Jube's pony. Bent tied the extra horses together and had the lead rope looped over his saddle horn as the sergeant in the lead rode up. The broad-shouldered, red-haired Irishman looked familiar to Jack.

The detail halted at command. The officer noticed the chief's pony, now tied in Bent's string, feathers in its mane and tail and with the paint marks of a warrior's mount. He saw an Indian girl dressed in buckskin, her blanket tied behind her saddle. Sarah was Indian, too. One cowboy was certainly white, but the fellow with him looked like a breed, although he bore himself and dressed like a white man. He looked over the assemblage, then rode closer to Bent.

"Looks like you're aimin' to take off. Have a good time here?"

"Yeah, lost a few races, then bet all we had left, an' it come out in our favor. You on patrol?"

"Jest lookin'! Your pard looks like somebody I might've run into once."

"His name's Jack Tate. His old man was Trader Bill Tate, but the Injuns called him Quick Hands."

"I know him," the sergeant marveled. "Met him a year or so back. I'll go say hello. I see a few drunks around. You bring any whiskey with you?"

"Naw, just a couple bottles of bitters an' a cure fer female troubles to swap to old Jube, the trader. He'll maybe show 'em to yuh."

"Jest two?"

"Maybe three. One had a picture of a black stud horse on it. There was one showin' a big feller in tights—that's the rejuvenator for gentlemen." The sergeant was smiling. "The one with the high-class lady on it—that's the one fer females. Jube an' the old chief're thicker'n fleas on an Injun's old blanket."

Jack grinned at the sergeant. "Last time I saw you was down where the skeeters almost ate us up. You had three fellers to haul back to the fort."

"Jack, it's good to see you. Heard you done all right with the ponies."

"I was down to my last one, so I put up everything but our boots, riding against the chief and old Jube. They got mixed up on the turn and I won the pot. You rode into what might've been a real argument. The tribe don't like seeing a feller ride off with something they want."

"Jack, you did us a favor once, you and old man Hill. We'll stick around awhile to give you a runnin' start. Say, you ever find out what all took place when those fellows were killed up near the river gorge?"

"I'm still working on it. The Indian girl you see there's the one the leader, Stubbs, shot. I won her in the race, and maybe she can tell me more about what happened. First time I've seen her since then."

"Let me know if I can help."

"Thanks. The gold and plunder that bunch took is probably scattered in this tribe."

195

The sergeant looked around, sensing the Indians' mood. "These fellers're gettin' nervous, maybe wonderin' what we're schemin'. Better ride off, Jack."

As Jack turned Booshway, Jubal came up and greeted the sergeant, who asked to see the bottles with the pictures. Jube began to snort and argue. Jack grinned at him and rode away.

The four left the Warm Springs powwow grounds at a fast trot. Jack rode alongside Teeah, and they cast wondering glances at each other. Jack could not keep back speech.

"Teeah, I thought you were dead. I saw Stubbs shoot you. When they took the others away, I couldn't see you. I saw Ort and Ace throw all the dead ones over the cliff. You weren't there. I got down the cliff and looked for you in the river camp. The chief said he'd trade you for the gun, but it was not you, it was Ahseeah and her baby. I thought you were gone and I'd never see you again." He waited for her reply.

"Jack, I thought you dead. I thought all of you dead. Looks For Sun saw the shooting, saw me kill Stubbs. I ran to the rocks and he picked me up and carried me off. We went to the place where the trail goes down to the river, and I stayed there with another brave. Looks For Sun saw the bad men throw the dead ones over the cliff. Others went to follow the bad men. Two days later they came back. I heard little, but they said two bad men were dead. They didn't say who killed them nor if you were alive."

"Teeah . . . we can talk about it some other time. I missed you always. I was afraid to think you might be dead."

"But how did you get away? I saw Stubbs shoot Mr. Turpin—and the others shot the boys."

They could not stop the questions.

"Did you kill Stubbs?"

"Yes, with the knife you gave me. I played dead . . . he kicked me, then turned me over, got down on his knees over me. I cut his neck under the chin. I heard shots on the hill, and I ran."

"Ace and Ort both shot at me. I hid and followed them. I killed them both and took the ponies. I buried the gold and the guns and saddles, but somebody stole them. They were gone when Mr. Hill and I went to look."

"How did you find the secret river trail?"

196

"This spring I camped at the place and followed every track or sign."

Teeah broke in. "Ahseeah is girl stolen on raid far away. She belonged to men who caught her. Where is she now?"

"She cooks for Bullhead Bailey. We stop there on our way to the John Day, where Jube and Sarah live."

Teeah seemed astonished. "Jube with us? He and chief bet against you!"

"Yes, Teeah, Jubal and Sarah are our friends. They helped me find you. Jube tricked the chief into betting you and my gun."

"Jack, I am happy to be with you. Will we go to the mountains now, maybe back to the Clearwater?"

"We will go to Bailey's, then to Elk Hollow. Jube will catch up to us. Sarah hasn't said where yet. We will camp as far away as we can ride tonight. The old chief is angry drunk. After Jube leaves, he might send somebody after us. He told me if I ever came back he would have me killed. He may figger he was double-crossed and be mad enough to follow us and steal you and my gun back. We must cross the river soon. The soldiers' coming helped us. It was a good thing."

30

They traveled until midnight under a full moon, and pitched camp by simply throwing down the packs, getting out enough food for a meal, then stretching themselves on the ground, the only thing to destroy their rest a few mosquitoes. They woke at daylight. New plans must be made. Sarah spoke to Bent.

"Bent, we stay here and wait for Jube. Let Jack and Teeah go ahead, see Bailey, go up to Elk Hollow cabin. If chief sends men, they not here. Jack listen to you. Needs Teeah now."

Bent found Jack near the ponies, picketed close by. "Jack, if I was in yer shoes, I'd saddle ponies and take the girl to Bailey's hangout. Sarah an' me'll wait here fer old Jube. By now the chief'll be comin' alive with a bad taste in his mouth an' a headache. He might trick Jube into follerin' us."

"What if they come and we're not here?"

"Sarah an' me'll think of some fish story. We had a good start, but Injuns on good ponies with no pack kin travel twicet as fast. They might git ahead of us in the narrow country ahead—we'd be easy meat."

Jack and Teeah were in their saddles ready to go within a few minutes. They let Pardner carry the pack; he trailed easy, with Booshway leading. Teeah rode Speck. As they left the camp, both turned to wave at Sarah and Bent; then they were alone on the trail, together once more.

At the powwow grounds, while the sergeant talked to Jubal, the chief grew belligerent. Hogan was willing to let it slide until Jube took the chief's part. Jubal Street didn't like the army either, and when the sergeant called for the bottles, tasted the contents, and searched the chief's lodge and found a jug, Jubal swore at the army, its officers, and even the lousy mules.

Hogan had had all he wanted. Jube was grasped from behind by two powerful troopers who wrestled him to the ground while others went through Jube's belongings. They found two more jugs; one still had some of the joy juice in it. Hogan tasted it: this was the same stuff he had found in the bottles. As he was about to announce that fact, he heard Jube say, "Iffen you was as smart as I think yuh are, you'd look at my right eye." Jubal winked a time or two.

The sergeant walked to where he lay. "Do that again, you old thief."

Jubal winked again. "That ain't all. Iffen you take me into court fer peddlin' whiskey, I'll have somethin' to say that'll surprise yuh, mark my words!"

"Pick him up and put shackles on him," Hogan directed. "Pack up his stuff for evidence. I'll talk to the chief."

Hogan scored the chief severely for letting whiskey peddlers sell the stuff to his people, then gamble with them. He would make sure Jube didn't sell or trade any more. Then he told the chief he had heard the tribe had blankets, guns, and other things taken from the travelers who had been killed across the river. He was not accusing them because he was sure bad white men had blamed it on Indians. To show his friendship, Hogan gave the chief the three bottles with pictures on them and spoke last words of advice. "Chief, don't drink this all at once. Make it last. It'll keep you feelin' good."

The sergeant turned away to gather his troop together along with old Jube and his outfit. Once they were alone, Jube looked at him and grinned. "Boy, yuh come jist at the right time! The chief was beginnin' to figger out what was happening. By mornin', he'd've made me take the trail with him after his favorite pony, the gun, the girl, an' all the goods he figgered as his."

"You and Jack must've whipsawed him good."

Jubal Street laughed as he told the story. "The pony still limped clear to the startin' line, but when Jack got off an' started rubbin', I'll be dad-blamed if it didn't begin to walk right."

"That how he won the race?" The sergeant was still puzzled.

"Naw, me'n the chief run into each other an' rolled off in the dirt. 'Course Jack won, easy-like, an' me'n the chief argued he stole the race an' was gittin' real hot about it when you boys come off the hill. Only way to git Jack and them away was to pitch into you fer a spell."

"I wondered about that. When you winked at me, I knew there was something I had better find out. There was a rumor going around the chief's band had some guns. I suppose you heard they're going to make this whole country into a reservation and run all the loose bands in here."

"Yeah . . . there's been a lot of squallin', but it'll be some time yet, won't it?"

"Don't think so. They'll keep us scoutin' around. Next big trouble, as I see it, will be with the Nez Percé over near the Snake and the Salmon. What do you wanta do, now that we're out of the chief's sight?"

"Stop somewhere fer a while, then take off."

"We'll cut back south and make a circle. Say, what did you fellows put in that jug, anyway? Did it really cure that pony's foot?"

Jubal shrugged. "All I know is, he lost his limp and run like an imp outta hell. Me'n the chief an' ever'body seen that!"

"Well, there's tricks in all trades. Jack can be tricky. He

ever tell you about how he and old man Hill did away with a buncha cutthroats down near the Klamath a couple years back?"

"Never said a word about it."

"Me and my men hauled the bodies back to the fort, all shot in the front, real rough outlaws. What's Jack and his girl gonna do now?"

"Derned if I know. We got a little bunch of stock atween us over on the John Day. He might decide to stick around there."

"That boy has a rough time ahead of him. Half white, half red, folks on both sides suspicious, and he can't go either way in peace."

Jube left the detachment an hour later, after swapping information with the sergeant about the killings near the gorge, and he did the best he knew how to convince the sergeant that the chief had taken advantage of Jack, and that the half-breed had wanted only to get the girl and his gun back.

Feeling pretty good, Jube rode along on the trail. His trading before Jack arrived at the powwow had been profitable. He had found some Indians in camp making earbobs from five-dollar gold pieces, larger coins being beaten and shaped into buttons. He traded his goods for the shiny coins and figured his possible profits. When he got Jack and Bent's first jug, he gave away a few sips, then gathered in coins like kernels shucked from ripe ears of corn. He might have enough money right now to get into the cow business in a small way.

He found Sarah and Bent at the night's campground, surprised to learn Jack and Teeah had gone ahead. He told the story of his talk with Hogan, and chuckled as he said, "I sure would like to know how Jack cured his pony's leg so quick. Bent, what made Pardner lame?"

"Jack never told me nothin'. I said he was crazy to run Pardner, but when he come in sound as a dollar, I knew Jack had tricked us some way."

"Well, we come out better'n I figgered," Jubal assured. "That old chief was close to guessin' our gamblin' game when the army showed up," and he told them how he had almost been nabbed for selling whiskey to the Indians.

They stopped at the forks. "You kin take Bailey's pony back to him, Bent," Jube said. "You got the chief's runnin' stock. Here's a few gold pieces to put in yer sock to make up fer all the workin' time yuh lost."

"Hell, Jube, I don't want nothin' from you! I went fer the good time an' to help Jack out. We had one whale of a time gittin' even with the old chief. You think he'll try to git revenge on Jack?"

"Hit's too late fer that. He'd ruther have the gun. There's wimmen'n girls aplenty in his camp. I got two guns I want Jack to look at. I figger they come from the cache he made. I'm dang sure the gold I traded fer is some Turpin had with him. Where else would those bucks git it?"

"So you an' Sarah're headin' fer home," Bent said. "You won't see me over there next year, or fer some time to come, I reckon. Jubal, if I was you I would never bet agin a lame pony! So long!"

Jack and Teeah bypassed Prine City; Jack didn't want to risk having someone stop them and ask questions. As they headed across country, following game and cattle trails, Teeah said, "Jack, remember when we were with Mr. Turpin and we talked about going up in the mountains just to be alone and do what we wanted to do? Can't we do that now?"

Jack recalled the times he and Teeah had talked and dreamed of such a thing. So far, there had been no chance to leave others and go on their own. Why shouldn't they do it now? Jube and Sarah would go to the John Day. Bent would go back to Bailey's ranch and ride for him, but Jack had made no promises to anyone except himself. He had kept that promise, searched and found Teeah. Now that he had her, there was so much to talk about, so many things to share.

They could head into the high green Ochocos, where mountain streams were clear and meadows cool, food plentiful. No one would bother them. They would live the summer in the Indian way, and when winter came, perhaps still stay hidden away from white men and their ways.

"Teeah, if you really want to, follow me. We'll head for the mountains to places where we can stay as long as we want. If you're sure, ride up close so I can rub my face against your cheek. Remember?"

Pardner sidled up to Booshway and stopped. The two riders leaned together, their long-held-back tears beginning to

201

fall. Terrible despair, the torture of revived hopes, and greater despair were ended. What the future would bring, neither Jack nor Teeah knew or cared. They had each other, and the present made up for the past.

ABOUT THE AUTHOR

MICK CLUMPNER was born in Wisconsin and moved to Northern Idaho at an early age. He lived in many places as his father followed his trade, working in sawmills, and later spent a number of years with the Forest Service and Bureau of Entomology in Idaho, Montana and Washington. During World War II, he logged and located timber for large mills and plywood plants. He has also owned and operated cattle ranches in Oregon and has carried on mining operations in Montana. He and his wife, Dorothy, now reside in Sebastopol, California, and have five grown children, four sons and a daughter.

This is his sixth published novel.